Isabella Mumphrey Adventures

Secrets of a Mayan Moon
Secrets of an Aztec Temple
Secrets of a Hopi Blue Star
Secrets of a Christmas Box

Secrets of an Aztec Temple

An Isabella Mumphrey Adventure

Book 2

By

Paty Jager

Windtree Press
Hillsboro, OR

SECRETS OF AN AZTEC TEMPLE

Contact Information: info@windtreepress.com

Windtree Press
Hillsboro, Oregon
http://windtreepress.com

Cover Art by Christina Keerins
CoveredbyCLKeerins

PUBLISHING HISTORY
First Edition by Windtree Press in 2013

Published in the United States of America

ISBN 978-1-952447-55-6

Special Thanks

These books and this character wouldn't have come to life so quickly without the help of Julie Drey and Danita Cahill. Thank you, ladies, for pushing me to go beyond my safe zone.

Chapter One

Augustino Konstantine—or Tino Rodriguez as he was known to drug lord, Paolo Garza—stood waiting in the inner sanctum of the drug lord's compound.

"You've been pushing to prove your loyalty. Today is the day." Garza sat behind a mahogany desk in the spacious office that only the few he trusted were allowed to enter.

"What am I to do?" Tino silently applauded himself as he stood at attention. During the five months he'd worked his way up the chain in Garza's organization, the drug lord had checked out all of his fake background. Garza would expect an ex-military sniper to show his respect by standing at attention.

"The Alvarez gang intercepted one of our shipments. I want the Alvarez brothers brought to me."

"Alive or dead?" he asked, filing away in his memory the newly garnered intel about the seven-foot safe door on the wall now directly behind him and the heavy door to his left. He'd bet his *abuela's* Bible that door was bullet-proof.

Garza's teeth curled back in a feral smile as he nodded his head. "I like your thinking, but I wish them alive. I need to set some rules the two *pendejos* need to learn."

"Does Cezar know where they are?" Garza's righthand man had been missing for the last hour. Tino suspected he was gathering information on the whereabouts of the brothers.

"Cezar is escorting a special guest here. But Hector has been following the two and called to tell me he lost them in the *colonias*."

"I'll start there." Tino turned to leave.

"Rodriguez."

Tino pivoted and looked the drug lord in the face.

"If you cannot bring them in, do not show your face here again."

The threatening tone punctuated what he already knew. If he didn't bring the Alvarez brothers back, he would be hunted down and killed because he'd witnessed and participated in illegal activities.

"I will be back with your guests."

Tino exited the office congratulating himself at having made it to Garza's inner sanctum, but now realized there were two more doors that would need breeched before he could find the evidence to bring in the Drug Enforcement Agency.

His mind wandered to the problem of finding the Alvarez brothers and gaining entry into the room behind the bullet-proof door. He stepped out onto the front portico. Cezar walked alongside a woman who carried herself in a familiar way.

Tino's blood iced with fear as he recognized the long hair, button nose, and wire-rimmed glasses. Another glance at the woman he knew so well and the ice melted, simmered, and quickened his heart. What brought his *querida* to the drug lord's Mexico City compound? Dread, desire, and regret collided as he blindly slammed into a cement pillar.

Coño! He pushed away from the cold, hard pillar and swept a hand across his stinging cheek, quickly scanning the area to see if anyone noticed his face plant into the column and the reason for his distraction. Allowing Garza or one of his narcos to notice his reaction to the appearance of Dr. Isabella Mumphrey would start a fissure in his carefully crafted identity. Fear for her collapsed his lungs making it hard to gather in air. He'd already lost his family to the man he planned to take down; he didn't want her to get caught in his revenge.

Isabella had changed his outlook on life less than a year ago and now she walked into a viper pit as innocently as she'd walked into the Guatemalan jungle and his heart. His feet stalled, but as vehemently as he wanted to hurry to her and keep her from entering the door of Paolo

Garza's home, he couldn't jeopardize her life or his chance at bringing down the person responsible for so many lost lives.

Tino continued his path along the edge of the courtyard, watching the slender backside of the woman he'd left six months ago in a bed in Guatemala stroll into his enemy's lair. Even in her drab, long, flowing skirt, pink school-girl top and sweater, doing nothing to hide the fact she was as flat-chested as he, he couldn't control the effect she had on his body.

His *miembro* tightened remembering the passionate days spent in the woman's arms. What was she doing here? He'd only had contact with her once after rushing from her arms to worm his way into Garza's confidence. Tino grit his teeth and forced thoughts of Isabella from his mind. Now wasn't the time to wonder about the woman.

He had a job to do that would bring him closer to his goal. Revenge.

Tino slipped into his SUV and drove past the open wrought iron gate, the only entrance into the adobe walled compound surrounding Garza's fifty-two-hundred square-foot vacation home. Two miles away, he pulled over and extracted a small surveillance detector from his backpack. One thing he'd learned while working his way into Garza's small circle; the drug lord was suspicious of everyone and liked to keep tabs on his underlings without them knowing. Just one of the many reasons he had to pretend he'd never met Isabella before. His background cover would not have put him in contact with the anthropologist.

Satisfied there wasn't a listening or tracking device in his vehicle, Tino pulled a Glock from under the seat and slid the magazine out. The ingenuity of the DEA's geek squad lifted his lips in a sardonic smile. If any of Garza's men searched his rig, all they'd find would be his older model Glock. He plucked the last bullet from the magazine and popped the ear bud out of the casing. Placing the small microphone and receiver in his ear, he placed the gun on the seat beside him and turned the vehicle back onto the road. In this upper-scale neighborhood his dark blue Tahoe wasn't unusual.

"Rico, do you have an eye on the Alvarez brothers?" Tino kept his SUV pointed south, heading toward the borough in Mexico City where only the desperate lived. His skin crawled every time he entered this area. It reminded him of his early years in the U.S. after his father secreted the family out of Venezuela. They'd lived in slums until his father acquired a U.S. teaching certificate and lifted them back up into the comforts a professorship offered them.

"*Sí*, they are conducting business at the Cantina de Los Amigos. Why?"

"Garza ordered me to bring them in."

Rico's soft whistle and curse loosened the bunched muscles in Tino's shoulders. "What *mano*? Are you worried I cannot bring them in?"

"You are as crazy as Garza. The last time Garza sent *three men* to capture those two Garza's men disappeared."

Tino tipped his head side to side, popping his neck. "You forget, I know how to take down my prey."

"I hope you have a lot of tranquilizer darts." The worry in Rico's voice added to the edginess Tino had been ignoring since seeing Isabella. More than his cover could be at stake. Now that the brilliant anthropologist stepped into his mission, he had to keep her alive.

Tino looked into the back seat of his SUV. The case holding his sniper rifle, modified to handle tranquilizer darts, sat in the seat along with a pistol that shot the same darts. When he started his career as a jaguar tagger for the Central and South American governments, he'd never known it would come in handy with his DEA work.

"They have three bodyguards, but the way the two are partying we should be able to lure them outside. Guadelupe and Bess are ready to roll into the cantina and catch Raul and Jorge's eyes." Rico chuckled.

"I thought you said they were conducting business?" Tino hadn't come up against these two before. They had just been picked up on Garza's radar as encroaching on his territory.

"Mano, that *is* how they conduct business. They *pachanga* with their distributors, showing off their product, and close the deal after an orgy of sorts." Rico snorted. "They will be drooling to get Guadelupe and Bess into their party. "

Tino shook his head. He didn't see the Alvarez brothers as competition to Garza if they partied more than they conducted business, but he had orders, and he had to bring the brothers in or risk losing the ground he'd made in gaining Garza's confidence.

"I will wander in myself and check things out. Will the ladies be wearing jewelry?"

"Hear you loud and clear, Tino." Guadelupe's deep sexy voice filled Tino's head.

"I am a block away. Make your move." Tino turned into the alley behind the cantina and parked. The area was empty. A chill chased up his back. Where were the guards? The Alvarez brothers couldn't be so cocky they didn't expect trouble. Not after hijacking a shipment of Garza's product and selling it in his area.

"Why is there no guard in the alley?" he asked Rico.

"You will find him inside the back door. They like to surprise unexpected guests."

That made more sense. "Are there cameras in this alley?"

"Not that we are aware of."

In case there were surveillance cameras pointed at him, Tino leaned between the seats, pulled out a bottle of Cervaza and sat in the driver's seat, pretending to drink. When he finished, he twisted around through the seats again and prepared his rifle and pistol, placing them under the middle seat before locking the vehicle and walking down the alley toward the front of the cantina.

It was four in the afternoon, when most businesses were starting back up after a two hour lunch break. The constant hum of voices from the pedestrians, the drone of engines crowding the street, and gagging exhaust folded around him, dragging him out of the pleasant thoughts of Isabella and into the present unsavory world he now revolved in.

Tino detested the cantinas in the colonias. While he came from a long heritage of male dominance in his culture, he'd acclimated to the American woman who didn't allow herself to be lorded over. The cantinas in the lower-class areas of Mexico City clung to the machismo attitude allowing few women into the establishments and filling the air with too much testosterone for his liking. While the men didn't appreciate their own women in the cantinas, they welcomed the half-dressed women who wanted to party for a small token. The air reeked of musky floral perfume battling men's spicy musk cologne, pheromones, and fried food. The music of the *trovadores* rattled and stomped in his head like a bad headache.

"You would think they could attract better musicians," Rico said in his ear.

Tino snorted. "Sí, their squalling is irritating."

Rico laughed. "Do you see the girls?"

Tino worked his way to the bar, ordered a Cervaza and peered around the establishment, searching each booth along the wall. He found Bess chatting with a group of men in a corner booth.

"You did not tell me Bess was wearing a flower garden."

Rico barked laughter, causing Tino to flinch. "It made her easy to find, no?"

"I am going to walk by so they know I have arrived and see what the Alvarez brothers have for back up." Tino picked up his glass and wandered through the middle of the room, stopping now and then to make eye contact and nod to the other patrons. He wanted to appear a local rather than an outsider.

A smiling, curvaceous woman in a short tight skirt and see-through blouse moved toward him. Not that long ago he would have easily played along with her, but no longer. His body and heart had been taken hostage by a tall, thin doctor of anthropology who could set him on fire with one look.

Tino's stomach churned when the woman grasped his hand and encouraged him to follow her to a booth. The only woman he wanted to spend time with in a dark corner was in Garza's compound. His stomach clenched. Whatever Isabella was up to, he hoped like hell she didn't get herself killed in the process.

Chapter Two

Isabella Mumphrey followed the muscled Cezar into the tall, well-lit atrium of Paolo Garza's home. Tino wanted Garza and had left her bed after a call about this man. When she'd been approached by Garza to visit his Aztec collection, she hadn't hesitated. Getting close to Garza might give her a glimpse of Tino. She scanned the hacienda, taking in the expertly displayed Mesoamerican artifacts. The reason she'd been invited.

"*Profesora* Mumphrey, I am happy you accepted my invitation." Paolo Garza walked down the winding staircase on her left, his hand extended in welcome. A dark mustache sprinkled with gray hovered above a toothy smile. His dark eyes crinkled at the edges with good humor.

How could this man be as violent as Tino suggested?

"Señor Garza, your invitation was too intriguing to turn down." She placed her hand in his warm one and was surprised by the gentle, yet firm, grip.

His laugh boomed through the tall atrium, echoing down the hallway. "What could be intriguing about my desire to show you my treasures?"

"One person's treasure could be junk to another person. That's why I'm intrigued. I've been told by many at the Museo Nacional de Antropología e Hisotria that you have an excellent collection of Aztec and Teotihuacán artifacts." Isabella spun slowly taking in the display cases and carvings on pedestals. "I don't believe I'll be disappointed by your tour from what I've seen so far."

He motioned to the nearest display case. He smiled but no warmth softened his eyes. Isabella walked over and studied the glassed-in collection of obsidian blades. "By the rough design and chipped edges, I'd guess these to be Teotihuacán tools."

"¡*Símon*! You are indeed as intelligent as I have been told." Señor Garza clapped his hands and then motioned to the large stone carving to their right. "And this was also found near the obsidian tips. What do you make of this?"

Isabella's hands itched to touch the smooth rock and dip her fingers into the rough, carved lines of a jaguar. Instead of touching with her fingertips, her gaze followed every etched line and rounded obtrusion. "I would say this was formed into the jaguar by a skilled Aztec artist. By the detail and reverence paid the stone I would think it was a gift to a jaguar warrior." The two words, jaguar and warrior, strung together brought up images of Tino. He would have been in the elite jaguar troops of the Aztec. No doubt, one of the most revered warriors.

"You are impressive, profesora." The tone in which Garza complimented her sent Isabella's senses shoving her thoughts of Tino to the side and peering at the man standing next to her. His dark brown eyes assessed her like a scientist studied an amoeba under a microscope. What was he searching for? "You view my stone not as a stone but of the history it has seen."

How had he recognized her gift so quickly when her mentor, Dr. Virgil Martin, who she and Tino thwarted in Guatemala, had been blind to her affinity to see the history in the artifacts and carvings she deciphered? Having the drug lord read her so easily set her nerves to jangling.

Composing herself, she forced a cheerful smile and waved a hand. "I am, after all, part Native American and believe that is why I've been drawn to study all Native American people."

"Interesting. Are you North, Central, or South American?"

Again, his scrutiny sent bubbles of wariness skittering under her skin.

"North. My mother is a quarter Hopi. My thesis is a proclamation that my ancestors at one time ventured down here and over to the Mayans to trade and perhaps intermarried. My department is in the process of acquiring funding to test DNA of all the southern U.S. tribes with that of the Central American peoples." Isabella moved to the next artifact on display, training her interest on the rock slab with a faded red depiction of a sacrifice.

"This is my favorite in this collection." Garza stepped forward, his attention on the image.

Isabella couldn't ignore the chill that arced through her body, causing her to gasp. Six months ago, she'd lain on a rock altar as her mentor tried to use her for a sacrifice. If not for Tino…She swallowed, forcing the panic crawling up her throat to remain trapped and gnawing in her stomach.

Garza placed a hand on her arm and peered into her face, more inquisitive than caring. "Are you all right?"

"Sí, I…" Did she dare reveal any of her past experience with the devil? Not a good idea. "No matter how many times I see depictions of sacrifice it unsettles me." Avoiding his gaze, she continued to stare at the image. "I believe they affect me so because an ancestor was sacrificed."

The hand still resting on her arm squeezed briefly and released her.

"I see. You are a very perceptive young woman. I think you and my wife, Karyme would enjoy visiting."

"Is she here?" Isabella found it hard to fathom a man who murdered and sold drugs would be married or have a family. But she knew from researching Garza, he had three daughters whom he doted on.

"She and my daughters will be arriving this weekend. How long will you be in our city?" Garza led the way into a room large enough to be called a ballroom. All around the edges were cases, stones, and carvings.

"Oh my!" She'd never witnessed so many artifacts in one place other than in a museum. Her gaze slowly swept the room cataloging the items. "Have all of these been authenticated and logged?" Two carvings she'd not seen in any books or museums caught her attention. She moved across the room not waiting for an invitation or an answer.

A deep chuckle sounded close behind her as she studied the first stone. "I believe I have found someone even more loco over my ancestor's history than my wife and myself."

"Where did these two come from? I've never seen anything like them before." Her hands burned to reach out and touch the stone and follow the chiseled lines to trace the image of what appeared to be an earlier representation of Mixcoatl, a god of war and hunting, believed to originate in the Northern Chihimeca groups who she believed could have been part of her ancestors.

"No, they are recent acquisitions." His softly spoken words drew Isabella's attention from the stone to the man. "You are a remarkable young woman that you could pick out this stone from all the others in the room and know it is something exceptional." He again studied her, making her uncomfortable, much as she had all through school when teachers realized her intelligence was beyond their knowledge and the other students considered her a freak.

He tapped an index finger against his lips and continued studying her, making her even more nervous. "You have a gift. One I wish to use." He turned her from the stone and started back across the room.

That's when she noticed Cezar standing inside the door. When he'd escorted her to Garza's home, he'd said little but sent her leering smiles when he'd caught her studying him. He was a few inches taller and broader than Tino with the same Ladino facial features. Only where Tino was smooth-skinned with classic contours to his face and dark smoldering eyes, Cezar had a pock-marked face, scar below one ear, and dark angry eyes.

"Cezar, tell Anarosa to prepare refreshments for myself and my guest." Garza placed a hand on Isabella's back, ushering her out of the room, back into the atrium, and around the staircase to what appeared to be a library.

"Profesora Isabella, I have a proposition for you." Señor Graza closed the library door locking them in and turned toward her. The glint of greed in his eyes gave Isabella her first glimpse of the man Tino sought to bring down.

Chapter Three

Extracting himself from the under-clothed, over-painted woman, Tino sauntered out the front of the cantina. He casually walked to the back of the building and climb in his SUV. The tranquilizer rifle and pistol rested on the window frame of his vehicle when Guadelupe and Bess walked out the back of the cantina with Raul and Jorge. Two body guards followed.

"Now," he whispered and shot the darts into the Alvarez brothers. Bess and Guadelupe sprayed something in the body guards' faces and whacked their purses into the men's heads dropping them like boulders.

"Well done, ladies." Tino jumped out of his SUV and loaded the brothers into the back seat, not bothering to make them comfortable. He hopped into the driver's seat, shoved the vehicle into gear, and drove a respectable speed through residential areas to avoid traffic jams and being spotted by any of Raul or Jorge's men. He stopped before entering the upscale residential area and replaced the ear bud in the Glock and the tranquilizer rifle and pistol in the case, sliding it under the middle seat.

At Garza's gate, he buzzed.

"Did you get the packages?" Cezar asked.

The urgent tone in his voice brought a triumphant smile to Tino's lips. If he hadn't brought the Alvarez brothers in, Cezar would have been sent to collect the rivals.

"Sí, the packages are ready to be delivered," Tino responded, peering at the still sleeping men in his back seat.

The gate swung open, and Tino drove the SUV into the open bay of the garage. Cezar stood at the front of the garage along with two more of Garza's men. The frown on Garza's righthand man sent Tino's senses tingling.

"How did you bring these two in when three men could not?"

Cezar's distrust was warranted. Tino wanted his job. He needed Cezar's access to Garza's office. It was the only way he could acquire the information he needed to bring down Garza's cartel and seek his revenge. But, so far, both Garza and Cezar kept him on a need to know basis while he proved his loyalty.

"Sometimes it is easier to sneak in among your prey alone than have the whole pack attack." Tino stepped out of the vehicle and opened the door to the middle seat. The two men in the seat flopped over one another like rag dolls.

"Are they dead? *Jefe* does not want them dead." Cezar snapped his fingers and the other two Garza thugs reached in and dragged out Raul.

"The boss will find them very much alive. I tranquilized them." Tino reached in, hauling Jorge out and flopping him over his shoulder. Cezar led the way out of the garage and into the hallway leading to Garza's office. Tino followed sniffing the aroma of spicy stewed meat and fresh baked bread wafting from the kitchen down the hall. His stomach rumbled. He hadn't eaten since the morning meal.

The double office doors opened, revealing no one in the room. Where was Garza? He'd expected the man to be waiting at his desk for the Alvarez brothers. Had he been detained all this time by Isabella? Could she still be here?

He plopped Jorge on the couch next to his brother and stood back his arms crossed, waiting to see what would happen next.

Garza strode into the room. His gaze took in the sleeping men and then studied Tino. "I see you have succeeded where others have failed."

The disbelief in his voice tingled the hair on Tino's neck.

"Sí. You sent me to bring these men to you. I have done as you requested." More information would be necessary to earn the man's trust. "They were partying. I paid two *prostitutas* to party with them and bring them out the back of the cantina." He raised his arms as if pointing a rifle at the two men. "Then I shot them with a tranquilizer."

Garza's eyes narrowed. "What of the body guards?"

Tino shrugged. "They were not a problem."

Garza tipped his head toward the door. "I have a guest who is ready to leave. Take her back to her hotel and then return."

Tino forced his facial muscles to remain impassive as his heart raced in his chest. The guest had to be Isabella. She was smart enough to not show she knew him. But could their attraction be hidden? As much as he anticipated seeing her again, he feared their relationship could bring her harm.

"Where is this person?"

"Waiting in the atrium." Garza moved to his desk chair, the conversation finished.

Tino walked slow and assured out the office door. Cezar closed the doors behind him. Tino stood a moment, but knew he'd hear nothing. He'd tried to listen in on meetings through the door before, but they were too solid to allow sound. Preparing for his meeting with Isabella, he blew out air and straightened his shoulders before striding down the hall to the atrium.

His body hummed at the sight of Isabella studying a case of small trinkets. She leaned slightly forward over the case. The pink sweater and tan skirt she wore gave her the appearance of a school girl; not a learned doctor of anthropology.

He cleared his throat and she straightened.

"Señorita, I am to escort you back to your hotel," he said, keeping his voice as neutral as possible.

Isabella's heart fluttered and her eyes widened at the voice she remembered so well. The words had been uttered in a flat tone. She slowly turned to the man she owed her life and gave her heart. The only indication he was excited to see her was the slight brightening of his eyes.

"What happened to my earlier escort?" She could pretend they didn't know one another. After all, she'd have him all to herself on the ride back to the hostel.

"He has been detained. I was instructed to return you to the hotel." He motioned to the front entrance.

When she turned and headed to the doors, he moved, as swift and gracefully as she remembered, to open the door for her. They walked side by side to a dark SUV sitting in the circular drive.

Tino opened the passenger door for her but didn't say a word. She followed his lead, climbing in and holding her questions. He rounded the front of the vehicle and slid into the driver's seat. His hand went straight to the ignition, and his face remained forward as they drove out the wrought iron gates.

"I—"

He cut her off with a shake of his head. Her heart now pounded in her throat. Why was he being so distant? Was the vehicle under surveillance?

"Where are you staying, señorita?" he asked, watching the street.

"The Hostel Catedral."

His gaze landed on her then. "Is it wise señorita to stay in a hostel?"

"It's where most of the archeology students stay while working at Templo Mayor."

"You are here then to help at the archeological site?"

The question in his sentence tickled her. He was fishing for why she was here without coming out and asking.

"Sí. I am here to write a paper on the people who built and lived at Templo Mayor."

Tino pulled the vehicle over once they were out of the elite residential area. He shook his head slightly and reached in the back seat for a backpack. He pulled out one of the latest devices for detecting surveillance equipment and swept it around the interior of the car, then stepped out and disappeared. She assumed he swept the undercarriage of the vehicle as well.

He slipped back in the driver's seat, returned the detector to his backpack, and grasped the back of her neck, dragging her lips to his.

She'd missed his kisses and virility. In the six months since they'd last been together, she'd resigned herself to the fact the gorgeous Venezuelan would find a more desirable woman and never think about her again. The body-humming, mind-scattering kiss dissolved all those fears.

He eased back, but his hand remained on her neck. "*Querida,* I have missed you. But it is not safe for you here."

"I know why you're here, and what I'm doing is much safer than what you're doing." Her heart thumped in her chest. Their one discussion on the phone five months ago had been brief. All she'd had time to ask was if he was safe and tell him she missed him. He didn't know she was the newest member of the Worldwide Intelligence Agency, and her assignment was to find out how artifacts were being spirited away from Templo Mayor after being logged and housed in the National Museum of Anthropology. She'd bet her survival vest the two pieces she saw in Señor Garza's collection were part of the missing items.

He narrowed his eyes and peered into hers. "What are you not saying?"

She huffed out a breath. He'd always been able to read her. "Can we go somewhere and eat and talk?" Isabella leaned forward placing a chaste kiss on his lips when she really wanted to drag him into the backseat and see if he'd learned any new tricks.

Tino released her neck and straightened his body behind the steering wheel. "Garza told me to deliver you and return. He might get suspicious if I take too long." His brown eyes darkened and his face tensed with anger. "If he realizes we know one another and care for one another, we are both in danger." His gaze softened. "I would rather keep my distance than have harm come to you." He grasped her hand in his. "I do not know why you were at his home, but promise me you will stay away. I cannot compromise my position by worrying about you. I am too close to my goal."

Isabella didn't like this Tino. The one who would die to bring about revenge for his family's deaths. The hatred and rage he possessed when talking about Garza scared her.

She put her free hand over his on her arm and squeezed. "I'm not here to jeopardize your mission. I've been sent here to find the artifacts missing from Templo Mayor." She held her breath as her words sunk in.

"Sent here to find missing artifacts? As in stolen?" He stared at her and cursed. "A doctor of anthropology does not chase stolen artifacts. What have you done?"

The dread lining his eyes and drooping the sides of his mouth, tugged at Isabella's conscience. She'd made her hasty decision to join her parents' organization without consulting the one person whose love and understanding she valued most.

"I joined WIA six months ago. Right after you made love to me and left me lying in a bed in Guatemala."

Rage, regret, panic swept across his handsome face as his hand gripped her arm then released and dropped to the console between the seats. "You put yourself in danger to punish me for leaving you?"

"No! This isn't to punish you. Heaven's no! I wanted to get closer to my parents. I'd hoped by becoming a member they would include me more in their lives and we'd have something in common." A seductive smile slid into place. "It also gives me access to areas where you are working."

"*Carajo*! For a brilliant woman this is the dumbest thing you could have done." He grasped her shoulders and held her face inches from his. "You have made yourself a target of every villain the agency has ever brought to justice and made my efforts to keep you a secret and safe that much more difficult."

Fear trickled down her back and sent her body trembling. Not once in the months of training or even when her father handed her this mission did she consider putting herself in more danger or more specifically, Tino, in more danger.

"Ezzabella." Tino folded her into his arms and held her to his hard, familiar chest. "Your impulsiveness will one day bring you harm. You should have waited until we could talk before you uprooted our life."

She liked the sound of "our life." It gave her hope that he would forgive her. "So much happened so fast. You took off and all I could think of was discovering more about my parents. Joining the WIA seemed like the best way to do that and perhaps see you more often."

He set her back in her seat and placed his hands on the steering wheel. "I must return you to the hostel and get back." He pulled onto the street. She watched his brow furrow as his eyes search all the mirrors and the roads intersecting with the one they drove on. Her news had heightened his surveillance.

A deep remorseful exhale slipped through her lips as she shoved her glasses up her nose. Her disclosure now had Tino more paranoid. "Will I see you other than from afar?"

His gaze slid to her face. Regret dulled his eyes. "I do not know. It all depends on what comes of the situation I put into play this afternoon." He returned his attention to driving as the Cathedral came into view. "You found something that links Garza with your mission."

The flatness of his words didn't alleviate the lump of dread setting in her stomach like a boulder.

"I won't know for certain until I go over the logs of the items found in the temple. But he had two carvings I've never seen and they fit the period of the missing artifacts." She cleared her throat as her heart pounded against her ribs. What she was about to say was only going to upset him more.

"Señor Garza invited me to a party he's hosting this Saturday for his wife. He believes she and I will hit it off."

Tino cursed again and slammed a hand against the steering wheel. "He is not doing this for his wife. He is doing it to watch you. Did you show an interest in the statues you believe to be stolen?"

She flinched and nodded. "Yes. They attracted my attention immediately. I didn't go to his house to find the artifacts. He is a huge benefactor of the museum, and the director insisted I should see Garza's collection."

Tino peered at her. "How long have you been in Mexico City?"

She knew that look. He was back in protector mode. "Two weeks. I haven't been looking for you. No one can connect us. I promise. Are you going by Tino Kostas here?"

"No, Tino Rodriguez. Why did you go to Garza's compound today?"

"This afternoon when I was helping a local anthropologist decipher a hieroglyph, Cezar arrived saying he was to bring me to señor Garza for a tour of his collection."

"He had two weeks to send out feelers to find out all he could about you. Now, he is keeping you close because of something he learned." Tino ran a hand over his face. "I do not like this."

It didn't occur to her Garza was checking her out until their conversation in the library. That transaction she'd keep to herself. If Tino knew Garza had more or less ordered her to return to his house next week and run tests on his carvings, Tino would find a way to stop her visits.

Chapter Four

As Isabella slid out of the vehicle in front of the Hostel Catedral, Tino remained in the SUV. He would have preferred to deliver her to the airport and place her on a plane back to Arizona. But knowing her as well as he did, she would have gone kicking and screaming and then found a way to get back to Garza faster than he did. When her mind was set on accomplishing something there was no stopping her. In this case a major flaw. Now, he not only had to bring Garza down, but he would also have to keep Isabella safe in the process. No easy task with her nosing around Garza's ill-gotten treasures.

"I promise to treat you like all the other macho pig men in Mexico City when I see you at Garza's." Her light tone wasn't reflected in her worried expression and probing gaze as she leaned in the window.

"I will have a phone delivered to you with my number installed. Use the name Juanita when you call in case someone else answers. I want to know everything you find and anyone who you think is suspicious." He peered into her eyes. His gut ached with regret. If he failed at keeping her safe, he might as well let Garza know he was a spy. "Promise me you will keep me informed, so we do not mess up each other's mission or endanger one another."

Her gaze remained locked with his as she nodded. "I promise."

He forced his downturned lips and thoughts into a smile. "I will find a way to be with you." He did want to spend time with her, but her safety overrode his desires.

"You promise?" The waver in her voice tugged at his heart.

"Sí. I will find a way to hold you."

"I'll wait for your call." She leaned away from the vehicle.

Tino put the Tahoe in gear and drove away, watching her stand on the sidewalk until the SUV was swallowed up in the chaotic traffic. He slammed the steering wheel with the palm of his hand and cursed.

Why did Isabella have to join the WIA? If he ever saw her father again, he would gladly beat the crap out of him. His poor parenting had brought about all of Isabella's poor choices in life. From the graduate student who crushed her tender heart to the mentor who used her for his own gain. A father should protect his daughter from such harm. And now, rather than tell her she could not join WIA, he sent her on a mission to a city where drug violence is at an all-time high.

¡Coño! Sí, if her father was within reach, he would indeed show him what he felt about the man's parenting.

His phone buzzed in his pocket. Staring at the slow-moving traffic, he pulled it out and looked at the number. Garza.

"¿Sí?"

"Why have you not returned?" Garza's voice as always held authority and a trace of condemnation.

"The traffic on Reforma is crawling." He craned his neck. "There has been an accident."

"There are more roads in the city. Get back here quickly. You must take the garbage away."

The phone clicked off and Tino grit his teeth. He hated taking orders from Garza. He'd rather slit the man's throat the next time he was alone with him but that would only take down the man, not the operation. His goal was the man; his job was to take down the operation. Once he had the records DEA needed, he would avenge his family and take Isabella away from this life of pretend and violence.

~*~

Isabella hurried into her private room in the hostel and changed into jeans and a T-shirt. After seeing señor Garza's collection and the two interesting figures, she wanted to check the logged in artifacts from Templo Mayor. A tingle at the base of her neck told her he had the missing artifacts. Not the ones on display. She had no doubt those were legitimate. A benefactor of the museum would not have stolen items on display in his home and then invite her over. But he was suspicious of her or he would not have set her up to come to his home so frequently where he could keep an eye on her. His demeanor while questioning her in the library and then asking for her assistance…that had been calculated and not a spur of the moment idea as he tried to make it look.

Señor Garza was up to something more than drug trafficking. And it, too, was illegal.

She slipped her arms into her survival vest. The many pocketed fishing vest held every item needed to get out of any situation. She may not be exploring a jungle or cave, but knowing her tin of survival items and first aid kit were handy made her feel less vulnerable. And keeping her passport, money, and visa on her, felt safer. The vest and all its contents had been folded in her tote bag when she'd visited the drug lord. One never knew when disaster might strike.

Isabella exited the hostel. The exhaust fumes from the bumper to bumper traffic made her sneeze and wish for a scarf to cover her nose and mouth. How could people live every day of their life in this toxic air? She tried to take small breaths as she walked down Argentina Street and crossed, entering the sacred grounds of Templo Mayor. She strode toward the museum intent on checking the archeology logs for the list of artifacts found at the same time as the two carvings in señor Garza's home. Tourists and employees moved in unison toward the secured area that led to the underground archeological dig. What could be of interest there?

Shifting her direction, she nudged her way through the crowd, picking up snippets of conversation about the possibility they finally found Ahuitzotl's resting place. Adrenaline pumped through her body. The quest to find the most feared Aztec ruler's burial spot had been going on since the religious site was unearthed in 1978.

She pulled out her temporary "Visiting Specialist I.D." and flashed it toward the guard at the opening. He allowed her entrance and the crowd behind her collectively groaned. There were perks to being an anthropologist studying Native American people.

The audience's dismay was real. The Mesoamerican people took great interest and were more connected with their ancestors than the Native Americans in North America. Through her studies she'd come to the conclusion it was because their heritage was not ripped from them as it had been from their North American cousins.

The cool air wafted around her as she followed the makeshift wooden stairs downward under the streets and buildings. In specific areas, the tunnel widened into stone chambers and rooms where squares of dirt had been excavated, leaving holes in the sides of the tunnel and the floor. The electrical lighting in the passage made it easy to avoid any dangers. If the power went out, she had her vest equipped with an LED flashlight, matches, and a candle which would allow her to still maneuver in the dark.

Excited voices drifted down the tunnel toward her. How had those on the surface known this excitement was brewing down here? She quickly covered the distance and stood inside the most recently dug chamber. The group huddled around an area and the flash of a camera continued every thirty seconds.

She walked up behind the man who appeared to be in charge. He pointed toward a recently dug rectangular hole at his feet and discussed the possibilities of what they'd found.

"This resembles the canine remains found several years ago. But notice there are more bells and the collar appears to be made of jade and obsidian."

Isabella stared down into the carefully dug area and peered at the skeleton of what looked like a dog and, indeed, there were gold bells about the feet and jade and obsidian at the beast's neck. It was common knowledge dogs—pets—were buried with the rulers.

"Does this mean you've found Ahuitzotl's burial site?" she asked, shifting her gaze to the man she'd been introduced to as Professor Lopez when she arrived.

The man's dark eyes behind his wire rim glasses sparkled. "With this discovery, we could be getting closer to Ahuitzotl." The man's excitement crackled in the air. The workers were all grinning as one handed a small whisk broom to the professor. He dropped to his belly and began gently brushing the dirt from the remains. The camera flashed again.

Isabella wanted to lie beside the man and brush away the centuries of dirt and feel the connection with the ancient world. Being new to the site and seeing the zeal in the other workers eyes, she knew that would be stepping on too many toes. As much as she wanted to remain and watch the hours of painstaking work it took to uncover the past, she had a mission.

Knowing her congratulations would go unheard, she dragged her mind back to checking out the archeological logs. On the return trip through the catacomb of tunnels and chambers, her mind searched through the photos and drawings she'd witnessed of other Aztec burial sites. The belief Templo Mayor was the center of the human sacrifices to the gods sent a chill down her spine. Having known the fear a sacrificial victim feels, gave her an affinity with all those who had died on the altars and steps of this temple.

She left the cold damp underground and noted the long shadows. It would soon be dark. Even though the director gave her clearance to be in the museum any time of the night or day, she'd been warned to not be out and about after dark. The museum was only a short distance from the hostel… She needed evidence to tie señor Garza to the missing artifacts by Saturday so she knew what to look for when she returned at his invitation to meet his wife. That only gave her tonight, tomorrow, and tomorrow night to go through all the logs.

Ignoring the little voice in the back of her mind telling her to go to the hostel, she pulled an energy bar out of her vest and walked toward the museum. The more hours she could get into searching the records, the greater her chance of finding what she needed before Saturday.

~*~

Tino pulled into the alley behind the Cantina de Los Amigos. Two men barged out the back door as he slowed only long enough for Hector, one of Garza's men, to shove the Alvarez brothers out. Tino sped away with Hector cackling in the back.

He resented Garza sending the lowlife Hector along to return the brothers. *Sí,* the brothers were awake and would have made driving and keeping them from killing him a problem had he done the task alone, but he wanted to meet with Rico and set his plans in motion for Isabella.

Hector squeezed between the front seats to plant his butt in the passenger seat. "*Amigo,* I could use a drink after that fun."

"*Jefe* will want us to return." He refused to carouse with this low man on Garza's chain of underlings. Now if Cezar had offered, he would have given in. That man had the knowledge of the information DEA needed.

"Jefe won't know. We will only stop for one," Hector said with more bravado than his posture exuded.

"You are an idiot if you think Garza will not find out." Tino shook his head at the other's stupidity. He'd witnessed a car following them after leaving the compound. He knew it wasn't DEA so it had to be Cezar making sure they had a clean drop. That same vehicle was five cars back.

Hector pulled his gun out of a shiny new shoulder holster and pointed it at Tino. "Do not call me an idiot."

Tino sneered at the man. "You are only proving you are by pulling a gun on me while I am driving. If you shoot me, you will end up in an accident and be caught for shooting me."

The man glanced at the traffic and waved the gun. "Then pull over or I will just shoot your hand."

¡Coño! Could there be any narco dumber than this one?

"How about I pull over and let Cezar who is three cars back come see what you are doing?" Tino jerked the car over into the bus lane and stomped on the brakes.

"Cezar is behind us?" Hector slammed his hands on the dash as he squinted into the rearview mirror.

Tino used the distraction to take away the gun and yank the vehicle back into the stream of traffic before Cezar could get through the lanes and see what happened.

"He has been following us ever since we dropped the brothers. Do you want to give him a reason to kill you?" Tino forced a friendly tone to show he cared about the man when he would have rather turned him over to Rico.

"You knew he was following us and did not tell me?" The red on Hector's face shone bright as the streetlights illuminated his round face.

"What would you have done had I told you?" Tino ignored the man's rage and navigated out of the traffic to hurry their return to the compound.

Hector sputtered and sniffed.

That's what he thought. The narco wasn't so brave when it came to Cezar and Garza. If he was to get Cezar's job, he needed to be just as feared. He cranked on the steering wheel, pulling over in a dark neighborhood. "Get out!" Tino waved his hand.

"Get out?" Hector's eyebrows slanted together above his nose.

"Sí. Get out. You pulled a gun on me. I do not work with people I do not trust. Out!" He pointed Hector's gun at him.

The man sneered. "Cezar will pick me up." He opened the door.

Tino shoved him and hit the accelerator. He'd lost Cezar several blocks ago. Hector was on his own to get back to the compound. For the first time in days, mirth slipped through his lips in a gut tightening laugh. The man was an imbecile, and it made Tino wonder about the men Garza surrounded himself with. How had he become such a feared drug lord when he had idiots around him?

He had fifteen minutes before he'd be back at the compound. He needed to make the most of them. Tino flipped open his phone and dialed Rico.

"Mano, deliver a phone with tracking to Doctor Isabella Mumphrey at Hostel de Catedral with my number loaded on it. Also put your number as her backup." He waited for the onslaught of questions.

Rico whistled. "You know a doctor? Mano, I thought you only hung out with lowlife drug dealers."

Pride swelled Tino's chest knowing he had the affections of the brilliant anthropologist, but he wasn't going to let Rico know any more than was necessary.

"This doesn't go beyond me and you. ¿Comprende?"

"Sí."

"She is WIA and knows I am DEA. Garza has asked her to his home to meet his wife day after tomorrow. She will work with us as long as it does not undermine her mission." That was all Rico would get. To tell him their connection would make them both vulnerable. He'd known DEA to use anyone they felt would work toward their end.

"Why keep this between us?" Rico was a loner as much as Tino, but he liked to follow protocol.

"Same reason only a handful know my real identity—Garza has spies everywhere."

"Sí. I will deliver the phone tonight, personally."

"Gracias. I am headed back to the compound. They worked the Alvarez brothers over pretty good. I do not think they will be moving into Garza's territory any time soon."

"Good, because word on the street is the Bohu gang intercepted an overland shipment last night. Garza may have more troubles than he realizes."

"I do not understand, how do these gangs know where to intercept shipments and we cannot find them to intercept first?" Frustration tapped at his temples. Six months of infiltrating the Garza organization and all they had to show for it was himself and one other DEA agent on the other end of Garza's operation and yet neither one had been able to find out the shipments. That meant someone close to Garza was leaking the information. Cezar. If he could prove it, he would get the second in command's job and finish the job of taking down the drug lord.

Chapter Five

Isabella uncurled and rolled her shoulders before removing her glasses and rubbing her eyes. She'd examined two ledgers of artifacts extracted from Templo Mayor. Five more volumes stood on the end of the table in the inventory room in the basement of the museum. Her stomach rumbled and she looked at her watch. *One*. Morning would come too fast.

Getting back to the hostel, finding something to eat, and sleeping were warranted with the way her body and eyes felt. The rest of the books could wait until morning. She wanted clear evidence of the missing items before Saturday. Once she determined Garza stole the artifacts, she'd tell Tino and then the director.

She stood, stretched her arms above her head, and turned to leave. A man stood in the shadows of a bookcase. Her heart thumped two hard beats as she swallowed a startled gasp. To show fear would give him the advantage. How had he entered without her hearing? Easy, she was so absorbed in the findings she'd blocked out all else. I'll have to work on staying alert at all times.

Slowing her breathing and studying the man who'd yet to move, she readied her stance for evasive actions. Years of taekwondo with the addition of her WIA training had her prepared for an attack.

The man walked out of the shadow and as soon as she witnessed his movements her heart raced not of fear but of anticipation.

"How did you find me here?" She stepped forward and welcomed the arms that wrapped around her.

"When Rico said you were not in your room at the hostel and he waited for you for several hours, I knew you would be researching." Tino's warm breath swept across the top of her head. He sighed and raised her chin. "I have wished for you in my arms every day since I walked out of that hotel room."

His mouth lowered to hers, and her body responded as it always did to his kisses. Her mind shut down to everything but the wonderful sensations of his lips and their bodies molded together. Unhurried, he eased out of the deep kiss, placing wet, gentle kisses on her eyelids, nose and forehead. Tino always made her feel cherished.

"How did you get in? The museum is locked." She didn't want to ever leave his arms but they both had jobs to do.

"There are many ways to enter a building such as this." He left an arm around her waist and drew her toward the door as her stomach growled once again.

Tino chuckled. "You still have an insatiable appetite I see." He led her down the hall toward the back of the museum.

"We can go out the front door." She stopped their forward momentum.

"You can go out the front as that is the way you came in and the watchman knows, but I came in this way and it is the way I must go out." He kissed her temple. "And this time of night I prefer you stay with me."

"What about the guard? Won't he find it odd he didn't see me leave?"

"He will think you left while he was on a break. Come. I will find you food, and we can catch up." Tino moved her up a set of steps and opened a door that was ground level without setting off an alarm.

They walked arm in arm down the street. Isabella enjoyed the coolness of the night but took small breaths as her lungs choked on the exhaust fumes hanging in the air. For the late hour, the street was full of cars and the sidewalks, while not as crowded as earlier, still bustled with pedestrians.

"Where do you plan to find me something to eat at this time of night?" She tucked her body closer to his and felt the shoulder holster under his jacket.

"Just up the street is Salón España. They will have food."

His tone was nonchalant, but his body was strung tight under her hand and arm, and his gaze scanned the side streets and watched the traffic and people.

"You think someone is watching us?" She turned her attention to studying all the shadows.

"I snuck out of the compound, but that does not mean someone did not see me. I took precautions on my way to the museum and found no one following me." He shrugged and kissed the top of her head. "In this town it is always a good idea to be vigilant."

Two blocks from Templo Mayor, Tino stopped in front of a loud but unpretentious salón. The noise seeping out into the street with the boisterous bodies consisted of voices more than music.

"This place is world renown for their many types of tequila." Tino placed a hand at her back, maneuvering them both into the busy establishment.

"But I need food not alcohol," Isabella said over her shoulder.

"Sí, they also have free food with the drink and inexpensive menu items." Tino said in her ear as he moved her toward an open spot near a tall table in the back of the room.

The laughter and good humor was deafening. But the mood couldn't help but tickle her lips into a grin and tap her toes to the undertone of music vying to be heard over the drinkers.

"Stay here and I will get the drinks and food." Tino hauled her toward him with a hand on the back of her neck and kissed her senseless before strutting toward the bar.

Shaking her head to clear the sex haze his kiss spun her into, she noticed several women looking her up and down before setting feral looks on Tino. They probably wondered what a man like that could see in the skinny, glasses-wearing, *gringa*. The women were decked out in short skirts, revealing tops, and caked with makeup.

Tino returned, followed by a male bartender carrying a plate full of food.

The young, good-looking man greeted her and settled the platter on the table. "*Disfrute de botanas.*"

"Gracias." She returned a warm smile to the man and picked up what appeared to be a tacquito. One bite and her taste buds exploded with glee.

Tino sat watching Isabella eat all but the four foods he sampled from the platter. He had frequented this place several times in the past six months and knew the food to be delicious. It was near Templo Mayor, a place that only fascinated him because he could sit in the plaza and feel close to the woman sitting across from him. He had been lured to the ancient Aztec ruins knowing it would hold an allure to the anthropologist he had fallen hard for in a short amount of time.

"I've dreamed of seeing your handsome face and talented lips again."

Isabella's soft-spoken comment warmed the area of his heart that held hope he would one day have a normal life.

"As I have dreamed of you." He picked up one of her hands, fiddling with her fingers. "We are an odd couple."

"Yes." She nodded her head toward a table of women watching them closely and not hiding their disapproval. "They don't like that such a fine Latino specimen is making time with a bookworm gringa."

"They can disapprove all they want. I have eyes only for you, and I want you to remember that." He rolled her hand and kissed her soft palm.

Her eyes sparkled and burned with the desire he had been holding at bay ever since watching her walk into Garza's home.

"Come. I need to return you to the hostel and sneak back into the compound." He tugged her to her feet and wrapped an arm around her. The feel of her tucked against his body burned in his mind. Her thin, athletic body was so different from his past conquests but fit his in every way perfectly. As did her brilliant mind and accepting heart.

They stepped out the door. His gaze swept the curb and his breath sucked out of his body as his chest squeezed in fear for Isabella.

The Alvarez brothers sat in a car parked on the street corner toward the hostel. Their bandaged heads and bruised faces proved the afternoon visit to Garza was fresh in their minds. They didn't know he was the one who kidnapped them, but they knew he delivered them back to the cantina.

He swung Isabella around and whispered, "We need to take the long way back to the hostel."

"Why?"

"There are two men on the corner that met with Garza's anger today, and they know me as one of his men." He propelled her quickly down the street to the end of the block and turned right. He didn't like the darker street, but it was better to chance walking here than in front of the Alvarez brothers.

He wanted to keep her tucked under his arm, but they could move faster hand in hand. He slid his hand down and grasped hers. He didn't need to say a word. She fell in step beside him walking faster. The sounds of the salón faded in the distance as did the obnoxious automotive sounds as they moved away from the more populated Argentina Street toward the museums and churches in the historical district. With less populated streets also came less lighting.

They turned the corner onto Correro Mayor, the street that ran alongside the Templo Mayor plaza. Tino continued his quick pace, not sparing a breath to talk. His right hand rested on the handle of the Glock in his shoulder strap. His left clutched Isabella's fingers.

A car revved its engine and raced down the street. His senses snapped to take in the shadows, the sound, the smell of burning rubber and high-octane fuel. Steadying his heart, he slowed his pace and dropped his hand from his weapon. As the car drew closer, he pulled Isabella into his arms and kissed her with as much passion as he could while eyeing the car moving by them slowly. He grasped her leg, drawing it up to hook her knee around his hip. Give the gawkers in the car an eyeful and they would eventually move on along.

Her damn vest ruined the image of a *chula,* out for a good time, but he knew asking her to go anywhere without it would be the same as asking her to walk naked down the street. Not a bad image. He deepened the kiss and was rewarded with her hands clutching his overly long hair and returning the kiss, stroke for stroke with his tongue.

The gawkers finally rolled on down the street, and he slowly lowered her leg as she moaned and clung to him.

"Querida, you play the part of a vixen well." He kissed the tip of her nose and slid her glasses back in place.

"I have a great leading man," she crooned and nipped his chin.

"Aiii, you are going back to the hostel, pronto. I fear for you on these streets." He grasped her hand and continued down the sidewalk. The sooner she was locked behind her door, the better for the both of them. He'd much rather be locked in with her, but he would be cutting it close as it was to sneak back into the compound without anyone missing him.

Her giggles lightened his heart. Even when they were in danger in Guatemala she'd found ways to lighten his heart. Soon, he would deal with Garza, and they could live in anonymity in the place of her choosing.

They turned the corner onto Moneda, and he spotted someone lurking in the shadows of the Museo Nacional De Las Culturas. "We have company," he whispered and slowed their pace so he had more time to assess the situation. His chivalry battled with his training. He wanted to move Isabella to his right side away from the man lurking, but to do that would hinder his movement to reach for his weapon.

"When I squeeze your hand drop back," he whispered as they moved within twenty meters of the person who wasn't doing a very good job of hiding. The stranger moved when they came abreast of him. Tino squeezed Isabella's hand, released her, and pulled his gun out with one fluid motion.

"We have no quarrel with you move on." His tone was hard and calculating. He'd been hanging out with lowlife men enough to know most were cowards when confronted.

"Were you two comparing notes?" Rico stepped out of the shadows a loco grin spread across his face. "It seems you know the doctor better than you let on."

Isabella stepped to Tino's side, but kept a respectable amount of air between them. "You know this man?"

"Sí. We work together. He was the person who was supposed to bring you a phone, but could not find you and called me."

Rico lifted a brow. "It seems you knew exactly where to look. How is it you know Dr. Mumphrey's habits so well?"

Tino ignored the man's jabs and took Isabella's hand, drawing her closer. "Ezzabella, this is Rico Montoya, the only other person in Mexico City who knows my true identity."

"Pleased to meet you, Doctor." Rico bowed and helped himself to Isabella's hand, kissing her knuckles.

"Do not let this man fool you. He is not half the man I am," Tino said as Isabella slid her hand out of Rico's.

Rico laughed. "Now, I see he has brainwashed you into thinking he is an honorable man. I can tell you, Isabella, he is no saint."

Isabella laughed and leaned her head against Tino's shoulder, warming another section of his heart to her.

"I know he's a bad boy. Haven't you heard good girls are drawn to bad boys?"

Tino choked on his laughter at the sight of Rico's confused expression.

"Why are you spying on me, mano?" Tino checked the street, it was unusually quiet.

"I still have to deliver the phone as you asked." Rico held out the cell phone.

Tino took the device and handed it to Isabella. "This is called a burner phone. It is harder to trace. My number is in there under Julio. You will also see Rico's name. If for some reason you need help and you cannot get me, call Rico."

"He's your backup man?" Isabella asked, slipping the phone into a pocket on her vest.

"Sí, as he has just proven he knows where I am at all times and he has now met you and knows you are to be taken care of." He stared point blank at the other man. Rico was a womanizing, partying fool, but he would keep his distance from Isabella. If things were strained between him and Rico, the mission would be jeopardized and Rico was head of the mission.

Tino looped his arm around Isabella and started to move down the street.

"It would be best if I escorted the doctor the rest of the way and you returned to Garza." The command in Rico's voice was the first time the man had pushed his authority.

Tino slowly spun to face his superior. "You are right. I also do not want to jeopardize Ezzabella." As much as he hated the thought of leaving her in the street with Rico, Tino had no choice when faced with her safety. He held her head in his hands and kissed her, long and deep. Her body sagged against him, and he ended the kiss, holding her by her arms until she stood on her own.

"Call if you need me." He peered into her eyes and saw what he needed to get through the rest of this mission. Her belief in him was what kept them both alive and moving through the cave in Guatemala when she'd rescued him.

"I will." She tapped the pocket holding the phone. "Same goes.

You need me, call."

He nodded and started down the street to find the alley where he'd left the compact car DEA kept parked several blocks from Garza's compound for side trips like this. Now, to get back to the compound without anyone noticing he'd left. Having witnessed Garza's temper, if he had an inkling of a spy in his midst's he'd gun the whole lot down and go out looking for other unscrupulous men ready to cause havoc.

Chapter Six

Isabella walked beside Rico. He was good looking in the classical Mesoamerican way, but he took second to Tino's handsome face. He was her height, with muscles hidden beneath a long-sleeved shirt and khaki pants.

"Have you and Tino worked together before?" she asked. He probably wouldn't answer her since they were DEA, but she wanted to get a feel for the men's relationship. Tino trusted this man with her so that was enough for her to trust him back, but as usual she wanted to dig deeper into the man.

"This is our first assignment together. But he came highly recommended when I was putting my team together." He flashed a mouthful of white teeth. "And you, how do you know Tino?"

It appeared Tino had kept her a secret. Flashes of her father telling them what he said in the cave in Guatemala stayed in the cave, had her smiling and forming a story.

"We met in Guatemala where I was consulting on a Maya excavation." They'd arrived at the entrance to the hostel. "Gracias. Not that I abhor your company, but I hope we don't meet again. Because if we do…"

"It would mean either you or Tino would be in trouble. I understand. *Buenas noches*, Dr. Mumphrey."

Isabella watched him walk down the street before opening the door and entering the hallway. Her room was on the second floor. Climbing the stairs her body began to feel the fatigue of her long night. She walked into her room as the morning sun cast the wall in a pink tint. A few hours of sleep and she had to get back to the museum and sift through the ledgers. Saturday was only a day away, and she didn't have a clue of what to look for when she re-visited señor Garza's home.

~*~

Tino's senses shot electricity through his body. He wasn't alone. Rather than let on he knew someone watched him, he snorted and stretched, slipping his hand under his pillow to grasp his Glock.

He rolled to his feet and placed the muzzle of his weapon against Cezar's chest.

"You are sleeping late, amigo," Cezar said, pushing the weapon to the side.

"Yesterday was busy." Tino grabbed his pants and pulled them on, keeping an eye on Cezar.

"No, you were out late last night. Diego saw you coming back at four." Cezar grabbed the straight back chair, spun it around, and sat, straddling the seat, his arms crossed over the back. He settled his chin on his arms and peered at Tino. "Diego said you looked like a content man." He wiggled a finger. "You know Jefe does not like us consorting with women. It is too easy to talk big and spill important information."

Tino's heart hammered in his chest. To deny he was with a woman would look suspicious but there was no way he wanted them to find out about Isabella.

"Sí, I was tense from all that went down yesterday and the best relaxation is…" He winked. "I picked up a hot *mamácita* at a cantina and we had some fun." Tino leaned closer. "If you want to go with me another time, she has a friend."

Cezar licked his lips, but he slammed his hand down on the chair back. "No! You will not leave the compound again. There is trouble brewing. We need everyone here all the time." He narrowed his eyes. "I do not know how you brought the Alvarez brothers in by yourself yesterday, but I plan to keep an eye on you. If you are that good, we need you here." He rose. "I will not tell Garza about your trip last night, but if you do it again, I will tell him and gladly give his punishment."

Tino nodded, but kept eye contact with Cezar.

"I do not trust you. Hector came limping back last evening saying you made him get out of the car at gun point."

He'd forgotten about the dumb bastard. "Sí. But he did not tell you, he pulled a gun on me first. He wanted me to stop for a drink after we dumped the brothers. I told him we had to get back, and he pulled his weapon. I took the weapon and made him get out so I did not have to deal with his temper." Tino shook his head. "His temper will get him killed soon. Either by one of his own or the enemy."

"True. He is related to Garza. There is nothing I can do to get rid of him. Except kill him."

The matter of fact tone shot Tino's gaze to the man. Cezar would kill Hector the first chance he had. The dullness of his eyes was a dead give-away.

Tino brushed past Cezar to buckle on his shoulder harness and retrieve a shirt from the peg on the wall. While Garza lived in splendor, his help had crude living quarters over the garage.

"Hurry to the kitchen and eat. Jefe wants us all in his office in an hour." Cezar stood, swept a gaze around the small area Tino shared with Diego, and left the room.

Slipping the Glock into his shoulder holster, Tino scanned the room for any evidence there might be hidden surveillance equipment. Tino was sure Diego had been sound asleep when he came home so the *rata* couldn't have told Cezar. Which led him to…Why did Garza's righthand man allow him this indiscretion? It was obvious Cezar wished to have something to hold over his head to make him…what?

Tino hurried down the stairs and into the kitchen. Anarosa, a fifty-something woman with a pleasant smile, robust body, and efficient manner turned from the sink.

"You are late." She pointed with a soapy hand to the counter adjacent to the sink. "The leftovers."

"Gracias." Tino picked up a plate and filled it with fruit, tortillas, and beans. He quickly ate even though he would have rather used this alone time with the cook to chat with her about the household. He placed the plate on the drainboard and left the room, heading toward the office.

Hector and Diego stood beside the door, waiting.

"Why aren't you in there?" he asked, reaching for the knob.

Hector grabbed his wrist. "No! They told us to wait here while they discussed something."

Tino sat back on his heels and scrutinized the other man. Perspiration beaded on Hector's forehead and his upper lip quivered a bit. Was he worried about the incident yesterday? Or, Tino glanced at the man's nervous hands, was he using the drugs? Tino shook his head. Only an idiot would use the drugs they transported. A clear head was needed at all times. Garza would expect that.

The door opened, causing Hector to jump backwards into Tino. He shoved the man forward, knocking him into Cezar. Cezar's nostrils flared, and he glared at Hector who worked at righting himself.

"What are you doing?" Cezar snarled, slapping Hector in the back of the head and propelling him deeper into the office.

Tino stayed one step behind Diego as he entered the room.

Garza had been seated but sprang to his feet when Cezar slapped Hector.

"What is the meaning of this?" Garza asked, his glare sweeping the room and focusing on Hector.

Tino remained beside Diego a good ten feet to the side of Cezar and Hector. He followed Diego's movements as he seemed a bit anxious.

"Uncle—" Hector began.

"I told you not to call me that!" Garza yelled and slammed his palm on the desk top. The sound cracked through the room like a gun shot.

Hector flinched and yelped. His eyes started jiggling in the sockets.

"Cezar tells me you arrived alone yesterday after leaving with Tino to return the Alvarez brothers." Garza slid a glance Tino's direction.

"Sí." Hector swung an arm toward Tino. "He pulled a gun and told me to get out of the auto."

Tino shook his head. The man was going to play on familial truth.

"Is that what happened?" Garza stared at him glare for glare.

"No. When I refused to pull over to get a drink, Hector pulled his gun on me. I took it away and then suggested he get out. I did not want to drive the rest of the way back worrying his anger would make the gun go off." Tino didn't allow his gaze to waver as Garza continued to stare.

"I do not understand what was wrong with having a drink considering what we had just seen and done," Hector said, drawing Garza's angry stare.

"Does my business make you squeamish?" Garza asked.

Hector held his tongue and ducked his head.

"Then perhaps you should go back to your father's and make roof tiles?" Garza pointed to the door.

"No! I hate making tiles. I want to make money." Greed glistened in the young man's eyes.

"To make money you must follow orders and do as you are told. No drinking, no women, and no consuming the product we sell." Garza peered at Hector and the young man started visibly shaking. "Am I clear, nephew?"

"Sí." Hector stood straight and stared at the far wall.

Tino felt a bit of the tension drain from the room, but Garza wasn't completely relaxed. The tick above his right eye proved he was still upset with his nephew.

Cezar moved to a round table beside the bookcase. "We need to strategize how the Alvarez brothers and now the Bohu gang have intercepted our drops."

Tino was as interested in this as Garza. There had to be a snitch in Garza's employ and that snitch could help him with his mission.

Chapter Seven

Isabella blinked at the strong stream of sunlight shining through her window. As the veil of sleep lifted, the noise coming from the street had her checking her watch. *Noon*. She'd slept away the whole morning.

She should have been back at the museum hours ago. Now, she'd have to work late tonight until she'd read through every page and entry in the ledgers. She walked into the small bathroom and splashed water on her face, tracing her fingers over her lips. Tino still wanted her. She'd feared he'd see a more curvy and beautiful woman and forget about her stick figure and plain features. But last night he'd washed away any doubts she'd harbored about him finding someone else. Being held in his arms, experiencing his hot kisses, and sultry words, she believed in the two of them and would wait as long as it took for them to be together.

The clothes from the day before lay in a pile beside the bed where she'd shed them. Isabella quickly dressed and took the stairs to the lower floor. She smiled at the clerk behind the bright blue semi-circle counter and followed the enticing aromas of spicy food into the restaurant. Her stomach rumbled as she took a seat in a wicker barrel chair by the window.

A waiter appeared. He was neatly dressed and sporting a wide smile. "Buenas dias, señorita."

"Good morning or barely morning. I'll have hot chocolate, *chicharrón en salsa verde, frijoles refritos, sopes*, and *crema de piñón.*"

The waiter grinned. "Señorita, that is a lot of food for one so small."

Isabella winked. "I have a long day ahead and need lots of energy."

The man chuckled and wandered off with her order. A young woman arrived with her drink and water.

The room buzzed with energy. Leaning back in the chair, she studied the travelers, the archeology students, and the locals who seemed to be hanging about. The locals caught her attention. Mainly because two men seemed to be unusually interested in her. Her plain appearance and lack of womanly attributes rarely garnered her a second glance. To have the two men watching, yet trying not to appear as if they were, made her edgy. Did she call Tino? What could he do? She couldn't call him every time someone made her feel uncomfortable.

She turned her attention to the street and the bustling activity of cars and pedestrians. Footsteps and the smell of food drew her attention from the outside. The waiter placed her large fare on the table and shook his head.

Isabella picked up her fork and dug in, giving the food her full attention until every morsel had enticed her taste buds and filled her stomach. She leaned back and sighed. That was the first large meal she'd consumed since arriving. Even though she'd taken precautions against the influenza that struck most tourists, she'd come down with a brief case of the flu. But her body was now acclimated, and she was going to take full advantage of Mexican cuisine.

The waiter walked up and stared at the empty plates. "You have a very good appetite, no?"

"Sí, I enjoy food." She handed him ninety pesos for the meal and his service.

"Señorita, please, come back again."

"I will. Gracias." Since she'd donned her vest and everything she needed was hid in the pockets, Isabella left the restaurant and the hostel. The day was warm and sunny, lifting her spirits even more than the food. If only the toxic exhaust would lift, the day would be perfect.

Tourists meandered in and out of Templo Mayor. I wonder if they did find the burial site? She started to head for the excavation site and turned her toes. There would be media and more crowds if they'd come across the old ruler's final resting place. She had to get through those ledgers.

Someone bumped her from behind. The sound of Velcro and a tug on her vest spun her around. Feet planted and hands in defensive placement, she confronted her assailant. It was one of the men who'd watched her so intently in the restaurant. She reached around and felt the pocket he'd tried to pick. It held her energy bars.

"If you need it that bad it's yours." She snatched a bar from the pocket and flung it at the man.

He caught the bar and stared at it as if unsure what to do.

"Not what you were after?"

The man's gaze drifted over her shoulder and he turned, running away from the site. She spun around to find a guard walking their direction. Unlatching a pocket, she pulled out her visitor credentials and met the man halfway.

"That man just tried to steal from me." She pointed to the crowd where the man had disappeared. She'd remember his face, but realized it was useless to try and have police do anything. "Never mind."

"You are Dr. Mumphrey?" The officer grasped her elbow.

"Sí."

"Director Bastante is looking for you."

"I really need to get to work." Without appearing rude, she extracted her hand from his grip.

"Doctor, I must bring you to him. It would not be good for me to not follow his wishes." The man turned and walked toward the museum.

Isabella fell into step beside him. Perhaps Director Bastante only wished to ask about her progress, which was little, and she could tuck herself back behind the ledgers.

They entered through the main entrance and headed to the elevator leading to the offices on the fourth floor. The security guard pushed the button and the doors dinged open. She stepped inside the elevator but kept enough space between them she could counter act any offensive move he might make.

You are paranoid. The security guard isn't a threat. But Tino's anxiousness last night and the man who tried to steal from her moments ago reminded her she wasn't in Arizona and she was on a mission to uncover dishonest people. She would be more careful.

The elevator bounced to a stop, the doors swished open, and the guard waited for her to alight from the conveyance.

Isabella stepped into the reception area and crossed to the secretary sitting at a large new age looking desk.

"Director Bastante is waiting for you," the young women said, pointing her long tangerine colored nails to the door of the inner office.

Had Isabella been fashion conscious, she would have asked where the secretary found the tangerine spiked heels. But she'd never understood the need to totter on the tiny heels and worry about sprained ankles.

The security guard opened the office door, and she entered. Before the man in the seat facing the director rose, she knew who it was. There was no mistaking the hair style, body language, and expensive style shirt Paolo Garza wore the day before.

"Dr. Mumphrey, Paolo was just telling me how much he enjoyed your visit to his collection yesterday." Director Bastante's small teeth reminded her of a piranha as he smiled and motioned for her to take the chair beside Garza.

She seated herself, noting the careful perusal Garza was taking of her clothing. His gaze lingered on the many pockets of her vest as if x-raying and seeing the items inside.

"Señor Garza has an impressive collection. It rivals the collection in this building depicting the Aztec history in wonderful detail." She set a fake smile on her lips when she really wanted to rise out of the chair and stand at the far wall. Until meeting with Tino, and feeling his anxiety and fear she would get caught in the drug lord's business, she'd been comfortable with the man. And watching his slightly raised eyebrows, her fear was being read by him.

"Indeed." Director Bastante smiled benevolently at Garza. If he knew of Garza's illegal doings, it didn't seem to bother him.

"Director, if you only brought me in to agree with señor Garza's impressive collection, I really need to get back to work." She put her hands on the chair arms to push out of the plush seat.

Garza placed a hand on hers closest to him. "I wished to speak with you." The tone of his voice said, "sit down".

Her desire to please, a trait many older students had used to their advantage when she tried so hard as a child to fit into the higher academics, took her back to her adolescence, and she sat. Hating the fact she acquiesced, anger blossomed. She was an adult and should stand up for herself. But to avoid a conflict with a man she knew killed people, she did the only thing she could do.

She retracted her hand from his and tangled her fingers together in her lap. "Is it something that can't wait until Saturday?"

"I would like to pay the museum for your time to help me catalog and identify some artifacts that I believe a dealer may have been dishonest with me about." Garza peered at the director who nodded.

She could have sworn she saw dollar signs glimmering in Director Bastante's eyes.

"I see, but I don't work for the museum. I'm down here gathering information for a paper I'm writing." She peered into the director's eyes. He didn't know she was also looking into the missing artifacts. She had to be in the museum and vicinity to discover how the artifacts were stolen.

"I would think some of what you see and learn at Paolo's collection will help with the writing of your paper."

This time the director gave her a look that put her theory he was greedy back in her mind and added him to her list of suspects. If he were the one stealing, he'd jump at the chance to pad his pockets and get her out of his hair. But Tino wouldn't be happy with her working in Garza's compound.

To hide the disgust she felt toward the museum director, she turned to Garza. "Is this the same project you discussed with me yesterday?"

He didn't show surprise at her directness. If anything, she saw a flash of admiration in his brown eyes.

"Yes, and more."

"I have documents I'm reading in the archives. I could spend my mornings here and come out to your house in the afternoons, if that would work." Tino was really not going to like this, but there was no way to get around it without raising suspicion.

Garza watched her intently and steepled his fingers under his chin. "I was thinking you could move into my house, keep my wife company, and show her how to catalog my discoveries."

Trepidation trickled down her spine and her stomach lurched. There was no way she'd become locked in the house of a drug dealer.

"I'm here on a grant. I can't squander my time by working only for you. I'll come over around noon and will work with your wife, but I'll not stay in your home." Her voice remained calm and firm.

His pleasant demeanor started to darken.

"I think that is a very workable situation, Paolo. I know Dr. Mumphrey is on a deadline for her paper, and I am sure you would not want her to lose her funding."

"I can pay you three times as much as your government is willing to pay you." Garza shifted in his chair, giving her his full-on glare.

"That may be so, but I still have many years I want to work for the university and if I take money from you and not write my paper, I'll lose my tenure. I've worked too hard and sacrificed too much to allow greed to shove me into anonymity in anthropology circles." Isabella glared back at him. As much as he scared her, she would not get herself locked up in his compound nor compromise a career she'd set her sights on at seven years of age.

Isabella stood. "I'm going to the archives," she said to the director. She walked to the door and stopped with her hand on the knob, and peered back at Garza. "I'll take a taxi to your residence when I finish today, unless you want me to wait until tomorrow when your wife arrives."

The dark hooded eyes and scrunched brow proved he was not used to people disobeying him. She sent a plea to all the deities she'd ever learned about to make sure Garza never discovered her connection to Tino. She feared for both their lives.

"Come to the welcome home party tomorrow to meet my wife. You can begin work after that." The sentences sounded forced almost as if he choked on the words.

"I'll see you then." Isabella slipped out the door, took a deep breath, nodded to the secretary, and headed for the elevator and the archive room. She had the rest of today and tonight to finish going over the ledgers of the retrieved artifacts from Templo Mayor. If she didn't see any artifacts at Garza's that corresponded to the ledger, she'd have to find a way to get out of there and search for other clues.

Chapter Eight

Tino sat in the tan SUV waiting for señora Garza's airplane to arrive. He'd been sent to the Toluca Airport to meet Garza's personal plane and pick up his wife's luggage. And her, if Garza didn't arrive before the plane landed.

This would be his first glimpse at the drug lord's wife. He'd tried to find out about the woman but all the narcos had refused to talk. He took that to mean someone in the past had mouthed off and ended up as vulture food.

The blue underbelly of the Learjet circled once above the airstrip at Toluca Airport and as the wheels touched the asphalt landing strip, Garza pulled up in his gold Mastretta mxt. Tino stood outside the SUV leaning against the hood. The mxt purred to a stop and Garza unfolded himself from the interior.

This was why I had to grab the luggage. It wouldn't fit in his toy.

Garza pulled off a pair of designer sunglasses and walked up to Tino. "I will take my Karyme to dinner before bringing her home. Please make sure Hadda unpacks for my wife."

Tino nodded. It appeared Garza was anxious to see his spouse. He was as antsy as a teenager about to walk up to his date's door.

This anticipation for the woman and knowing Garza was one of the few drug lords who was faithful to his wife, showed a softer side to the man that Tino refused to acknowledge. He turned his back, pretending to fiddle with a loose mirror.

This was the problem with getting close to your mark, you saw them as people instead of the parasites they were and that clouded one's judgment. He slammed his mind to what he'd just witnessed.

The jet pulled to a stop in front of the vehicles. The door came down and Tino watched as Garza climbed the steps and extended his hand. Out walked a very beautiful Latino woman with light tan skin and soft brown hair. She hugged Garza, her face glowing and her lips curved in the suggestive smile of a lover.

Tino spun from the sight. The man didn't deserve this kind of happiness after ruining so many lives of other families.

He waited until the man and woman roared off in the sports car before striding over to the airplane and walking up the stairs. Sticking his head in the cabin, he found a woman cleaning up the lavish interior.

"I am here for señora Garza's things."

The woman grinned brightly. "They are here. Where is Diego? He usually picks up the señora's belongings?"

"He was detained on other errands." Tino took his time scanning the inside of the plane. Most wives knew their husband's dealt in illegal activities. Especially when they flew from country to country on a private jet.

"This is a nice plane. Do you always tend to señora Garza?" Tino sat on the arm of a chair and used his *abuela* smile—the one that always made his grandmother or any woman respond—on the petite, average-looking woman.

The woman motioned to two large bags and two small ones. "There are her things."

Another loyal minion on Garza's payroll.

"Gracias." Tino picked up the small bags under his arms and the large bags in his hands and exited the plane. Did Garza threaten his employees to keep their mouths shut or was loyalty the key to their thoughts and feelings? Whichever didn't matter. He would find the way into the man's graces and take him down. He owed it to *his* family.

~*~

Isabella rubbed a hand over her tired eyes. She now knew

everything about the missing artifacts and believed the statues she drooled over at Garza's were not them. But that didn't mean they weren't somewhere in his house. The artifacts he'd purchased from a dealer and believed were fakes had captured her curiosity.

She stumbled out of the archive room and into a dark basement hall. A glance at her watch showed the hour to be ten o'clock. She'd eaten an energy bar a few hours before when her stomach had rumbled and she'd only had one more ledger to go through. Her stomach set up a ruckus that echoed in the silent hallway as she headed for the stairs to the main level.

Strolling down the hall, her gaze fastened on the thin line of light shining under a door. Who else was down here? And what was in that room? She stepped toward that side of the hall and the light disappeared.

Someone was coming out.

Even though she had a legitimate reason to be in the museum, if the person coming out of the room didn't belong here, it was a sure bet they were up to no good and being found wasn't satisfactory.

Isabella quietly retraced her steps and ducked into the recessed doorway of another room. She peeked around the edge and watched as the night guard locked the door and sauntered to the stairs, taking them two at a time.

Why was the guard in that room? Why did he leave when she left the archive room? *Surveillance cameras.*

She thought back to her first day and the tour the curator, Delgado, took her on. Was that room in the tour? She shook her head. No. He'd only shown her the rooms he felt she would need to discover the missing artifacts. Delgado was the only person who knew her true mission at the museum.

Her fingers clamped around the door knob and she twisted her wrist. Even though she'd watched the guard lock the door, a teensie hope glowed that the door hadn't really locked.

Nothing.

She blew out air and marched to the stairs. Food, sleep, and tomorrow morning she'd discover what was in that room. At the top of the stairs, she pushed the door open and headed down the hall to the front doors.

The guard jumped when she walked up behind him.

"Where did you come from?" he asked in Spanish.

"Archive," she replied studying the surprise on his face and the quickly closed down expression.

He'd thought she'd already left. Was that because he saw her put the books away and head out of the archive room? Or did he think she'd left hours ago like all the other museum employees?

Satisfaction tipped her lips as she headed out into the square and immediately missed the purified air-conditioned environment inside the building. Tonight the exhaust fumes hung even thicker in the cloud covered sky. Coughing, she quickly walked across the square. The area wasn't empty. People milled around and sat on the short cement walls. She preferred the quiet solitude of the archives to the dark shapes of people loitering around Templo Mayor.

Lengthening her stride, she hurried across the street and into the hostel. Seeing the clerk, Felix, behind the counter smiling and welcoming her, Isabella slowed her pace.

"Buenas noches, señorita."

"Buenas noches. Is there a chance I can find something to eat in the restaurant?" She eyed the dark area where she'd eaten breakfast.

The clerk grimaced. "It has closed for the night. We have a kitchen for guests but you are to use your own food."

Her mouth watered thinking about the *disfrute de botanas* at the Sálon España. Was it safe for her to walk the several blocks and find something to eat? She'd be safe in the crowded establishment, wouldn't she?

The phone Tino gave her vibrated in her pocket. Anticipation of hearing his voice carried her to the far side of the lobby as she flipped the phone open and answered.

"Hello?"

"Querida, are you still in the archive room?"

"No. I'm standing in the hostel lobby starving, but the restaurant is closed and I don't have any groceries to make my own food in the communal kitchen." She peered out the window. "You don't happen to be nearby to escort me to Sálon España, do you?"

He sighed heavily. "No, querida, I am nowhere near you and will not be able to come see you. They caught me sneaking back in last night. I must stay close to the compound." He cursed. "I have to go. Stay safe."

"You, too." The phone went silent before she could tell him she loved him. Flipping the phone closed felt like closing the door on Tino. But she couldn't call him back and couldn't stand in the lobby mooning for him. They both had work to do and right now she needed to find food.

She walked back over to the counter. "Is there a place that would deliver food to me?"

The clerk stared at her a moment before offering. "My cousin, Alphonso, would do this for you for a small compensation."

"How soon can he bring me food?" Her stomach rumbled loudly as she pulled an energy bar from her vest pocket.

"I will have him pick it up and deliver it within the half hour."

"Perfect. Call your cousin. I'll sit here and go over some notes while I wait." Isabella plopped down on an overstuffed chair by the lobby window and pulled out her journal. She'd made specific notes on the recently found Aztec items and had a brief list of the pieces, Tomas Delgado, the curator, believed were missing. With this information she should be able to determine if anything Garza had in his possession were the stolen items.

Running the list she'd read in the inventory logs over in her mind, she thought about the security guard sneaking out of the other room. Could he be in on the missing artifacts? It was evident he was up to no good if he used his security key to sneak into a room. The man would have access to the whole building including all the boxed artifacts waiting to be disbursed.

She flipped to the last page of her journal and wrote down "night security guard." Tomorrow she'd ask señor Delgado to get her information on all the museum employees and have them run through WIA's computers. This led her to wonder why the local authorities hadn't been called in. Did Delgado believe the local police could be part of the problem?

"Señorita, your food has arrived."

Isabella looked up and nearly choked.

Felix's "cousin" was the man who tried to steal her energy bar earlier in the day. Recognition flit across his face as she stood and walked to the desk.

What to do? The clerk had offered his cousin's services with good faith. The cousin had come through from the look of the bag dangling from his hand.

She reached for the bag, took it, and considered the contents while trying to decide how to handle the predicament.

The young man shuffled his feet as Felix's expression changed from eager to please to staring hard at his cousin.

"Alphonso, have you and this lady met before?" Felix asked in Spanish, his voice dropping an octave and accusing.

They carried on a short exchange, obviously, believing she couldn't understand them. But she knew enough of the language to understand Alphonso was letting the family down by hanging out with the Bohu gang. It sounded like the other person who had been with Alphonso had put him up to trying to take her money, only with all the pockets on her vest, he'd gone for the one that looked like it might hold a wallet.

She cleared her throat and both men looked at her as if she'd committed a cardinal sin.

"I hate to interrupt this family discussion but how much do I owe you for the food?" The Velcro on the inside right pocket ripped as she pulled out a handful of coins.

"Five dollar American," Alphonso said.

"Good. I'll pay you for the food you brought, but not your time since you think your time is only valuable for stealing. If I need more food and your cousin calls you to run the errand, I'll pay you for that errand." She placed the payment in his hand and nodded toward the clerk. "Where is the kitchen?"

Felix pointed down the back hall, and she and her rumbling stomach found the kitchen. Isabella prepared her food, ate it alone, standing in front of the sink, and took the remainder of her food with her up to her room.

Sleep was a long time coming as she went back and forth over what she should wear to meet a drug lord's wife and how to broach the subject of a possible untrustworthy guard to señor Delgado without the guard getting wind of her checking him out.

Chapter Nine

Tino wondered at the excitement of the Graza household staff as
they hustled around preparing for the welcome home dinner and party
for Karyme Garza. From the chatter among the staff, that didn't go on
when the woman wasn't around, it would seem the mistress of the
house was more down-to-earth than her husband.

This knowledge worried him. Isabella would like señora Garza
and it would put a strain on their relationship, with her knowing his
plans. She could feel a need to warn the woman which could end up
hurting everyone.

He had to find a way to speak with Isabella tonight. He had to
make her see staying away from the Garzas was in the best interest of
their relationship and missions.

"Rodriguez! Go help Hector, he cannot even figure out how to
park cars."

Cezar's command and derision for Hector could give him his
chance to talk to Isabella. If he helped park cars, there was a chance he
would be at the front of the house when she arrived or better still keep
her company while waiting for a ride to pick her up.

Tino hurried out to the garage and then the circular driveway.
He'd been warned by Diego that only Cezar was allowed to mingle
with the guests. They, the lower pecking order, were delegated jobs to
blend in and still be handy in case any enemies infiltrated the party.

He found Hector, drawing lines on a diagram of the compound.

"What are you doing?" Tino asked, peering down at the small hash marks all over the circular drive.

"I have to do this right or my uncle will send me back to making tiles." Hector spit on the ground. "I do not like making tiles."

"You cannot park all the vehicles in the drive. You will have to take them over to the side yard and park them." Tino placed his finger on the flat area west of the house.

"Sí. Why did I not think of that?" Hector scratched his head and continued to peer at the diagram.

"Because you are worrying too much. Cezar sent me out to help you." At that moment a delivery van arrived.

"More flowers?" Hector said, slanting his gaze toward a van that came from the back of the house.

Tino spied Rico driving the flower van. Ahh, so DEA would have eyes and ears planted, literally, in the party. Unless the ever-vigilant Garza had Cezar do a sweep of the rooms before the guests arrived. Tino glanced at his watch. The first arrivals would pull into the driveway in half an hour. Would Isabella be early or late? He'd guess late. She knew he didn't want her here and she'd procrastinate, debating about coming at all. A proprietary smile curved his lips. He knew his *pichon,* little dove, well.

~*~

Isabella stood in the lobby of the hostel waiting for Director Bastante to pick her up. When she was leaving the curator's office earlier in the day after requesting records of all the employees and asking about surveillance cameras, the director had cornered her. He informed her, he and his wife would pick her up for the party at Garza's. He'd also told her to purchase a nice outfit if she didn't bring one with her. He implied that Garza parties were the same as a Hollywood party in her country.

She'd dumped the employee files and tapes from the surveillance cameras in her room and took a taxi to one of the upper scale clothing stores, Palacio de Hierro. She purchased a long dress that wrapped about her body like a sarong, tying behind her neck, and sandals with a two-inch heel to dress the garment up. Also bangle bracelets and an obnoxious large beaded necklace that the saleswoman at the store insisted made the dress. She felt overdressed and yet, naked, venturing

58

out without her vest. No matter how hard she tried, finding a way to bring her vest along had ended in futility. The only bag she brought with her that would accommodate the folded-up vest looked tacky even to her untrained fashion sense.

She stood in the lobby waiting, and feeling vulnerable.

"You look stunning tonight, Señorita," Felix said, smiling.

Isabella smoothed a hand down her dress. "Gracias." She eyed the restaurant. "I think I'll get something cold to drink. When Director Bastante comes in would you let him know where to find me?"

The clerk nodded and turned his attention to another guest hovering near the desk.

Walking slow so as not to step on the long dress or fall off the wedge-shaped heel of the sandal, Isabella entered the restaurant. All the tables appeared to be full. As she peered about, a hand rose and waved to her. She pushed her glasses up tighter on the bridge of her nose and recognized the clerk's cousin, Alphonso.

What would he want? She crossed the room, her gaze taking in the other man and two young women at the table with him. They didn't look threatening though the other man didn't exude hospitality.

She peered back out at the lobby where Felix was in a conversation with a guest.

"We have room for you to sit." Alphonso squeezed the shoulder of the young girl sitting next to him and pulled her across the bench seat to scrunch up next to him.

Was he using her as a ploy to get close to this girl? Isabella studied the girl. Her makeup was on too thick and her clothing too tight and skimpy for one so young.

"If it's all right with your friends?" She turned her attention to the couple across the table. The man was five to ten years older than Alphonso, but the girl clinging to his arm was just as young as the one Alphonso clutched to his side. She wanted to tell both the girls to go wash their faces and go home to their families.

The older man nodded and motioned with a hand for her to sit.

"I'm Isabella," she said, extending her hand across the table.

The girl just nodded and the older man looked at her hand before saying, "Alphonso, how do you know this gringa?"

Her shoulders ached from the tension bunching her muscles.

"There you are." Director Bastante walked up to the table. His eyes widened when he noticed the man across from her. He grabbed her upper arm, dragging her from the seat. "We need to hurry. We are running late."

Isabella didn't bother saying good-bye. She was still trying to figure out what had compelled her to walk toward Alphonso when he waved at her.

"Do you know who that was you were sitting with?" the director hissed in her ear as he continued towing her out of the building.

"Not everyone. Alphonso ran an errand for me last night." She stopped, jerking her arm from his grasp. "I'm perfectly capable of walking at a fast clip. There is no need to haul me around like a recalcitrant child."

"I'm sorry." The director ran a hand over his face. A man held the door on a limousine. It looked like she and the director and señora Bastante would be arriving at the Garza's in style. He waved the man away and shut the door. "Do not tell Paolo about the men you were just with."

The hair on the back of her neck vibrated. "Why?"

"If he found out you were talking with his enemy…" The director opened the door, again. "Get in. And there will be no more talk of this."

Isabella took the seat opposite señora Bastante. The woman's dress made Isabella feel like a peasant. It looked to be the kind of party, where once again, she would feel out of place. Her quivering lips proved hard to press into a smile. Behind the smile, she dissected the conversation with the director. He knew what Garza was capable of. And he knew Garza's enemies. That made director Bastante more than an acquaintance of señor Garza. It made him an accomplice.

After being led to Guatemala on a promise of money for her department only to learn she'd been lured there to be used as a sacrifice, this new development between Garza and Bastante had her wondering about the stolen artifacts. She knew that Delgado asked for her specifically. Was he also in cahoots with Garza and Bastante?

With that thought and her insides churning, she gripped the arm rest on the side of the car and tried to stay focused on the conversation in the car. It appeared señora Bastante considered herself one of señora Garza's best friends. Her haughty tone and condescending stare made Isabella wonder how Garza could believe she and his wife would get along if this person was so chummy with señora Garza.

The limousine pulled up to the compound. A guard at the gate waved them through after Bastante lowered the window and conversed with him. As the vehicle neared the house, Isabella swallowed the lump in her throat. What was she doing mixed up with this type of people?

The car circled the drive, and her heart picked up speed. Tino leaned toward the car opening the door. The Bastante's exited. She took her time, allowing them to walk away. Tino took her hand, helping her out of the car.

She squeezed his hand, wanting him to know how much of a lifeline she considered him.

He leaned into the car while she stood beside him still holding his hand.

"Park on the west lawn," he said to the driver, then stood next to her.

"We cannot talk. Someone might see." He peered into her face. "What is wrong?"

"I-I'm wondering if this is more than I was told."

His gaze hardened. "What have you learned?"

"It's not so much as what I've learned as what has been happening." She glimpsed someone walking toward them. "We need to talk."

"I will find a way." He squeezed her hand and dropped it.

"You will find the party through the front doors and straight back in the ballroom," he said loudly and turned to help the people from the next arriving car.

She turned and found Cezar watching her and then Tino. She rubbed her hands up and down her arms, wishing she'd purchased a shawl to cover her shoulders and headed into the house.

Passing Cezar, she met his eyes and smiled. "Buenas noches," she said in greeting, hoping he'd think she was one of those women who talked to and smiled at everyone.

"What were you and Rodriguez talking about?" Cezar put a hand on her arm, stopping her.

"Who is Rodriguez?" She peered straight into his eyes and tried to look nonchalant.

"The man who was holding your hand." The coldness in his eyes caused a shiver to ripple up her spine.

"My there is a chill in the air tonight." She rubbed her hands up and down her arms again. "So, the guy who helped me out of the car is Rodriguez? He didn't tell me his name when he drove me back to the hostel the other day. He'd given me some tips on good restaurants and asked if I'd had a chance to try any of them."

She looked down at his hand still on her arm. "He detained me much like you are doing. What is it with you domineering Mexican men? As an independent American woman, I don't like it." She pulled away from his grasp and walked with authority to the door and entered when a young woman held it open.

Garza and a very beautiful woman in a champagne-colored, silk dress stood in the middle of the foyer greeting the guests. The Bastantes were there now. From the forced smile and head bobbing of the woman who must certainly be señora Garza, Isabella had to snicker. Señora Bastante was not a favorite of her hostess.

The couple moved on, and Isabella walked forward.

"Karyme, may I present to you the woman I have been telling you about. Dr. Isabella Mumphrey, may I present my wife, Karyme Garza." Garza held his wife's hand as he did the introductions. It was evident by their glowing faces and eye connection the two were deeply in love.

How could one love a drug dealer?

Isabella extended her hand to the woman. "Señora, it is wonderful to meet you. Your husband has a high regard for you."

Laughter crinkles formed at the sides of the woman's dark brown eyes. "Dr. Mumphrey, I am my husband's one weakness."

Garza laughed and squeezed his wife around her waist. "This is true. Karyme has a way of making sure I keep my full attention on her when she is around."

Señora Garza laughed pleasantly and patted her husband's hand spanning her mid-section. Then she walked out of his embrace and linked arms with Isabella. "Come, I want to hear about the work you do and where you live in the United States."

Isabella found señora Bastante glaring at her, but she didn't care. She liked the straightforwardness of señora Graza even if she was married to a drug lord. They sat on a couch large enough for only two.

"Please, call me Karyme. From what Paolo says, we will be

working together. It was his love of Aztec and Mayan artifacts that brought us together. I was working at a site that he visited. We talked all night about the history of his people and why I found it all so interesting."

"So, all these artifacts displayed in your home are not just for his pleasure." Isabella didn't like the way her mind was going. If Karyme also loved Aztec art and lore, she could be the one stealing from the museum.

"Sí. I started collecting and insisted they be displayed. What good is having something if you can't display it and enjoy the beauty of it?"

"I agree. But that is what a museum is for, to allow the public to see the wonders. Here only you and your friends and family are able to view the pieces." She waited in anticipation of the woman's reply. It might give her a clue as to Karyme's part, if any, in the missing pieces.

"Oh, we share. You will be helping me box up the carvings in the foyer to send to a museum in London. They will be on loan there for six months." Karyme leaned closer. "Isabella, I would never dream of harboring my ancestor's work for my own. It belongs to the people." The sincerity and earnestness in her voice gave Isabella the impression the woman was trying to impart something more than her feelings about the artifacts.

All during their conversation the guests mingled among one another, stopping in and saying hello to señora Garza and finally coming back by and saying buenas noches.

Isabella gazed around the room while Karyme talked with a couple that was about to leave. The Bastante's had left. She didn't see any sign of her ride among the handful of people who remained. How would she get back to the hostel?

With that thought fresh in her mind, she stood.

"Isabella, is something wrong?" Karyme touched her arm.

"It's late and my ride has left." She looked around and spotted Garza watching the two of them.

"You can spend the night. We have lots of rooms."

"No! I mean, I need to return to the hostel. I have a lot of work to go over tomorrow."

"But it is Sunday. Surely, you could get started later. Anarosa makes the most delicious *chicharrón*." Karyme stood and waved her hand. Within seconds, Garza was by their side.

"What has you two women looking so upset?" he asked, snaking an arm around his wife's waist.

"Isabella's ride has left. I offered her a room, but she insists she must be at work early tomorrow." Karyme rested her head on her husband's shoulder.

"But it is Sunday. A day of rest." Garza peered at her.

"A day of rest for those who aren't working to keep a university department open. If I'm to come help you each day, that shortens my time researching for my paper. I really need to get back, get some rest, and get up early tomorrow to work."

Garza continued to watch her.

"I like your dedication." Karyme turned to her husband. "One of your security men could drive her home."

Isabella's heart raced, hoping he'd picked Tino.

"Most of the guests have left. I could spare one man to drive Dr. Mumphrey." Garza pulled his gaze from her and motioned to Cezar.

When the other man walked up to them Garza turned his attention back to Isabella. "Cezar, have Hector take Dr. Mumphrey back to her hostel."

She kept her expression neutral and nodded her head in thanks. Was he watching to see what her reaction was to who he picked? Did he already suspect her and Tino? Nerves buzzed around inside while she worked to remain calm and detached on the outside.

Cezar nodded. "Dr. Mumphrey, please come with me."

Karyme clasped her hands. "I am looking forward to working with you on Monday."

"I'll be here around one," Isabella answered, releasing the woman's hands and following Cezar's broad back to the front of the house.

Out in the cool air of the evening, she shivered.

"Wait here while I find Hector." Cezar gave her a pointed look and walked toward the garage.

If tonight was any indication of what coming here every day would be like, she wasn't sure her nerves were going to be able to hold up. She'd studied ancient people and languages her whole life. Trying to decipher what modern day people said and thought was much harder. Especially when you knew your life and the life of your lover were in the balance.

Chapter Ten

Tino watched Cezar and Isabella walk out of the house. It appeared Cezar was taking Isabella back to the hostel. He resented it but knew he couldn't offer. Not after witnessing Cezar grill Isabella when she'd talked with him at her arrival.

Cezar left Isabella standing at the edge of the walkway and strolled over to where Tino stood near the garage waiting for Hector to return from a smoke.

"Rodriguez, take Dr. Mumphrey back to her hotel." Cezar's eyes were calculating as he watched Tino.

"It is late and Hector is in charge of the guests coming and going, have him take her." Tino remained leaning against the garage doorway. He'd never had to pretend as hard as he was now. It was the perfect set-up for him to speak with Isabella, but he refused to let the man watching him so intently know that.

"Jefe said you were to take her."

Tino slowly pushed away from the wall and straightened. "Then I guess I have no choice." He walked over to his SUV and climbed into the driver's seat hiding his excitement. Tino pulled the vehicle up to where Isabella stood. Cezar had returned to her side. He opened the Tahoe's door and Isabella's eyes narrowed.

She faced the narco. "Señor Garza said Hector was to take me home. You told me this man was called Rodriguez."

Rage and fear collided inside Tino. What was Cezar doing? "I am Tino Rodriguez. Cezar, you told me Garza asked for me to take the señorita home. What is going on?"

He wanted to watch Isabella to see if she gave anything away, but believed this game by Cezar was his way of determining a connection between Tino and Isabella. Garza's righthand man was trying to catch them off guard. Trying to discredit him. Tino had to act like he didn't have an interest in the woman.

Cezar's phone buzzed. "Sí?" He stepped away from the open door.

Isabella stood on the spot, her gaze searching his face. He had to keep his expression chiseled as if in stone. If Cezar spun around and caught either of them communicating, they were dead.

Cezar pushed a button on his phone and turned to them. "Take her to the hotel. I will tell jefe I could not find Hector. Which is the truth. He is missing." Cezar sent Tino one hard look. "Hurry back. I have a feeling the rest of the night will be long."

Isabella climbed into the SUV and slammed the door. She continued staring at Cezar as Tino pulled the vehicle out of the driveway.

When they'd put several blocks between them and the compound, she asked in almost a whisper, "What was he doing?"

"Seeing if we knew one another better than we let on." Tino took her hand and kissed her palm. "Querida, you are a superb actress."

"Is this safe?" She still whispered.

"Sí. I have been close to my vehicle all night. I know no one has tampered with it." He pulled over before getting into the busy traffic. Tino knew it was risky but he had to kiss Isabella. He could see she was shook up by the events.

He leaned over. "Come here, *mi pichon*. I have been dreaming about this since our last parting." Placing his lips on hers, he held her head in his hands, cherishing the exotic scent he'd learned so well in the jungle and tasted the sweetness of her lips. Slowly, with reluctance, he drew back but held her head and peered into her eyes. The light of the moon wasn't strong but it was enough to see her within the vehicle.

"Now, you have met señora Garza you will finish your mission at Templo Mayor and go home. I do not think I can go through another meeting like tonight."

She turned her head and kissed his palm. "I'm sorry, but you're going to have to. Señora Garza has asked me to help her box up artifacts to be sent to museums."

He pulled his hands back and sat in his seat, staring at the onslaught of cars on the road. "Do you believe the missing artifacts are at the Garza home?"

"No…I'm not sure…They could be, but I'm not positive." She placed a hand on his arm. "I don't like going there either, but I was ordered by Bastante to help them. Garza offered the museum money for my help."

Tino slammed his hand against the steering wheel. "That is because he wants to keep you close. What is it he sees in you that he feels he must keep you under his surveillance?" Isabella's arriving when she did hurt his investigation and it placed her in danger. Rage over his impotency to keep her safe without jeopardizing his mission nearly strangled him.

"I don't understand it either. This is my first assignment. He can't know I'm WIA."

The reason hit him as hard and fast as a covert missile. "Carajo! He knows you are the one who helped captured Don Miguel and his drug shipment."

"No! Daddy said my name was kept out of all the records."

"But what if he didn't ask about the shooting. What if he asked about the people who were at the dig? The other workers would have said your name and then he'd wonder why you weren't in the reports."

"How would he get the reports?"

Tino scoffed. "He has the money and power to get his hands on anything he wishes."

This new information made Tino nauseous. "You have to call your father and have him replace you with someone else."

Isabella shook her head. "No. I had a feeling earlier today that this wasn't what I was sent to do. There is something else going on that's deeper than missing artifacts. Someone else would only be looking for what they were sent here to do. I can puzzle the pieces and discover the truth."

"Ezzabella, querida. You could end up dead. That is not a risk I am willing to take." Tino grasped her arms, making her peer into his face. "You must leave. Tonight. It is too dangerous."

"What about you? If Garza learned about me from the other people at the dig you would have come up, too. What makes you think he hasn't figured out who you are?" She put a hand on his cheek. "You are in just as much danger as I am. Are you going to pull out tonight?"

He remained silent and dropped his gaze to the large necklace moving up and down as she breathed.

"I thought not. Don't tell me what to do if you aren't going to follow your own warnings."

He knew short of kidnapping her and hiding her out until he was through with his mission, he had no way of making her stay away. The knowledge weighed him down like a boulder the size of his SUV.

Tino pulled her into his arms and kissed her as if they would never see one another again, because if either one of them wasn't vigilante at all times that was exactly what could happen.

Isabella savored the kiss, tangling her tongue with Tino's and taking as much as she gave knowing this would not happen again for them until their missions were complete. They couldn't risk moments alone like this knowing Garza could be watching their every move.

Tino pulled out of the kiss first. "I have to get you back to the hostel and return to the compound."

"I know. I don't want harm coming to you because of me." She straightened in her seat as her heart ached for what she couldn't have. She'd put this strain between them by signing up with the WIA. At the time, she'd been positive it was a good way to use her intelligence. Now, seeing what it was doing to the only man she loved and trusted, she believed it to be one of the biggest mistakes of her life.

"Can I still call you?" The desperation in her voice made her cringe.

Tino took his eyes off the road and nodded. "Sí. We must know what the other is doing to avoid more complications." They had entered a busy street. He turned his attention to the traffic.

"Good. I'd hate to think I couldn't contact you at all until this is all over." She stared at his profile etching every plane and angle into her memory.

"Querida, if you are in trouble call Rico. He can get to you faster than I can. If you need to discuss things, call, but I may not be able to answer you right away. Just leave a message that no one else would misinterpret as a code."

Her head was spinning with all the things that could go wrong. "Tino, we will get through this and be together."

His gaze locked with hers. "Sí, querida. That is all I have thought about since leaving your bed in Guatemala. I will make it happen."

The conviction in his words helped ease the panic that had started to settle in her chest. "I'll make sure it happens as well."

He kissed her knuckles and parked in front of the hostel. "I wish I could follow you to your room and make love to you, but I must get back. If Hector is missing, I must help find him. He is Garza's nephew."

She leaned toward Tino. He shook his head, his eyes dulled with sorrow. "There are too many eyes here, querida."

Isabella nodded and opened the door. "Gracias." She closed the door and watched Tino drive away. When will I get to see you again?

Chapter Eleven

Tino cursed every person in Isabella's life including himself. She should not be here in the middle of what he now believed to be a showdown between the drug lord, the gangs stealing his goods, and DEA. He wove in and out of traffic, his foot pressing the accelerator to the floor as he sped back to Garza's compound. He wanted to charge into the house and confront the man but that would only get him killed and perhaps Isabella as well.

He punched the button on the call box at the gate and was buzzed in. Everyone, including the staff, milled about the grounds. Tino parked his vehicle in the garage and strode up to Cezar.

"Why is everyone walking around?"

"We still have not found Hector." Cezar motioned toward the house. "Perhaps you should go in and tell jefe all you know about where Hector could be. I told you to watch him."

Tino shoved the man in the chest. This was an excellent way to work off his rage. "You did not tell me I was to babysit."

Cezar shoved back. "You knew he was incompetent."

Tino stood in front of Cezar ready to shove a fist in his face, when he caught sight of Garza watching. He pressed his arms down to his side, clenching his fists. "I did not think he could screw up parking cars." Shaking out his tense arm muscles, he nodded toward the house.

"I'll go see Garza now."

Without another glance at Cezar, Tino walked into the house and followed Garza into the office. He shut the door as Garza settled himself behind the desk.

"What do you know about Hector's disappearance?"

Tino stood at attention. "Nothing. The last I saw him he said he was going to smoke a cigarette. That was ten minutes before Cezar brought the doctor woman out and asked me to take her to her hotel."

Garza stared at him, his hands steepled under his chin. "Did you notice anything unusual about Hector tonight?"

"Each time after he'd go for a smoke he was more agitated." Tino figured the man had been taking hits of something when he disappeared. How he received the substance, he didn't know but planned to find out.

Garza's eyes narrowed. "Did you ask him what he was doing?"

"Sí. He told me to 'Fuck off'." It had surprised Tino to hear such a vehement and American remark from a man he'd believed a Mexican National. Now he wondered if Hector wasn't either another DEA agent or something else; a plant from a rival gang in the U.S.

Garza sat back in his chair and stared at Tino, his eyes darkening as his bushy dark eyebrows pinched together.

"Tell Cezar to get in here. You get out there and help find Hector. And when you find him, I want him brought immediately to me."

Tino nodded and left the office. Garza had looked ready to grab an AK 47 and lay everyone low. Had he come up with the same conclusions about Hector?

He'd have to get to Hector first. It was the only way the man would stay alive long enough for the DEA to interrogate him.

Cezar was handing out flashlights to the other guards. "Spread out and cover the whole compound," he instructed.

"Garza wants to see you," Tino said, taking a flashlight.

"Where are you going?" Cezar yanked the flashlight back.

"Where I was told to go. To find Hector." Tino yanked the flashlight back and struck out toward the parking area. That was where Hector wandered to when he took his "breaks". He thought back to the last trip Hector made. Had a vehicle left after he'd disappeared? No, only him taking Isabella back to the hostel.

Swinging the light back and forth in a sweeping motion, he

watched the ground. After covering all the area where the cars had parked, he moved to the area closest to the fence. He looked back at the tower where he knew a man was stationed at all times to watch the perimeter and noticed a blind spot. Either Hector was smarter and more calculating than he let on or someone else with intelligence had told him what to do.

Tino drew a visual line from the blind spot on the tower to the fence. Then set a course straight for the adobe wall. Halfway between where the cars were parked and the fence, he spotted a cigarette butt. Scanning the area with the beam of the flashlight, the ground revealed two sets of prints, toes pointed toward the house. Hector had met someone and talked about…what? Was he working against his uncle from the inside? But how would he have known about the shipments that were intercepted? Hector was lower down and had barely had access to the office…or had he? He was after all family. Could he have been allowed into the office even though it was clear Garza didn't think highly of his nephew?

Tino shook his head. This didn't make any sense. Even if he had access to the room, how did he get into the other room which held the vital information? He had to find the man and learn how he could get in and steal the secrets.

The two sets of prints walked toward the wall surrounding the compound. At the wall, Tino shone the light on the adobe. At the top, at the right distance apart for a rope ladder, there were marks on the wall. Why would Hector leave now? He'd know his disappearance would cause turmoil.

He flipped his phone open and called Garza.

"Did you find him?" Garza snarled.

"No, but I think he went over the wall with another person. I am at the west wall." He hung up. Within minutes, two vehicles and half a dozen men along with Garza pulled up to the wall.

"What did you find?" Garza stepped out of the SUV before it stopped completely.

Tino waved his flashlight up to shine on the marks on the edge of the wall. "I followed two sets of prints to here."

Garza cursed and snapped his fingers. "Get a ladder up there and see what's on the other side."

A ladder was slapped against the wall and Cezar climbed up and peered over the top. "Looks like a body on the ground."

Tino groaned inside. If it was Hector, he'd just lost his inside source to information.

"Drop down and check it. Diego, you and Tino drive around." Garza waved his hand.

Tino hopped in the Jeep with Diego and they raced toward the gate.

"Do you think it is Hector?" Diego asked, barely stopping for the gate to open.

"I do not think it could be anyone else." Tino held onto the dash as Diego spun the vehicle to the left.

"This is not good. Hadda and Hector have been seeing one another. I do not want to be around when she is told." Diego whistled and slammed on the brakes.

The vehicle's headlights shone on Cezar bending over a body. He turned it and there was no mistaking Hector. Tino cursed and stepped out to get a closer look. A bloody hole in the middle of his forehead seemed to be the only mark on him. It appeared Hector was expendable, but why? Did whoever he was working for have all the information they needed? And what information would that be? Now that Hector was dead, he was pretty sure the shipment schedule would change. Garza was smart enough to suspect Hector as the mole inside his operation.

They loaded Hector into the back. Cezar took the passenger seat, so Tino hopped into the back with the body. He took the opportunity to search Hector's pockets, stuffing everything he found into his own.

When they pulled up to the house, señora Garza hurried down the stairs and held her shawl to her mouth as they lifted Hector out of the vehicle.

"No! Paolo, who would do this to Hector?" she asked, her eyes glistening with tears.

"Karyme, go back inside." Garza turned her from the sight. "Anarosa, give my wife a nice cup of hot tea. I'll be right in."

Tino took the sight in. It appeared Garza's wife wasn't usually around when the seedier side of her husband's work happened. He found that curious.

They hauled Hector's body into the garage and up to his bed.

Garza planted a finger in Cezar's chest. "I want you to check the body over, then call Dr. Guiterrez and have him check for any evidence that could help us find Hector's killer."

Garza turned from instructing Cezar and waved his arms. "Everyone out but Cezar. You," he pointed to Tino, "take two men and search the area where the body was found. See if you can find any evidence to tell us who did this."

Tino nodded. He would have rather stayed with the body and heard what the doctor had to report but to refuse now would draw suspicion. Tino snagged Diego and Cruz, taking them back out the gate to the bloody area where they found the body.

While searching the area, he listened to the two talk about Hector. He had his opinions but wanted to hear from the men who conversed with him on a daily basis. Tino now wished he'd made more of an effort to friend the narcos, at least to be in their confidence. He'd kept his distance, so no one asked him personal questions and to keep all emotion out of his taking down the operation. If he became friends with one of the men it would make his job harder to do.

"Hector was hot-headed," Cruz said. "I am not surprised he did not get any older."

"Sí. He and Hadda were arguing yesterday before the señora arrived."

"Whose nephew was Hector? On the señora or señor's side?" Tino asked.

"The señora's. He was her brother's son." Diego, who had been with the Garza's for many years had the most useful information.

Ouch! How did Garza tell his wife and her family their relation was dead because of his drug dealing? The family had to know what he did. Everyone on the streets connected Garza's name with drug trafficking. Not to mention weapons and people. He was powerful and any family member would know the seedy side of his operations no matter how much money he tossed around toward philanthropic projects.

"Were Hector and Hadda sleeping together?" He was pretty sure that was against Garza's rules but then again, Hector was family and maybe he didn't have to follow all the rules.

"He said so, but she denied it when I asked her," Diego offered.

Tino found nothing to tie Hector's death with anyone or anything. He'd doubted there would be any proof. The person who lured Hector over the fence had everything well thought out.

"There is nothing here." Tino climbed into the Jeep, motioning for the others to do the same, and headed back to the house. If he couldn't learn anything from the doctor, the next person to be investigated was Hadda, the cook's daughter and household maid.

Chapter Twelve

Isabella had trouble falling asleep. Could Garza have brought her here under false pretenses? There were two ways to find out—either ask him or do some digging of her own. As soon as the sun filtered into her room, she pulled out her cell phone and dialed Eunice Isakson. Other than calling her father and asking for Pedro, the cook/operative's, phone number, Eunice was the only other person at the Guatemalan dig who she knew how to contact and ask if someone had come around asking questions about the people at *Ch'ujuña*.

The phone buzzed several times.

"Come on, Eunice, have cell service." Isabella mumbled as her stomach grumbled.

"Hello!" Eunice sounded out of breath.

"Hi, Eunice, it's Isabella."

"Well, hello. I haven't talked with you since Guatemala. You disappeared into the jungle without a trace. I asked around and learned you'd returned to work, but I didn't stop worrying about you until I called and confirmed it. I told the officials who showed up at the dig that you were missing, but they didn't appear worried." Her tone held a scold and relief.

"I'm sorry. I just had to get away from Virgil. I didn't understand his attitude and… well…"

"I understand, he wasn't himself at all during that dig and to think his irrational behavior got him killed."

There was an awkward silence.

Eunice blurted. "I was surprised you weren't at the funeral."

"I was out of the country and couldn't get back." She hated lying to her friend. She'd been in training at the WIA institute. Even if she hadn't been busy, she would never have been able to go to the funeral of the man who betrayed her so openly.

"Are you back in the country? We could meet for lunch today. I'm at a dig not far from your university."

"Bad timing. I'm actually in Mexico researching for a paper." And she meant it. Lunch with Eunice would have been heavenly after all the chaos in her life lately.

"That's a shame. What did you call me about?" The curiosity in the woman's voice couldn't be missed.

Isabella collected her thoughts. She had to ask without it seeming as if she were hunting for information. "I just wondered if someone contacted you, too, about our time in Guatemala."

"I heard that private investigator talked to everyone. Well, everyone but Virgil, for obvious reasons."

Her heart pounded and vibrated in her chest like a bass beat at a rock concert. "Do you happen to still have his card? I lost mine and I remembered something he asked about."

"Sure, just a minute. It's on my bulletin board in the office."

The sound of Eunice's breathing and her walking resounded in Isabella's ear. Her hands shook scrambling to find a pen and paper. Someone *had* been investigating. Now she needed to discover if he was working for Garza. She couldn't call and tip her hand that she knew Garza was investigating her. Her next call would be to Daddy. Her father could send someone to discreetly find out who was the investigator's client.

"Here it is. Joseph Pintauro. He's out of Tucson."

Shamutz! He lived and worked right in the same town as she did. He'd, no doubt, also talked with her colleagues and the staff at the university. He'd know she was the same person the people from the dig talked about and that she was right now in Mexico City.

"Thanks. I forgot he was local." To draw Eunice's thoughts away from this topic she asked, "What are you doing in my area?"

The discussion focused on the dig where Eunice was taking photographs of the artifacts for categorizing and photos of the dig operations for an archeological magazine.

"That's wonderful. Maybe I'll still get a chance to meet up with you for a cup of coffee or a meal when I return." Isabella glanced at her watch. They'd talked for half an hour.

"That would be wonderful." The welcome in Eunice's voice brought tears to Isabella's eyes. This was the only real friend she had besides Tino, and she couldn't even tell this woman about the man she loved. Maybe by the time she returned to Arizona she could tell Eunice all about Tino. That little bit of hope sparked a renewed effort to decipher the puzzle for the true reason she was in Mexico and to help Tino get the information he needed so they could both be tucked away safe in the states.

"It's been great talking with you, but I need to go. I have work to accomplish today."

Eunice chuckled. "You're always working, young lady. You should take a vacation some time and find out it can be good to sit back and enjoy life now and then."

"That sounds like wonderful advice, and I'll take you up on it one of these days. Perhaps went I get back home. See you then."

"I'll be looking forward to the meeting. Bye."

"Bye."

Isabella tapped the end button on her phone and stared at the notes she'd jotted down. As much as she hated to bring her father into her assignment, if she and Tino were right, they needed to know what Garza knew.

She scanned her contacts and dialed.

Voice mail.

She sighed and after the beep said, "Daddy, I need to talk to you. It's important." She tapped the end button and dressed.

Folding the dress she wore the night before, she uncovered the employee files and surveillance tapes. The only way to watch the tapes was to have a video player brought up. She picked up the phone in her room and called down to the desk.

"This is Dr. Mumphrey in room 211. I'd like to have a video machine that will hook up to the television delivered to my room as well as breakfast."

"Señorita, we have cable for the television."

Isabella's heart raced. She hoped they had what she needed. "Sí, but I brought videos with me I want to watch."

"Ahh, we can help you. I will have that to you in thirty minutes."

"That will be fine, gracias."

Isabella stacked the video tapes on the dresser and picked up the stack of files. She used the list of occupations with employee's names to find the security guard files. She pulled those out and sat down in the chair. One by one, she opened the files and read. Two people, the night guard and one of the day guards, started at the museum within weeks of one another. They also had a large backlist of references. That alone was a red flag.

Either the two moved from job to job a lot or they padded their resumes with places of prestige. Either one was a reason to have them looked at further. She added their names to a list she titled suspects.

Director Bastante was the next file she read. He'd been the director for five years. Before that he was at a smaller museum for ten. He had degrees in archeology and business. Both made sense given his chosen profession. She pulled out a small laptop and began searching his background some more. When she couldn't find him listed under the awards he stated having received in college, she added him to the suspect list.

Knocking at the door interrupted her search.

"Just a minute." Isabella closed her laptop and tossed her dress across the files. She didn't need some nosy bellboy saying she had files scattered around her room. With everything she'd learned, she knew enough not to trust anyone.

She opened the door and was surprised to see Alphonso.

"What are you doing…?" Her question trailed off when she saw the video player under one arm and a tray of food in the other hand.

"I didn't know you worked here." She took the tray, set it on the dresser by the door and then took the video player from him.

"I was downstairs when my cousin was looking for a boy to bring up what you ordered." The smile he gave her felt genuine, but his gaze roaming about her room, made her uneasy.

"Gracias." She grabbed up her vest and pulled out a five-dollar bill. "I appreciate your cousin's diligence." Handing the money to Alphonso, she pushed him to the other side of the threshold and shut the door.

Wonderful! Now it appeared she had become a person of interest to the Bohu gang. Was there anyone in this city who wasn't watching her?

She set the video player on the table next to the television and connected the cords. After popping in a video from the archive room dated during the week before the curator noticed the first missing artifacts, she sat down with the tray of food on her lap and watched.

The film was grainy and hard to distinguish who went in and out of the room. From what she could tell, it seemed to be the same five or six people throughout the day. Then the lights were shut off and the video camera seemed to sleep, until light made the camera come alive once more. She leaned forward in her chair, setting the tray to the side and peering intently at the television.

The way the person carried himself she knew him. But who was it? The film was too grainy to get a good glimpse of his face. He didn't wear a guard uniform. He was dressed in a baggy shirt and pants and wearing a ball cap. To get into the building at night he would have either sneaked in or been an employee that was trusted. He walked up to a specific crate and… She moved closer to the television. The person was adhering shipping labels on two crates.

That's how the items came up missing. They were shipped. No one carried them out stealing them; they were carried out by employees to be shipped. But the address would have to be something that didn't set off any alarms in the person delivering them…unless the person who delivered the shipments was the person who put the label on the box.

She ejected the tape, placing it on top of the files of the people she wanted her father to check out. Why hadn't he called back?

She plopped back down in the chair and finished off the tortillas and cheese, leaving the papaya and bananas for later.

The theme song from Indian Jones invaded the quiet of the room. Isabella chewed on her lip and picked up her cell phone from the table. Now that Daddy had called, she didn't want to come across as a newbie agent.

"Hello?"

"How are things in Mexico?" Daddy's jovial voice brought a weak smile to her lips.

Too bad he wasn't here to infuse more of that her way.

"Getting more and more complicated every day." She pushed her glasses tighter on her nose and peered at the name she'd scribbled on the note pad.

"This is just a simple job of discovering how the artifacts were stolen." The tone of his voice instantly took her back fifteen years to when she was eleven.

"I discovered how that was accomplished—"

"Good, send me the report and get back here."

"I can't." She held her breath waiting, and it came.

"What do you mean you can't? That's not a request as your father that's an order as your superior."

"There is more going on here than stolen artifacts."

"Isabella, you're in Mexico City for crying out loud, of course, there is more going on than stolen artifacts. It's a city teeming with every black market there is. And that's the best reason for you to get back here."

"Now you sound like Tino." She hissed out an exasperated sigh.

"I knew I liked that boy."

"I need you to check out a private investigator in Tucson. His name's Joseph Pintauro." She heard an intake of breath. "Mom, are you listening in?"

"Yes, Isabella, I am. Joesph Pintauro did work for us several years back. What makes you suspect him of the artifact theft?"

"I don't. Someone has him interviewing everyone who was in Guatemala when I shot Virgil."

"How do you know this?" Her father's hard tone proved he'd shifted to work mode.

"Tino and I have our suspicions that I was brought down here for a reason besides the thefts. He suggested Paolo Garza, the drug lord he's infiltrated, knows about my connection with the circumstances surrounding his friend Don Miguel and the shooting in Guatemala. I contacted Eunice Isakson, and she confirmed this Pintauro has been asking questions about the Ch'ujuña dig."

She heard her mother talking on another phone.

"Your mother is looking into who hired him right now. Write your report and bring it and your evidence back to me tomorrow."

"I can't. I promised someone I'd help with something, and I'm not leaving here until I've had a chance to talk with Tino." She rarely defied her father and never defied a boss, but this time, she was going to listen to her gut and it told her she needed to stay and assist Tino.

Chapter Thirteen

Tino had been brought into the locked room off Garza's office as the sun rose over the east wall of the compound. He tried to see everything without Cezar or Garza noticing his surveillance. Hector's death had the drug lord shaken up but not enough he wouldn't still be vigilant when introducing someone new to the hub of his drug organization. The fact an intruder had infiltrated Garza's compound during a party for his wife, murdered his wife's nephew, and left without being observed had the drug lord fuming.

Tino had overheard señora Garza on the phone earlier telling their daughters they would stay in Columbia and not come to Mexico City as had been planned. From the conversation on the señora's end, the daughters were not happy to be left behind. But with the security having been breached so easily having their daughters here would make them easy targets for whoever was toying with Garza.

"Rodriguez, tell me again everything that happened last night." Garza stood in front of a large white board with grids. Dates, names, and weights filled in much of the grid.

Tino went over the evening again, as he had every hour since the doctor arrived and verified what type of bullet had killed Hector. When the doctor pronounced him dead, Cruz was left to sit with Hector until he was prepared for burial. No officials were called. Only Hector's family.

"How many times did Hector go for a smoke?" Garza asked.

"Three or four times. It was about every half hour."

"And you did not ask him why he was smoking so much?" Cezar turned an accusing gaze his direction.

"Ever since I came here, Hector has worked harder at getting out of work than doing a job. I figured he was just using the smoke as an excuse to do nothing." Tino shrugged. Neither man could find fault with that assumption. It was true. Hector had been lazy.

Garza nodded. "And why would anyone be interested in Hector? He knew nothing, I made sure of that."

"He must have known something that got him killed," Cezar said, still eyeballing Tino with ill-will.

Tino wasn't going to mention Hector's closeness with Hadda. With luck Diego would keep quiet about his knowledge of Hector and Hadda's relationship long enough for Tino to question the girl. He wanted the information for the DEA and not Garza.

"Maybe Hector went for a smoke and walked into something he was not supposed to see?" Tino ignored Cezar and spoke directly to Garza. "Prehaps someone had come over the wall and was sneaking to the house when Hector came upon him. To keep Hector from alerting the rest of us, he was knocked out and dragged over the wall, then shot where they could make a faster get-a-way if they were found." It was highly implausible, but he had to throw suspicion outside the compound in order to talk to the people inside the compound before Garza.

The drug lord stared at him. Tino could see Garza's mind working. Would he fall for the false lead or did he already realize it was false? Frustration paralyzed Tino's thinking. He'd never been in a situation where the person he was bringing down could possibly know he was an agent.

A knock drew all their gazes to the thick door.

"Answer it!" Garza directed Cezar.

Señora Garza marched into the room. Sorrow for her nephew pulled on her face adding extra years, making her look her true age.

"Family has started to arrive and the man at the gate will not allow them in." She stopped in front of Garza. "You cannot keep my family out. Either let them in or let them take Hector so we can be with him until he is buried."

Garza motioned to Cezar. "Go man the gate, you know Karyme's family. Only let in family. No friends."

Cezar left the room. Tino shuffled his feet waiting to be excused. But Garza seemed to have forgotten him so he took this opportunity to scrutinize the room one more time. The grid was a visual of Garza's drug routes and what product and amount was being moved over each route. This was the room that needed to be breached and the information confiscated. That was his mission for the DEA. His private mission was to take the man down completely.

Garza captured his wife's hands. "I only want to keep everyone safe. Whoever killed Hector came into our home and did so. We have to be extra careful. I do not want you leaving without me or Cezar with you." His attention flew to Tino.

"Rodriguez."

"¿Sí?"

"Go see if they need help laying out Hector." Garza pulled his wife into his arms as Tino walked out of the room.

Tino strode out the door with mixed emotions. He'd found what he was looking for but seeing Garza and his wife together, played chaos with his sense of justice. He knew the cold, hard side of Garza. He'd witnessed the goodness in the señora and didn't like to think about how he would upend her life when he brought down Garza.

Walking down the hall, he caught a glimpse of Hadda in the dining room. He stood in the doorway watching her dust around the keepsakes and religious items on the massive altar display built into the corner of the dining room wall. A painting of the Virgin de Guadalupe sat on an easel in the back of the display. Hadda placed a photo of Hector in the front and lit the candles on the sides.

Tino stepped into the room, blocking her from leaving when she turned from the altar.

Quietly for her ears only he said, "I heard from Diego that you and Hector were friendly."

Hadda's dark brown eyes widened. She glanced about before whispering, "No one is to know."

"Why? Señora Garza does not seem like the type to worry about classes mingling."

She stared at her feet.

Tino moved closer and dropped his voice even more. "I would

like to help you. If someone killed Hector and you know why, you could be next." Tino hoped the woman would come to her senses without making him give up his cover.

Her face scrunched up as if she were going to cry.

Tino pulled her into his arms, holding her. She was too young to be mixed up in whatever Hector lured her into. "I can help you, but you have to tell me what you know."

She shook her head.

He put his mouth next to her ear for only her to hear. It was a huge risk, but he had to find out who she was helping. "You and I are after the same things, no? To find out about the shipments."

Her body froze. She peered at his face with tear-filled eyes. Raising on her tiptoes, she whispered in his ear. "You are working with Luis Bohu, too?"

This was who had discovered the information to help the Bohu gang. But what about the shipment the Alvarez brothers intercepted? Did Hadda help them as well?

"No. I am after information for another." He pulled back in time to see a flash in her eyes and a faint smile slip from her lips. Would she turn him over to Garza?

He eased her away from him. "Did Luis kill Hector?"

She shook her head. "No. Luis was not here. I do not know who killed him. That is why I am so scared, but I cannot tell señor Garza what Hector and I have been doing."

"Sí, you may be Anarosa's daughter, but he would not care knowing you are a traitor." Tino squeezed her hand. "Keep this to yourself. I will see if I can determine who killed Hector, so you will feel safe."

"Gracias." She sniffed and wiped at her runny nose with the hem of her shirt.

"Rodriguez, why are you not helping with Hector?" Garza's voice boomed through the room.

Tino winked at Hadda and spun. "Hadda asked me to hold the Virgin de Guadelupe so she could dust and prepare the altar."

"Get to where I told you to go." Garza's dark stare watched him leave the room.

Tino hustled to the living quarters over the garage and discovered Diego and Cruz dressing Hector. Someone had cleaned him up and filled in the hole in his head with flesh tone putty.

He couldn't wait for this day to be over with and Garza to lighten up the security. He needed to speak with Rico, and he was worried about Isabella now that they both felt she was lured to Mexico City.

The three carried Hector's body down to the casket sitting on a stand in the grand salon. Relatives had already taken up seats and filled plates with food. The chatter was gay and one young man sat to the side strumming a guitar.

The last wake Tino had attended was for his family. He'd not been allowed to return to Venezuela for his abuela's funeral. His only consolation had been the knowledge he'd spoken to her three days before a stroke took her away.

Once Hector was placed in his coffin, Tino made his way slowly back to the doorway. On the way, he caught a glimpse of everyone present. It wouldn't hurt to know who the family members were in case he came across someone snooping.

The museum director rushed into the room and straight for señora Garza. Was he family? If so, he could be the connection that brought Isabella down here.

Tino moved in the direction of the director and the señora, offering condolences to people he'd not met before. Diego and Cruz had left as soon as they deposited Hector in the coffin. Would the others think it strange he stayed behind?

"Karyme, I'm so sorry for your family's loss," Bastante said, clasping her hand.

Ahh, so that was the man's game. It appeared the director had aspirations to perhaps fill Garza's shoes one day. Any fool could see the director had more than friendly feelings for the woman.

Tino backed away. Why did Cezar allow the man in when Garza had firmly stated only family?

His idea would either get him in thicker or shot sooner.

Once outside the grand salon, Tino hurried down the hall to the office. He knocked.

"*Entrar*," Garza called out.

His eyes narrowed when Tino slipped into the room.

"What do you want?"

"Is Director Bastante related to your wife?" Tino watched the storm cloud of anger build in the man's eyes.

"No. Why?"

"You told Cezar to only allow family; yet, Bastante is consoling your wife."

Garza sprang out of his chair, stormed around the desk, and swept him aside to leave the room.

Tino trotted on Garza's heels. He wanted to see the outcome of his little scheme.

Bastante stiffened the minute Garza entered the grand salon. The director couldn't move fast enough away from señora Garza.

Garza jammed a finger in the director's chest. "My office! Now!" He spun and his gaze landed on Tino. "Send Cezar to me, now!"

Tino nodded and headed out the front door. Was he to keep guard on the gate? He hoped not because he could use this latest development to contact Rico. It appeared more than DEA wanted to take down the Garza empire. He needed to know if the director was working with the Bohu gang and how young Hadda fit into the arrangement.

Chapter Fourteen

Isabella watched all the surveillance tapes and discovered the person returning to the storage area in the museum three more times and labeling crates. How did he know which crates to label? And why did he look so familiar?

She wandered down to the restaurant with all this information tumbling around in her head.

Felix greeted her. "Did the machine Alphonso brought you work?"

"Sí. I was able to watch my movies. Gracias."

She continued into the restaurant and took a table by the window. It was mid-afternoon. Staring out at the crowded streets and sidewalks made her cringe. She'd have to navigate through the throng to get to the museum and do her research.

Several wait persons hovered around her table filling her glass with water, taking her order, and supplying her with appetizers or *botanas*. The flurry of people inside and outside was enough to make her wish for her peaceful apartment and the quiet coffee shop on her block that she frequented on Sunday mornings.

Unable to endure any more, she dug pesos out of her vest pocket and left the restaurant. At least the archives at the museum would be peaceful. The exhaust filled air, leached into her lungs causing her to cough. How could people live in this? Today the air seemed unusually thick and toxic.

She fell in step with the wave of people heading toward Templo Mayor. Once through the entrance, she nudged her way through the people and peeled off at the museum entrance. Breathing in the filtered and cooler air, she again broke from the wave and headed to the basement stairs.

Closing the door, she leaned against it a moment before descending the stairs and pushing through the door into the hallway. She preferred the stairs to the elevator. Counting the steps was more calming than hurling downward in a closed box.

Once inside the archive room, she breathed in the musty scent of old papers. Her second favorite scent behind glued book bindings. A vision of a man popped into her mind. Perhaps they both now took second to the earthy scent of Tino.

Her lips heated and her body quivered thinking of Tino. When they both left Mexico, she planned on showing him how much he meant to her and hopefully persuading him to give up hunting down Garza and working for the DEA.

She pushed away from the door and headed to the section in the archive area that held the information she needed to write her research paper. Basically, she'd finished her WIA mission. Her goal was to determine how the artifacts were stolen. She'd discerned that from the videos. But why hadn't anyone else looked at the videos and determined it themselves?

Prickling sensations crawled up her back. Why indeed? Were the law officials in the pocket of whoever was stealing the artifacts? She knew the curator, Delgado, had connections with WIA and had requested someone help determine how the items were disappearing. Had the officials not even been brought in on this?

All the conversations she'd had with señor Delgado he'd never mentioned the local authorities. With Bastante not knowing she was WIA, it led her to believe Delgado had reason to suspect the director may have something to do with the missing artifacts. The more she thought about all the people who could be involved it became a kaleidoscope of possibilities.

The only positive lead she had on the missing artifacts was the videos showing someone labeling crates after hours.

She played the videos over in her mind. The person who labeled the crates hadn't come in from the door. The sensor that tripped the lights and the camera came on when the person was in the middle of the storage room. If they'd come through the door, it would have been tripped at the door.

I have to look inside the storage room.

Isabella left the archives and walked down the empty corridor to the storage room. Her footsteps echoed in the silence. The noise made her flinch and search the corridor behind her. No one followed. Why paranoia had a hold on her she didn't know. She was the only person in this part of the building. All the tourists, guides, and guards were in the upper floors. She was the only one skulking about the basement.

The storage room door had a push button lock. Holding her breath, Isabella punched in the date Bastante took over the position of museum director. The light continued to blink red. She scanned through her memory to other important dates in his life and tried those.

The light blinked green and a click signified she was in when she used the date of his first dig experience. Having read all the information on the man, she'd discovered he liked to keep track of events in his life. The reason she had memorized all his important dates.

She opened the door, releasing cool, musty, underground air into the corridor and across her face. The air was reminiscent of her recent exploits in Guatemala. Stepping across the threshold the overhead lights blinked on. That was what should have happened if the midnight labeler had entered through this door.

There were rows of stacked crates, some open crates with wood shavings spilling out, and material stacked to one side to make more crates. To the left was the service elevator. He hadn't used the elevator either.

Isabella extracted her LED flashlight from her vest pocket and began a thorough search of the walls of the basement. There had to be another way into the room. She stopped and surveyed the room, replaying the video in her mind.

The labeler had his back to the camera when approaching the crates. She scanned the upper corners of the area searching for the surveillance camera. There. In the corner opposite the door and elevator. The person had to come from this area.

Several crates were piled against the wall. Investigating the area around them, she found scrape marks on the concrete the width of the boxes. They'd been shoved. She pocketed her flashlight and pushed on the crate. It moved easier than she'd anticipated. She fell to her knees when the crates slid to the side and revealed an opening four foot tall and three feet wide.

She pulled her flashlight back out, shining the beam into the passageway. Footprints in the dust proved someone had recently used it as entry to the basement storage. Where did it lead to? It had to be an extension of the tunnels being excavated in Templo Mayor. Who found this and why did they keep it a secret?

She mentally thunked her forehead. It was a secret because whoever found the tunnel used it to steal artifacts found in the temple. The people using the hidden entrance to label specific crates had to be part of the museum or part of the archeological groups or a combination. There could be a multitude of people involved.

The flashlight shone down a straight passageway leading…She ducked her head and entered the area. Logic told her to go back and research when the excavation near this passage was done. That would give a clue as to who could know about the tunnel. Then she could check on the whereabouts of all the people involved. But the adventure seeking part of her, who adored Indiana Jones movies, wanted to follow the passage and see where she came out.

Hunched in the secret passage, debating with herself, Isabella gave in to the logic and stepped out of the passage. Shoving the crates back against the wall, she wiped the dust from her hands and left the storage area.

Back in the archive room, she searched for the records and maps of the first excavation teams at Templo Mayor.

~*~

The house was full of Hector's family. Or those who told him they were family members as Tino manned the gate when Garza ordered him to send Cezar to him. Eventually, Diego relieved him. Rather than return to the house, Tino used the upcoming funeral and chaos to slip away in the darkness. He hurried to the car DEA had stashed for him and headed to his rendezvous with Rico.

Satisfaction hovered on his lips driving through the congested streets. Once he filled Rico in on the new findings, he'd find Isabella and spend some time with her. Try, one more time, to talk her into returning to Arizona.

Tino cursed the Sunday traffic and couldn't even conjure up a hint of a laugh while watching a mime entertain the people in cars as they crept through the main thoroughfare. He should have taken side streets to the cantina where he'd asked Rico to meet him.

An hour past the time he'd planned to meet Rico, Tino walked into the dark cantina in the Bohu gang's territory. He didn't want to be caught in the Alvarez's *distrio* and he wanted to get a feel for the mood in the Bohu distrio.

The music was loud, the lights low, and the room crowded. He'd called Rico while sitting in traffic and knew his contact would be waiting, what he didn't know was where in all these people Rico would be.

It took several moments for his eyes to adjust to the bodies and dim lighting. During that time two women walked up to him, each slipping an arm through his and drawing him deeper into the room.

"I am looking for a friend," he said, smiling and trying to withdraw his arms from their hold.

"Sí," said the voluptuous raven-haired beauty on his right arm. She was the kind he'd favored before Isabella. She curved her plump, blood-red lips into a seductive smile and continued moving him to the back of the establishment.

He scanned the people as the crowd surged around them. His mind began all types of scenarios where he ended up dead. The two stopped in front of a booth in the corner. They extracted their arms at the same time bodies moved, and he spotted Rico chatting up another exceptionally well-endowed *chica*.

"Mi Amigo, have a seat." Rico waved his hand toward the vacant seat at his booth.

Both girls slid in with Tino, sandwiching him between them. In the days before Isabella, he would have wrapped an arm around each woman. Now, he hoped their strong perfume didn't seep into his clothing.

"I see you have found a way to be entertained while waiting for me." Tino stared directly into Rico's eyes. He wanted privacy to speak, yet the man had surrounded them with women who could be informants for the Bohu gang. He was beginning to wonder if Rico wasn't playing two sides.

"Señoritas, bring my friend a cervaza then give us some time to conduct business." Rico kissed the woman next to him on the cheek when she pouted.

Tino gladly hip-bumped the woman on the outside of his booth, pushing her to her feet and standing to allow the other woman out. Once she vacated the seat, he plopped back down on the edge so there was no space for one of them to decide to sit back down.

Rico laughed as the three sauntered off. "Mano, you are not very convincing that you are a single man out for some fun."

"I have too many things on my mind to enjoy a woman's soft body." And he wasn't single in his heart. In his heart, he was already married to Isabella. This acknowledgement to anyone but himself could cause her harm and be used against him.

Rico's expression hardened. "What has happened in the compound? There have been rumors señora Garza's nephew is dead."

"This is true. Sometime toward the end of the party last night someone slipped into the compound and met with Hector, lured him over the wall, and killed him. Garza is pissed and going crazy trying to figure out who it was and how it happened."

Two of the women returned with the drinks and lingered at the end of the table, swaying to the music and smiling.

"Vamos," Rico said, swatting the one closest to him on the bottom. She pouted, again, and he grabbed her hand, dragging her down into his lap. He kissed and groped her for what felt like an hour to Tino as he watched the people around them. No one seemed to be especially interested in them. He also didn't see any activity that appeared gang related.

When Rico released the woman, she blew him a kiss, and strutted off. The encounter must have allayed her worries he would forget about her after their meeting.

Rico slowly drew his gaze from her swaying hips and narrowed his eyes on Tino. "You saw us leaving before the party. We planted several listening devices and cameras in floral arrangements. We were unable to pick up anything. Do you have any idea why that was?"

Tino nodded. He'd guessed right. "Garza does a sweep of the house anytime anyone other than his employees have been in the house. He probably found the devices and disposed of them."

Rico cursed. "I do not have enough of a budget to lose that much equipment."

"You would be smart to not bother bugging his house."

"Do you have any idea who killed Hector?"

"My first thought was Alvarez brothers. Payment for being roughed up. But I learned that someone in the household has connections with the Bohu gang."

Rico nodded his head. "That is why you wished to meet here. In their distrio."

"Sí. If they know who works for Garza, my appearance here should stir the pot a bit."

"And put your head in the noose if Garza finds out."

Tino shrugged. "If I need to use lowlifes to take down Garza I will. Anyone is expendable when it comes to stopping him."

"You are very determined to stop Paolo Garza. What makes him any different from any other drug lord?" Rico stared intently at him.

Tino had kept his secret desire to rid the world of Paolo Garza from the DEA. If they knew he was on a one-man mission, they would not have allowed him to join and put him in the exact place he wanted to be.

"Nothing. But you take down one of his reputation and it will make the others extra careful and perhaps slow their business for a bit."

Rico continued to study him. He wasn't buying Tino's answer. He finally lifted his gaze, peered around the establishment, and smiled sardonically.

"I think you are getting your wish.

Chapter Fifteen

Tino knew all the major players in the Mexico City drug scene and the man stalking toward their table was the head of the Bohu gang. Four of his flunkies lined up behind him like a low budget movie scene.

"What are you doing in our distrio?" Luis Bohu asked, stopping at the end of the table, crossing his arms, and staring with unbridled hatred at Tino.

Tino spun the glass of beer in front of him and peered into the man's eyes. "Visiting with a friend."

At that moment, the three women returned. One climbed over Rico's lap and the other snuggled up to his side and the third one shoved Tino over, draping her body against his side like a blanket.

Luis narrowed his eyes. "Carmelita, how do you know these two?"

The woman who Rico had kissed with passion earlier and had just climbed over his lap snuggled closer to Rico. "He is the second cousin of Rosita and this is his friend." She nodded toward Tino.

Luis shook his head. "Sister, you are being far too friendly with someone you only know as Rosita's cousin."

Tino used his best effort to not snap to attention at the word "sister." Rico was playing Russian Roulette using Luis's sister.

Since it was obvious Luis already knew he worked for Garza and he was still alive, a few questions to Luis might just get him some answers.

"Who would want Hector Martinez dead?" Tino asked, playing with the beads dangling between the ample breasts of the woman draped over him.

Luis waved his hand. "You, women, go! Now!"

The ladies scurried out of the booth and away from the area in a flash and the men behind Luis closed in close and tight, their scowls tapping away at Tino's confidence.

Luis slapped his hands on the table and leaned toward Tino. "Is that why you are here? To see if I killed Hector?"

"No. I am confident you did not kill him. But you may know who did." Tino leaned back casually and took a sip of his drink.

"Why would I want to help you or Garza?"

"You would not be helping Garza. It is Hadda who needs help."

The surprise and fear that flashed across Luis' face told Tino all he needed to know. The girl and he were lovers. That was why she would risk so much to help him.

"What do you know of Hadda?"

Tino wanted to see if Rico was against him spilling what he knew to Luis. To make eye contact with his superior could tip Luis they were working together. Getting his suspicions aroused would not only put them in trouble but possibly the man's sister. For the sake of so many, he kept his gaze riveted to Luis.

"I was told Hector and Hadda were close by one of Garza's men. When I spoke with Hadda she let slip her connection with you. Given the recent developments of a missing shipment that landed in your hands, if Garza learned of Hadda's conspiracy she would never be seen from again." Tino studied the man. His scrunched brow and narrowed eyes revealed he was deep in thought.

"Why are you not telling this to Garza?"

"Hadda is a sweet kid who got herself messed up with the wrong person." He stared point blank at the man. "I do not want to see her suffer for someone else's stupidity."

Luis's face darkened in color and contorted in anger. "You just called me stupid."

"What would you call asking someone as young and inexperienced as Hadda to steal information from a man known to kill people for lesser blunders?"

Luis stared at Tino for several heart beats. His color lightened and he straightened his body, relaxing the threat.

"All I need to do is tell you who killed Hector and you will keep Hadda safe?"

"As safe as I can. I cannot guarantee if Garza finds out and he sics Cezar after her that I can save her but I will try."

Rico stirred on the other side of the booth. Tino glanced over and notice him watching someone who had just arrived.

He recognized the person at the same moment Luis let out a curse.

Cezar was moving through the crowd.

"Stop him," Luis ordered his men.

Tino slipped out of the booth heading for a back door. How had Garza's righthand man tracked him here? Before he could find Isabella, he needed to check his clothing and hardware for tracking devices.

Seconds from opening the door to the alley a hand grabbed the back of his shirt and hauled him into the men's *baños*.

He spun around and encountered Rico.

"What are you doing? You set up a meet in Bohu territory and then have Garza's righthand man follow you here."

Tino didn't answer. He handed his gun and phone to Rico. "Check those for devices." Then he started striping, feeling the shirt tail and thick places on his clothing for a transmitter. He picked up his shoe and found the small transmitter in the sole.

"¡Coño!" Now he'd have to do some fast talking with Garza knowing he came to Bohu territory. Tino pulled out a knife and pried the device from his sole, flicking it into the toilet and flushing.

"It appears mi amigo that your boss does not trust you." Rico handed back his phone and gun.

"He does not trust anyone." Tino shoved his gun into the back of his pants and flipped open his phone. He pressed the icon for Juanita. He should hustle back to the compound and see what kind of trouble he was in, but he wasn't about to miss a chance to see Isabella.

~*~

Isabella blinked and raised her head from her palm. There it was again the trill of a phone. Her arm tingled as she unbent it to reach into her vest pocket for the phone Tino gave her. Moving her stiff neck and tingling arm, she pushed the button.

"Hello?" her dry throat scratched as she spoke.

"Querida, are you all right?"

The concern in Tino's voice tipped her lips into a smile.

"Yes. I must have fallen asleep reading all these old reports." She smoothed loose strands of hair out of her face and was relieved to find her arm beginning to work better.

"Then you are at the museum?"

"Yes." Her heart raced. "Can we meet?"

"Sí. I will be behind the building in fifteen minutes."

"I'll be waiting."

The phone went silent. She closed hers and stretched her body and arms toward the ceiling. How long had she slept? A glance at her watch said twenty minutes. The information she was searching for should have kept her awake. The long hours and quiet must have played a part in her sleepiness.

Isabella returned the log to its place on the shelf, closed her journal, and studied the area to make sure she didn't leave any clues to what she was really researching. From the information she'd gathered before falling asleep there were many different parties over the years who worked on the digging. Both archeologist and government employees. The archeologists would know the significance of the artifacts but the government employees would be the ones most likely to steal from the people and stuff their pockets.

She walked out of the archives and shut the door. Another click registered moments later farther up the corridor. Pressing her body into a door recess, she peered down the hall. The same night watchman was leaving the room near the elevator again.

Isabella slipped back into the archive room and searched for a camera. That was the only reason she could think of for the man to always be leaving the office when she left this room. There had to be a camera that fed directly to that room and wasn't part of the regular security system.

A quick peek at her watch had her ending the search. Tino would be there in three minutes. She exited the room and the building using Tino's method of bypassing the security system at the back basement door.

Out in the exhaust filled air she sneezed.

"Bless you."

She squeaked and jumped at the voice only a few feet away in the shadow of the building.

A car drove by slowly.

"Don't look at me. Start walking to your left. I'll stay in the shadow and join you when the car goes by."

Isabella turned to her left and walked casually down the sidewalk. The car moved on around the corner and Tino arrived at her side. He took her hand and continued walking.

"I'm glad you had time to see me. It's silly but when we were thousands of miles apart, I didn't feel as lonely as I do knowing we're in the same city and can't see one another." She leaned her head on his shoulder.

"I know. But it is for your safety I must stay away." He released her hand and slipped his arm around her waist, drawing their bodies close.

"My head understands. It's my heart that has a hard time." She hadn't planned to confess this much to him. It had to be as hard for him as it was her, and she wouldn't compromise both their missions because of her female yearnings.

He kissed her head. "Your big heart is what attracted me to you. But use that fascinating head of yours to keep safe."

"I'm trying. How much time do we have?" Her stomach was working up to a rumble, but if they could squeeze in time to be alone, she wanted that more than food.

His arm tightened and she felt his steps falter slightly.

"I am not sure. I may have blown my cover tonight in which case I would like to spend tonight in your arms."

The resignation in his voice stopped her forward motion. "What's happened?"

"Not here. Rico has reserved a room for us." He stopped beside a dark colored, older, small sedan. "This is my car."

He held the door as she slid into the passenger side.

Once in the vehicle, he leaned into her seat, kissing her with the same desperate need coiling in her. When they were both breathing hard, he drew away.

"We have the night, but only if we get off these streets."

The statement landed heavy and hard in her belly. It was as if he didn't believe he would be around tomorrow. The thought made her chest ache.

"You sound as if you may be gone after tonight." Pushing the air up her throat to say the words added to her pain.

"I will do everything in my power to be here tomorrow and many days afterward. Things have happened in the last twenty-four hours that have made the players hard to identify."

She placed a hand on his thigh as he drove. "What's happened?"

"When I returned from dropping you off last night Hector was found killed outside the compound. They didn't call in any authorities. I learned who the snitch was inside Garza's organization and it caught me off guard. I promised to protect her and when I met Rico in the Bohu distrio, Cezar showed up. I found a tracking transmitter in my shoe." He glanced her direction as they moved with ease through the lessening traffic.

"Garza?" Fear for Tino had her fingers digging into his leg. When his muscles flexed, she released her hold, scolding herself for allowing him to witness how the news affected her.

"That would be my first guess. But I do not understand why he was tracking me unless it was a test. He allowed me into the locked room that is the hub of his drug trafficking. The device could have been planted to see how soon I ran to someone like the Bohu or even Rico to see if I would leak the information." His rambling conversation led her to believe he was talking through the problem. It was something she did with her cockatoo, Alabaster, a time or two.

That he trusted her enough to run all this by her made Isabella feel good. She recognized the street name. "Where are we going?"

"To the JW Marriott. They won't think to look for either of us here and it isn't in anyone's territory that I've been connected with." He brushed fingers down her cheek. "I want to spend time with you to tell you everything to keep you safe without having to watch over our shoulders that someone may be spying."

She kissed his hand. "Me, too."

He parked the car in front of the tall professional looking building. A valet opened her door. Isabella stepped out and waited for Tino to hand the keys and a tip to the valet. She knew walking into such an upscale hotel with no baggage would appear odd but this wasn't a time to worry about appearances.

The vibrant colors of the furniture and plants in the lobby along with the marble floor added a posh feeling.

"May I help you?" asked a young woman professionally dressed in a suit with a Marriott name tag. She stood behind a registration counter to their right.

Tino approached the counter and handed over a credit card. "Therese, we have a terrace suite reserved."

Gauging from his request, Isabella reasoned, Tino had stayed at this hotel before. Was it this trip or another time?

Therese slid his card through a machine and flashed them both a bright smile. "Mr. and Mrs. Konstantine we are pleased to have you as guests in our Mexico City establishment."

Tino scribbled on the paperwork and took the key card from the young woman. "Send up two medium-well steak dinners, por favor."

He captured Isabella's hand and led her to the elevators. Once inside, he pulled her into his arms. His hands were everywhere at once. The upward movement of the elevator and his kiss made her light-headed. She pushed back, gulping for air. At that moment the elevator stopped. Her empty stomach bounced up into her throat.

"Querida, are you ill?" Tino held her chin in his hand as he studied her face. The elevator doors whooshed open.

"No. Just the upward movement, you taking my breath away, and an empty stoma—"

Tino swept her up into his arms and carried her to a door. He slid the keycard into the slot and turned the latch.

Her first glimpse of the room stole away all her words. A long bank of windows framed Mexico City's night lights. Tino placed her on the over-stuffed, green sofa. He closed the door then knelt on the floor in front of her.

The concern and love in his eyes made her misty with emotion. Could their hearts survive the lives they lived?

He unbuttoned her vest and slid it off her arms. "We have twenty minutes to take a shower before the food arrives."

The thought of lathering his muscled body forced her empty stomach to the back of her mind.

"I think we can get showered and be ready for dinner."

Tino stood, drawing her to her feet. "You do know I plan to do more than shower with you." He placed a kiss on her nose moments before plucking her glasses from her face.

Her body quivered with anticipation. "I was hoping you had other ideas."

They walked through a room with a king-sized four poster bed and into a bathroom with a large glass shower.

"You first." Tino slipped her cotton shirt over her head, kissed her bared nipples, and unfastened her khakis sliding them and her panties down her legs to her walking sandals. He left her pants bunched around her shins as he, one by one, took off her sandals and slid the garments over her feet. Standing naked in front of him, she was glad her father talked her into laser surgery on her eyes. She was able to watch his gaze leisurely travel from her toes to the top of her head. A feat before surgery she would not have been able to witness in focus.

Tino placed his hands on her shoulders and spun her. His fingers nimbly scaled her braid and soon her thick wavy hair cascaded over her shoulders.

"Get in the shower." Tino's command came out harsh sounding due to the emotion constricting his throat. How this woman, unlike any other he'd fancied before, could have worked her way into his heart and his very being still astounded him.

She peered at him coyly over her shoulder and sauntered into the glass shower. The illusion she was on display for him jolted his miembro.

The water sprayed her body. He slowly undressed watching her soak up the cool water and peer out at him, her intelligent eyes drinking in each inch of skin he revealed. His mind went back to their meeting in Guatemala. She was nearly blind without her glasses.

"Querida, how is it you see so well now?"

"Daddy insisted I have laser surgery so if I lose my glasses again, I can see. I still need them for reading but it has been wonderful, like now to see things, I didn't before." She opened the glass door. "Do you want me to wait for you to start soaping up?"

Her question was all innocence but the gleam in her eyes was pure passion.

"You may start without me." He turned from the shower to open a complimentary toothbrush and use it. He turned back around and was struck again at how this woman surprised him. Her front was covered with lather. Her eyes were closed as her hands ran slowly up and down her body, dipping between her legs.

He wasn't going to torture himself any longer. He opened the door quietly and placed his hands over hers, guiding them to her breasts. Her hands slid out from under his, and he enjoyed the feel of her slickened skin under his fingers. Her small breasts fit in the palm of his hands, the peaked nipples hard. He ran a hand down her belly to the curls at the juncture of her legs. She sighed and leaned her head on his shoulder.

Not one to miss any opportunity, he kissed her neck, jaw, and temple.

"Turn around."

She spun and he rubbed his front against her as he lathered her back with the earthy scented soap. Soon his front was as frothy as Isabella was all over.

He captured her luscious lips in a kiss and backed her against the shower wall. Without releasing her from the kiss, he grasped her bottom and slid her up the wall far enough he could ease her down over his throbbing miembro.

Entering Isabella was like returning home from a long trip. The last six months apart, he'd been restless and felt like something was missing. The missing piece was this woman. He realized it the day he drove her back to the hostel. Ever since the day she walked into the hotel in Guatemala his life had gone from empty and filled with revenge to a desire to rebuild his family and be faithful to Isabella. Now he understood the things his abuela and mother had told him about finding the person who makes you whole.

Isabella took control of the kiss, wrapping her legs around his waist, giving him deeper access for his strokes.

"Oh!" She pulled out of the kiss, her head resting back against the wall.

"Querida, do you wish to finish here or on the bed?" He kissed her neck and licked the water from her jaw.

She shuddered and her body clenched him. Her orgasm brought him to completion as well. He pressed her body to the wall when his legs started to shake.

"Stand and I will rinse you." He kissed her eyelids and moments later they fluttered open.

"I forgot how making love to you can make my heart and body

soar." She drew in a deep breath and slowly released her legs from his waist.

Once she stood without wobbling, Tino nudged her under the spray of water, making sure she was thoroughly rinsed. She did the same for him, only taking more care with certain areas on his body that were coming alive once more from her attentiveness.

Knocking echoed from the other room.

"Our dinner." Tino wrapped a towel around his waist and exited the bathroom. He would have rather helped Isabella dry, but he'd heard her stomach growl several times since picking her up at the museum.

After the earlier surprise this evening, he snatched up his gun as he walked through the bedroom. At the door, he left the chain attached until he was sure it was indeed room service. A young man dressed in a uniform of the hotel showed uneven teeth as he smiled and waved a hand at the rolling cart covered with dishes.

Tino opened the door allowing the man to enter. He closed and locked the door as the waiter pushed the cart to the chairs in front of the window.

"Ezzabella, bring me my pants, querida," Tino called not wanting to leave the man alone in the room. Being paranoid would keep them both alive.

Isabella came out of the bedroom wearing a white robe with the hotel logo on the breast. She handed his pants to him. He pulled out a tip for the waiter and signed for the food.

"Gracias." The man smiled and walked toward the door. Tino followed, unlocking and letting the man out, then relocking and bolting the door.

He turned back to the room. Isabella sat in one of the chairs, lifting lids and inspecting the food. The aromas made Tino's stomach growl. He couldn't remember when he ate last. Since finding Hector's body he'd been on duty until he walked out tonight to meet Rico. His stomach squeezed with uncertainty. By now Cezar would have reported that he'd met with Luis Bohu.

Either his cover would be completely blown or he would have to come up with a believable excuse for his apparent desertion from Garza.

"Hey," Isabella's quiet voice invaded his thoughts.

"¿Sí?" He walked over to the chair across the cart from her.

"You look lost. What are you thinking about? Us?"

The fear and uncertainty in her eyes shoved his other concerns to the back of his mind until later. When she was fully sated.

But he couldn't quell her fears just yet. He placed a finger to his lips and picked up the backpack he kept in the DEA car. He pulled out a device to check for transmitters.

Sweeping the device all around the cart and doing a visual inspection, he came up empty. The fact it was clean led him to believe that tonight he could enjoy time with Isabella and forget his problems for a few hours. Something he hadn't had the opportunity to do for six months.

He replaced the device and cupped the back of Isabella's head, drawing her lips to his for a soft, romantic kiss. He drew away and sat across from her.

"To answer your question. No. I have only happy thoughts when I think of us." He took her hand and kissed the knuckles. "I was thinking about how I will get back on Garza's good side after Cezar caught me with his enemy tonight." He shook his head. "I will worry about that tomorrow. Tonight is for us."

"Eat. I heard your stomach on the drive here." Knowing the suite was safe, he planned to focus on Isabella and their future tonight. Having found a woman to complete him, he wasn't about to let anyone keep them apart.

Chapter Sixteen

Isabella lay in the big bed feeling truly loved for the first time in her life. Tino had taken her to heights she thought only angels soared, and treated her so tenderly, tears came to her eyes. He'd fallen asleep quickly after their last round of loving. She'd known the first time she'd laid eyes on him in Mexico City that he wasn't resting well. How could he be at his best and stay one step ahead of the man who wanted to kill him when he was exhausted?

If she thought she could talk him into it, she'd ask him to stay with her, here, secluded for one more day. But she knew he'd be itching to find out where he stood with Garza. And she was due at the Garza's this afternoon.

Guilt burned in her heart as she peered at Tino's sleeping form. She had to tell him. That way he wouldn't be caught off guard when she arrived at the compound. But she already knew he would be against it.

His arm slipped around her waist. She willingly slid against him, spooning her bottom against his body. He kissed her neck as one hand cupped her breast and the other slipped between her thighs, his thumb grazed her throbbing nub. All he had to do was touch her and her body wanted his with a ferocity she found both exciting and frightening.

He sucked on her earlobe as his fingers one by one entered her body and his legs spread hers.

"Querida, your body opens to me like a flower to sunshine. This welcome makes my heart ache with happiness."

His words filled her heart. "Tino… Oh!" His clever fingers were increasing the throb, sending sensations to her extremities, and sparking rapturous sensations in her brain.

He rolled her to her back. His mouth captured hers at the same moment he slid into her, eliciting more spirals of electric sensations through her body. She clung to him, watching the morning sun slowly rise, knowing this could be their last intimate moment until they returned to the U.S.

His thrusts grew faster and harder as his kisses grew hotter, more needy. She lifted her hips taking him deep and clung to his body as she matched his movements and kisses, passion for passion. Her climax shook her body. She moaned and bit down on Tino's shoulder as sparks flashed and her mind went black.

Tino thrust deep and whispered her name before collapsing, covering her body with his and dropping small kisses all over her face. "Querida, you are my heart. Whatever happens you have given me back a life worth living."

Tears burned at the back of her eyes. "You have given me unconditional love."

He laughed gruffly, moving off her still lethargic body, but drawing her into his arms as he rolled to his back. She lay on him, peering down into his blue eyes.

"We make quite a pair. Do you think we could live a life that is not filled with danger?" She'd thought about this a good deal the last few days. Was their need for one another just an adrenaline high they both thrived on?

His face grew somber as his gaze heated. "I believe that no matter how we spend our lives, we will always crave the other and have passionate love."

His words were exactly what she needed to hear. They could live like regular people and not lose the excitement of one another. She leaned down, staring into his honest eyes, and kissed him with the sincerity she felt.

His arms tightened around her, and he deepened the kiss. Drawing her thoughts away from everything and holding her in the bliss of the moment.

The faint strands of a Mariachi band invaded her bliss.

"¡Carajo!" Tino swore, pulling out of the kiss and rolling to the side of the bed.

Isabella pulled the sheet up as a chill chased down her back. Tino sat on the edge of the mattress and flipped the phone open.

"¿*Hola*?" He listened.

She couldn't see his face but the muscles in his back visibly bunched. Sliding behind him, she massaged his neck and back listening to the conversation. It was Garza and he sounded angry.

"Sí." Tino tossed the phone into a chair and turned, drawing her into his arms, her legs wrapped around his waist as she sat in his lap and molded her body to his.

"Garza is not happy I have disappeared, but he is happy I am at least answering the phone. It seems Cezar has also disappeared and is not answering his phone." Tino's mind raced. Did the Bohu gang kill Cezar so he would not rat him out? If so, Hadda meant a lot to Luis Bohu and it would be in his best interest to keep the girl alive to not only take down Garza but to stop the drug activity within the Bohu gang.

He kissed Isabella soundly on the lips as her naked body, pressed to his, played havoc with his thoughts. The dread that had hounded him last night until he'd exhausted himself loving Isabella, now lifted. He would not die this day. At least not the way he had worried about. If Garza didn't know he went to the Bohu distrio then Cezar had planted the transmitter and Garza knew nothing of the meet.

Sí, today would be a good day. "Querida, I wish I could love you more, but you must get dressed so I can return you to the hostel and I can continue with my job."

Isabella leaned back. The cool air filling the space between them chilled him as much as the uncertainty shining in her eyes. She placed a hand on his chest, her fingers sifting through the dark spattering of curls.

"I've been acquisitioned to help at the Garza's in the afternoons."

The words sunk in and his fear for her escalated. Tino grasped her arms. She sucked in air and looked at him.

"Helping them is foolish. You know he kills without flinching, and he is most likely the person who orchestrated your being here." His fear for her life outweighed his own. "You will get on a plane and go back to Arizona. I will come as soon as I finish my assignment."

"No."

The defiant, independent nature that he loved in this woman was going to get her killed. "Querida, you have accomplished your assignment. You discovered how the artifacts are being stolen. Take the report back to your father and stay safe."

She slipped from his arms and his lap. Isabella paced the bedroom, naked.

"I don't see why I should slink off to Arizona when I can also figure out who is doing it and keep an eye on you to make sure nothing happens."

Her logic was illogical. "You are not my partner—" The minute the words hit the air she flinched and wrapped her arms around her thin waist.

"Querida." He crossed the room, gathering her stiff body into his arms. "You are my partner in everything but my job. I will not risk your safety to make my mission easier."

"You won't be risking my safety. I can learn things you may not be able to. A wife knows everything about her husband. I can gain señora Garza's confidence and supply you with added information." She stared into his eyes. "Garza adores his wife. If she likes me, he wouldn't dare harm me." She kissed his chin. "Just as you adore me and would never want to do something to upset me."

Her argument was not falling on deaf ears. She could be an asset if she were safe and didn't snoop beyond the boundaries Garza allowed her. But he couldn't let her know she was wearing him down.

"I might adore you, but I would not worry about upsetting you if my actions kept you out of danger." He narrowed his eyes in his best "don't mess with me on this" look.

Her hips swayed, rubbing her mound of curls against his miembro. Her hands squeezed his butt and moved on up his back. "I think we could make this work, just like we've made our relationship work."

He grasped her firm backside in his hands and pulled her hips tight to his.

Her breathing quickened and she whispered, "I'll ignore you at the Garza house and you ignore me."

"If we are to ignore one another—there can be no touching, no secret meetings at the compound, and no eye contact that isn't reasonable."

The hitch in her breathing when he backed her against the bed, made his heart race and his body ache for more. "This will have to hold you until we can find a moment to be alone again." He gently pushed her backwards. She fell upon the bed, her knees at the edge, splayed, revealing the treasure Tino could not explore enough.

He lowered himself over her, entered, and captured her mouth in an all or nothing kiss that brought him to completion seconds before she moaned in his mouth and her body clenched his miembro. He remained in her, holding her longer than he should. But there was no way of knowing when they would be together again.

Garza was already mad, so a few minutes longer wouldn't change anything with him. And the extra time with Isabella meant everything to Tino.

~*~

Isabella wore one of her long, colorful, tiered skirts, a white peasant top, and her walking sandals. She'd witnessed Karyme's fashion aplomb and wanted to fit in. She stepped out of the cab wondering what Tino had told Garza about leaving the compound and if he was now looking into Cezar's disappearance.

She walked up to the front door. Before she could ring the ornate bell, the door opened and Karyme met her with a welcome smile that didn't glow in her eyes. "I've been watching for you. I am excited to get your thoughts on the carvings and box them up."

Isabella was ushered into the atrium. A man standing inside the door made a grab for her newly purchased tote bag.

"Manuel, there is no need to search Isabella's purse. She is my guest and I will vouch for her."

"Señor Garza said no one, even our own people, are allowed in without being searched." The man's voice was objectionable, more like a child telling his teacher what his parent had told him.

"I will speak to him. Isabella is not a devious person. She is a scholar. Her only weapon is her brain."

Isabella's smile wavered a moment before she caught herself. How did Karyme know about her aptitude? Had Garza told her everything he'd dug up on her?" The thought the woman knew her intelligence and perhaps more was unsettling. Was the wife in on the scheme the husband had planned? She'd told Tino a wife knows all the sordid things about her husband even if she pretends to not.

Karyme shot her a smile that twinkled in her dark brown eyes before she started walking up the stairs.

"I thought we were going to look at the carvings in the ballroom?" Isabella said, following and clutching her tote, which held her survival vest, to her side.

"The ballroom holds Paolo's treasures. I want you to see mine first. They don't impress guests like the statues and carvings downstairs." They turned to the left and entered a room set up much like the archive room at the museum. Only at the museum there was an area where the items were tested, photographed, and studied.

"As you can see, these are fragments that are found around whole pieces. Many I'm uncertain of their original use, but they must be something that was used by the Aztecs to be buried with or near the other antiquities the museums keep." Karyme's eyes lit up as she scanned the shelves and then grasped Isabella's hands. "My favorite part is discovering how old the item is and what it was used for."

Karyme walked over to the shelves and picked up a small elongated piece. "This was part of a ritual spear."

Isabella crossed the room and looked down at what looked to be petrified wood. "How did you come to that conclusion?" Was Karyme mad? The piece of wood might be a splinter from a spear shaft, but it was highly unlikely it could have been from a ritual spear. There were so many variables that would need to be discerned and then it was highly unlikely it was what the woman believed.

"I ran carbon dating tests, wood classification, and under a ultra-violet light found traces of coloring and blood." The woman's eyes gleamed.

"But how do you know it was a ritual spear? Did you do comparison tests to make sure your outcome was conclusive?"

"That is why I want you to help me with my latest project. You know the questions to ask that will help me discover the truth about the carvings and my latest acquisitions."

"Where do you get these from?" At least what she was helping Karyme with wasn't the missing artifacts from the museum. Those had been intact statues and carvings…like her husband collected.

"I started out to be an archeologist. When I married and had children, I gave that up. But I still have contacts within their circles. They gather up the items too small to take the time to deal with and send them my way. If I discover something that is museum worthy, I pass it along. Otherwise, they stay right here where I can handle them and get close to my ancestors."

That perked Isabella's attention. "You are descended from the Aztecs?"

Karyme's frame straightened and she smiled. "Sí. It has been said my family is from the goddess Tlazolteotl. She was the goddess of sexual excess and childbirth." Her eyes glazed over for a moment. She shook her head and smiled. "So you see I have a very strong reason for wanting to learn all I can about the Aztecs. My people."

Isabella knew about that need to learn all about heritage and genealogy. She'd been doing that since she learned of her Hopi heritage.

"I heard about the death in your family. Was it a blood relative?" She hoped news like this was something that did make the rounds and she wouldn't have to lie about where she heard the news.

"Did Geraldo tell you?"

"Who?"

"Geraldo Bastante, the director of the museum. He paid his respects yesterday."

"Oh, yes." Why was the name Geraldo Bastante flashing through her memory? It wasn't just from researching the man. She'd read the name elsewhere.

"It was my nephew Hector Maritnez who died too young."

"Martinez?" Her mind was flashing even faster now.

"Sí, my brother's son."

The names Geraldo Bastante and Karyme Martinez were connected on one of the reports she'd read.

Chapter Seventeen

Tino walked into the cantina in the Bohu distrio that he'd walked out of last night and apparently Cezar had not.

Garza had grilled him about where he'd gone last night. Being halfway truthful he said to find out about Hector's death. Which is what had taken him to the Bohu cantina. When he told Garza he'd not learned anything yet, he'd also been given the task of finding Cezar.

He was pretty sure if he found Garza's righthand man; Cezar wouldn't be alive.

Luis stood at the bar talking with his flunkies. His gaze met Tino's in the mirror behind the bar when he'd crossed half the nearly empty room.

"Now what do you want? You cause me nothing but trouble." Luis turned to Tino as he walked up to the bar and pointed to the counter in front of him.

The bartender slid a shot glass into his hand. Tino downed the tequila and faced Luis.

"Garza can't find his righthand man. Do you happen to know where I can find Cezar? The last I saw him was in here."

Luis's eyes narrowed. "Did you tell Garza?"

"Why would I do that? It would also tell him I was in here. I have no plan to rat out Hadda, but I do plan on taking Cezar's place. I need to find him."

Luis laughed. "You can find that bastard in an alley in the Alvarez distrio."

"Dead?"

"Sí." Luis snapped his fingers and a shot of tequila slid in front of him. "That bastard grabbed my sister and thought he could persuade me to tell him who my informant was inside Garza's organization." He looked Tino up and down. "I would have fed you to him if I had thought you would not turn Hadda in to save your skin."

"Luis, by killing Cezar you did both of us a favor. I can control what Garza knows and keep Hadda safe, and you will have an inside man instead of a young woman, feeding you information." Tino backed away. "Could you give me a street to start my search?"

"José Martí."

"Gracias."

Tino exited the cantina and on his way to the Alvarez distrio called Garza.

"Señor Garza, I have reason to believe the Alvarez brothers have Cezar. I will let you know what I find out."

"Is he alive or dead?" The unemotional question told Tino he had a chance of becoming Garza's new righthand man. Garza expected loyalty from his men but he did not return it.

"Word has it he is dead."

Garza cursed and hung up the phone.

Tino smiled and dialed Rico. He filled him in and asked him to pay a couple prostitutas to keep the Alvarez boys busy until he located Cezar and retrieved his body. He really didn't want to run into their thugs and have to battle his way out of the area with Cezar's lifeless body slowing him down.

The fourth alley in the Alvarez distrio off José Martí, Tino found Cezar's beaten body. He couldn't tell if there were any bullet holes in him, he was so puffy and discolored. The only reason he knew it was Cezar was the clothing. The body had the same outfit the man had worn when he came into the cantina the night before.

He loaded the body into the back seat of his SUV and headed back to Garza's. He punched in Rico's number. "I have the body."

"You know you should give it to the authorities."

"Sí."

"But you are not."

"No, I am not. If I take this body back to Garza, I will be his new righthand man. I will know everything he is doing in his organization, and we will take him down." For the first time in a very long time Tino felt he was finally going to seek the revenge he'd ate, slept, and breathed for so many years.

"As an officer of the law, you are sworn to turn that body in." Rico's voice didn't condemn but it held a note of authority.

"Forget I talked to you today." Tino pressed the end button on his phone and smiled as he swung the vehicle up to the compound gates. Soon, very soon he'd be out of Mexico and basking in the Arizona sun with Isabella.

He shot a glance at his watch. Three. She was probably still in the house somewhere. His gut clenched. He had to avoid her. They couldn't chance a meeting with Garza around. He dissected everyone around him watching their actions and translating their motives.

Tino parked the SUV in the garage. Diego and Cruz walked up to the vehicle. The hesitation in their steps and fear in their eyes proved they'd been told what he brought back.

Opening the side door, Tino stepped back. "Did Jefe say what to do with the body?"

"Put him in his bed and the doctor will be here to examine him soon," Diego said, making the sign of the cross over his chest.

"Then help me carry him up the stairs. He is not light." Tino grabbed Cezar's arm and pulled him out the door. His body dropped to the concrete floor. He didn't see a need to be too careful with the man. His body was already badly bruised, and he hadn't been a nice man while alive.

He picked up one arm and motioned with his head for the other two to grab something. They both cautiously closed the distance between them and the body. Diego took the other arm and Cruz took the feet. With a shuffling gait they packed the hefty Cezar up the stairs and dumped him onto his bed. He was the only one who had a separate room.

Tino scanned the room. This could be his as soon as the body was removed. Would they have another sit-in here at the compound until the burial?

"Did Cezar have family that should be notified?" he asked Diego.

"He never talked of any. But Garza will know." Diego was edging his way to the door.

"Shouldn't one of you sit with him?" Tino doubted the custom of sitting with the dead was ignored because the dead person was bad.

They both shook their heads.

"I have to report to Garza, so one of you needs to at least watch the outside door until the doctor arrives."

Cruz nodded and stepped to the side, allowing Tino and Diego to exit.

Tino hurried down the stairs and into the main house. Purposeful strides took him through the atrium and down the hall to the office. He knocked and waited for a response.

"¿Si?" Garza's gruff voice told of his unfavorable mood.

Tino entered the room, shut the door firmly behind him, and advanced to the front of Garza's desk.

"You brought Cezar back?"

"Sí. He was in an alley in the Alvarez distrio."

"Did you encounter any of their people?"

"No, it was not far enough in and I was cautious as I searched."

Garza ran a hand over his tired face and slammed a fist onto his desk. "What was Cezar doing in their distrio? He would know going in there alone was stupid."

"Perhaps he was the one who leaked information to the Alvarez and Bohu gangs. If the Alvarez brothers learned he had also been working with the Bohu's, they would want him dead." Tino didn't know the truth and didn't care the small gangs were stealing Garza's product. He only wanted to stir the pot and get Garza so riled up he made mistakes. Ones the DEA could use to nab him.

As his suggestion rolled around in the drug lord's mind, Garza's eyes glazed over and his face reddened. "He and my wife are the only people, other than you the other day who have access to the business schedules." He slammed his fist on the desk again. "How stupid I have been not to see his duplicity."

His gaze smoldered as he peered at Tino. "You are my new righthand man, but be warned, I will not allow you as many privileges as Cezar had. I have learned foolishly that you can no longer depend on loyalty in a world of greed."

Tino nodded solemnly as inside excitement flipped around in his stomach like a slippery fish. "Did Cezar have family that needs to be notified?"

"Once the doctor has examined him, we will call his family and they can take the body away." Garza peered at him. "Could you tell the means of death?"

"His body was badly beaten and bloody. I could not see a bullet hole but his body was misshapen, so it was hard to tell."

Garza smiled. "Then he received what he deserved for being a traitor."

A chill chased down Tino's back at the man's perverse pleasure in Cezar's painful death.

The drug lord shuffled papers on his desk. "We have a shipment coming in tonight. I want you and Diego to make sure it arrives without problems."

Tino nodded and tried hard to listen as Garza filled him in on the latest shipment. After all these years, tonight could be the night he finally took down his family's killer.

~*~

Isabella found Karyme's excitement over her bits and pieces of the past to be contagious. She hadn't realized the time until a young maid appeared at the door and said dinner would be served in ten minutes.

"You must stay for dinner. I know Paolo would not mind." Karyme replaced the shard of a bowl back in the slot she'd extracted it from.

Isabella's stomach twisted with dread at the thought of sitting through a meal with Garza watching her every move. "Thank you for the offer, but I really have to return to the hostel and type up the notes I made this morning for my research paper. I only have one more week, and I'll return to the university. I need to have all my facts and information legible so I can write my paper."

Karyme studied her. "My husband makes you nervous."

She couldn't lie about that. "Yes. He has such an intense stare it makes me nervous."

Karyme laughed. "It was that intensity in his eyes that made me want to make him laugh. And when he did, it was like the angels had fallen from heaven and given me a gift." Her eyes turned dreamy. "I hope that someday you find a man that makes you feel the same."

Isabella thought of Tino and knew she had found her gift. "Me, too," she said and slung her tote bag over her shoulder. "I'll see you tomorrow. We need to get to the carvings."

Karyme's face stilled a moment before she smiled. "Sí. We will box up the carvings tomorrow." Karyme followed her out the door and walked beside her as they descended the stairs.

At the bottom of the staircase, Karyme placed a hand on her arm. "Wait here, and I will find someone to drive you back to the hostel."

"That's not necessary. I can call a cab." Isabella drew the phone Tino gave her from her pocket.

"No, I insist. You should not be spending money for a taxi when I have invited you here to help me. Wait. I will find someone quickly."

Isabella returned the phone to her pocket and walked toward the door. Through a window alongside the door she noticed what looked like a black hearse backed up to the garage. Had Tino found Cezar dead? She moved closer and stared out the window, watching a covered body be slipped into the vehicle and several men including Tino talking to a man holding a doctor's bag.

A shiver slithered up her spine, and she spun from the sight. Garza stood on the stairway watching her. His brows were drawn together and his lips formed a firm line. Was looking out the window a transgression in this house?

His silent observation annoyed and scared her.

Feeling a need to explain her presence at the door, she said, "Your wife went to find someone to give me a ride back to the hostel." Her tone while not as strong as she'd have liked rang a bit on the confrontational side.

"I am surprised to see you here today. I thought Karyme called and canceled due to the death in her family." Garza slowly descended the last three steps giving her the feeling he was a cat on the prowl of his next meal.

"I heard about the death at the hostel, but when Karyme didn't call and cancel, I came and she was happy I did." Isabella shored up her back and didn't budge as he stopped nearly toe to toe with her. His mustache twitched like an animal testing the air.

"There you are, Paolo." Karyme walked into the atrium. "I would like one of your men to take Isabella home. She refuses to stay for dinner, and I refuse to let her spend her money on a taxi." She slipped her arm around her husband's and smiled up at him.

"I am a bit short on men right now, Karyme. But I could take her back to her hostel."

Isabella's stomach nearly jumped up her throat at the thought of riding in a car alone with the man. Not to mention the chance Tino would go ballistic and ruin his cover.

"I really don't want to be an inconvenience. I'll call a taxi." She pulled out the phone and tried to focus on the contacts. Rico had put in several numbers of places she might need. A taxi service was one of them. She punched the number as Karyme stepped toward her, reaching for the phone.

"No, it is not necessary."

"I don't mind. And I don't want to interrupt your dinner." She backed away as someone answered her call. "Sí, I would like a taxi to pick me up at señor Paolo Garza's."

The voice on the other end sounded familiar as it rattled off the address.

"Sí." She kept her expression neutral as she turned the phone off. "They have someone only five minutes away. I'll wait at the gates so I don't further delay your meal."

"That is not necessary." Karyme waved toward the door. "The person at the gate will allow the taxi in. We will wait with you on the veranda. It is lovely this time of evening."

Isabella wasn't sure where the veranda was, but hoped the taxi she called came quickly.

"Splendid idea." Garza started into the ballroom with Karyme on his arm and his wife, tugging on Isabella's arm.

The girl named Hadda appeared.

"Hadda, bring sangría out to the veranda. We are going to sit with Dr. Mumphrey until her taxi arrives," Karyme said as they continued through the room and out a door on the left side.

This was an area Isabella was unfamiliar with. But now remembered these doors and the doors across the room were open the night she'd visited for Karyme's party. She'd sat and visited with the woman and not milled around, otherwise, she would have known where the veranda was located.

The tiled porch was shaded with a breeze blowing through a bush with fragrant magenta blooms. A patio table and four chairs sat in the middle of the shaded area.

Paolo held a chair for his wife and then moved to one by her side, indicating for Isabella to sit. She did, making sure she didn't touch the man for fear he'd feel the nerves skittering up and down her skin.

Hadda returned with a pitcher of the fruity drink and three glasses.

"Gracias, Hadda." Karyme filled one stemmed glass, straining the fruit, and handed it to Isabella. "Isabella is anxious to see the carvings we are to package for shipping."

The matter of fact way she commented sent more chills up Isabella's spine. Why had her mention of the carvings upset the woman? Was it because she showed more interest in the carvings than her bits and pieces?

Garza's intense stare shot her heart up into her throat. "Did you tell her we were told they were from the Aztec Triple Alliance in the 1400's?"

Isabella sat forward in her chair. "You have carvings of Itzcoatl, Nezahualcouotl, and Totoquilhauztli?" Vibrations of excitement shoved her jittering nerves to the side. "That was a historic period in Aztec history."

Karyme chortled. "You are well educated in our history. Your enthusiasm is admirable. We are hoping you can tell us if what we have is truly the three kings."

"Have you done carbon dating?"

"Sí. They are old enough, but we want to make sure the carvings are of the alliance and not some other historical event." Karyme sipped her drink.

Isabella nodded. There would be a huge difference in the price and historical significance if the carvings depicted the alliance. She would need reference books to help her discover the truth about the carvings. A thought struck her.

"If I am helping you box them to send somewhere, why not have that museum authenticate the pieces?"

Señor Garza cleared his throat. "If they are more valuable than we first thought, I need to secure more insurance, and we may want to request higher security for them while they are on display."

She agreed. If they were from the alliance, they would be worth millions and every archeologist and anthropologist interested in the Mesoamerican history would want to study them.

"I'll bring books with me tomorrow to help research the authenticity."

Hadda walked onto the veranda. "The taxi is here."

Isabella stood. Her nerves had dissipated with her excitement. She smiled at her hosts. "Gracias. I will see you tomorrow at one."

"We'll send a car for you and make sure you have a ride back," Karyme said.

"That isn't—"

The woman scowled. "It is necessary." The scowl softened and she smiled. "If you discover what we believe to be the truth, we will owe you considerable."

The woman was showing more sides to her today than she had at their initial encounter. Was the stress of losing her nephew wearing on her? She'd shown more hard edges and not such a soft demeanor.

Isabella followed Hadda to the front door. Her step faltered when her gaze landed on Rico leaning against a cab. That was the voice she'd recognized. Did he sit in the neighborhood in a cab waiting for her to call?

He jumped to attention as she exited the house and opened the back passenger door.

"Gracias," she said when she had so much more she wanted to ask. But she knew to show any sign of recognition, even though señor Garza was in the back of the house, could put them both in danger.

Rico sauntered around to the driver's door and dropped into the seat as if he had all day. He started the car and pulled out of the driveway. The hearse was gone and the only person she saw was the man standing guard at the gate. Once they pulled onto the residential street, she let out a sigh of relief and peered into the rearview mirror. Rico's chocolate brown eyes peered back at her.

"Did you have a nice time with the Garzas today?" The censure in his tone added to the anxiety that had washed over her during some of the conversations today.

"Not really. It's hard to watch what I say and analyze their words and actions. It's downright exhausting. I don't know how Tino can live like that."

"You get used to it. Did you learn anything to help you?"

He was prying to find out what she was here to discover.

"I'm not sure. How is it you happened to be the taxi on my

phone?" She raised an accusing eyebrow.

He merely grinned a toothy, and any other time, charming smile. "I added that number so you would have a secure taxi. I figured Tino would owe me for keeping tabs on you." He winked.

"I appreciate the fact you are looking out for me, and I'm glad I could feel safe on the ride home." She shivered.

His eyes narrowed. "What's wrong?"

"Señora Garza said she would send a car for me tomorrow and it would take me home as well." She stared into his probing gaze. "I don't like them having that much control over my activities."

"I know the agency they use. I will get one of our men to be the driver, but you cannot talk to him as you are talking to me. He will know nothing of your connection to anything other than the museum."

The relief of knowing she wouldn't be in the hands of someone the Garza's controlled gushed through her like a wave of warm air. "Gracias! I don't like feeling watched all the time."

He pulled to the curb at the hostel. "Be careful with those two. The wife has a reputation for being sweet, but it's hard to believe a sweet woman would be married to that man."

Isabella stared at him. "That's my feelings. And today…a couple of times she dropped her cover, and I saw a more calculating side to her. I will not underestimate either one."

Rico twisted, putting an arm across the seat and looking into her eyes. "You need to keep that attitude toward everyone you meet."

His warning brought up someone she wanted to know about. "There has been a young man hanging around the hostel. His name is Alphonso. He's the cousin to the desk clerk, Felix. I think he's part of the Bohu gang and for some reason he's always ready and willing to do errands for me."

Rico nodded. "I will look into this man." He spun to the door and exited, coming around to her door. He opened it and held out a hand to help her.

"Gracias. I have lots to do before I go back to the Garza's tomorrow. I appreciate the ride and the visit."

"*De nada.* If Tino trusts your instincts and you can help us take down the Garza Empire, then I will be at your service." He closed the door and walked to the driver's door.

Isabella didn't watch him drive away. She would eat while she was here, then change and head to the museum. From her conversation with Karyme today, she believed she knew who was stealing the artifacts.

Chapter Eighteen

Tino and Diego sat in a Jeep three hours from the city waiting to meet up with a drug shipment and escort it to the drop-off site. He understood Rico's line of thought, but he wasn't happy with it. They were to keep the shipment safe and let it be delivered. Rico wanted to build Garza's confidence in Tino as his new righthand man. Six months ago, Tino would have agreed.

Now, he wanted to get this job over and start a new life with Isabella. He'd hoped tonight would be the night he finally took Garza down.

"You do not look like a man who is now the righthand man of señor Garza," Diego said as they sat in the darkness alongside the road waiting for the sport utility vehicle carrying the drugs.

Tino snorted and took his gaze off the quiet highway. "Hector, Jefe's nephew and Cezar, the last righthand man are dead. I do not feel my move up will be good if I want to live long." He didn't believe he was a target, not yet anyway, but he couldn't help the depressed feeling shrouding him. Letting the man think it was due to his fear of dying and not a desire to be with Isabella would keep them both safe.

The lights of a SUV came toward them. It was the right color and had the right plates. He flicked on the Jeep's ignition and followed at a discreet distance. Both stolen shipments had been taken within an hour of Mexico City. Diego slumped in his seat as if dozing. As much as

Tino wished he could take down the shipment tonight, he searched the side roads keeping an eye out for anyone trying to intercept the vehicle in front of them.

He'd relish someone trying to take the drugs. The skirmish would give him a good cause to exert the frustration he was feeling. Rico knew the route but had said they would stay far away. Tino would be on his own whatever happened.

His headlights glinted off something shiny on the side of the road moving alongside the SUV.

"Wake up!" Tino smacked Diego in the chest. "Call Garza and tell him we just passed through Puebla and someone is following the SUV besides us."

Diego called Garza and handed the phone toward Tino.

Tino batted the phone away. "¡Coño! I am busy!"

He heard Garza curse and took the phone being waved beside him. "I do not know what we have but there are two motorbikes following beside the SUV. Sí, we will catch up and grab them." He tossed the phone to Diego and slammed his foot down on the accelerator, surging the vehicle toward the shipment. The adrenaline rush he'd wished for kicked in.

The motorbikes had moved to the front of the SUV. Tino drove around the SUV, cutting tight in front, forcing the bikes off the road. He thought about following the bikes to see which group was after the shipment tonight. If it was the Bohu gang, he'd read Hadda all wrong. She was not as innocent as she portrayed. Sending two bikes to stop the shipment didn't make sense. His gut said to stay with the SUV in case there were more. Twenty kilometers ahead two more bikes burst onto the highway in front of the SUV and two behind Tino.

This was the outlet he needed. He could care less about the shipment other than saving it placed him deeper in Garza's confidence. But the battle to save it…he was looking for an anger release. Tino slammed on his brakes, turned quickly, and aimed his pistol out the window, shooting one biker. The ring of rapid-fire shots and flashes of orange proved the thieves had AK 47 assault rifles. Tino flipped the light switch making his vehicle slightly harder to see.

The SUV with the shipment roared to life running over a bike and rider in its path.

Again, he left the banditos to continue following the SUV. It ate at him to not be able to grab one and find out who was trying to steal the shipment. But this small battle would surely not be their last try at the drugs. He'd wager it was the Bohu gang since Hadda was still in the Garza household. As much as he didn't want to believe the worst in the girl, there was no one else alive to find the information. But who had tipped off the Alvarez brothers? And they still didn't know who killed Hector.

Diego's phone rang as Tino spotted two more bikes alongside the road. Sparks flew from the SUV as gun shots cracked through the night air. He would not allow this shipment to be stolen. His and Isabella's future depended on him finishing this mission. He slammed his foot to the floor and sped toward the gunfire.

"Drop the phone and shoot!" he ordered Diego as Tino drove one handed and shot with his left. He had to give credit to the banditos they didn't give up.

He shot one and Diego shot the other. The SUV continued down the road.

"That was Jefe. See the flashing lights ahead? That is three others to help escort the shipment. He said to pick up anyone we can and bring them to him."

Tino pulled out a high-powered flashlight and aimed it at the two wounded bikers.

"Throw your guns or I will shoot you again!" he shouted. A volley of bullets and bursts of orange light zinged their direction pinging off the metal of his vehicle.

"¡Cono!" He shot them both in their gun arms. One screamed while the other tossed his gun. "Take care of the idiot screaming," he instructed Diego and grabbed a roll of tape he'd stashed in the vehicle for this reason. Tino strode away from his Tahoe training his Glock on the quiet man. He crouched to restrain the bandito. The young man glared out of a pale, sweating face.

"Which gang do you belong to?" He doubted the man would reply but the colors he wore told Tino what he wanted to know. The man was part of the Alvarez brothers' gang. He didn't have to worry about Hadda being implicated. He hoped. Tino taped the man's mouth and his wrists together. The bandito winced and cried out but the tape muffled the sound. He walked the man to the Jeep as Diego dragged the other one up. Once the second man's hands and mouth were taped, he forced them to climb into the Jeep. He taped them to the roll bar and headed back to Garza's. The boss would want to have a word with the two.

Tino cringed inwardly. While bringing the two in worked in his favor, Cezar had been the one who inflicted the wrath of Garza on the Alvarez brothers. As the righthand man it would be his job to beat the answers Garza wanted out of these men. They were just as apprehensible as Garza, but he only liked beating on someone to save his own skin. If he refused, Garza would become suspicious.

The weight of what lay ahead settled on him as heavy as a marble pillar.

~*~

Isabella slapped the book closed. She had remembered it right. The director and Karyme had been on three digs together as archeology students the last one was here at Templo Mayor. They both had knowledge of the tunnels and artifacts. Were they working together? She couldn't see the jealous Garza allowing his wife to work closely with another man. While Bastante came off as simpering around Garza, she'd witnessed a shrewdness in his eyes several times during Karyme's party when the director looked at Garza.

Everyone she suspected had two sides to them. She rubbed her throbbing temples and leaned back in her chair. Where were the artifacts shipped to? She sat up straight in the chair. There had to be a log of where all the crates were sent. Another hour passed as Isabella searched the room and came up empty. She'd have to ask Delgado tomorrow for a list of all the addresses of the shipped artifacts over the last year to be able to distinguish which were oddities or to see who signed for their release. The person who signed would have known if an unusual address was assigned to a crate.

She still needed to find the information for her visit to the Garza's tomorrow. If they had carvings from the Aztec Triple Alliance…excitement skittered across her skin. What a find! And she could write about it in a paper and double her notoriety in anthropology and archeology circles.

But what if the carvings are part of the stolen items? The time period is correct for the missing pieces. There wasn't a very detailed description of the missing items. She tapped her fingers on the table top. Surely knowing her aptitude, they wouldn't have her look at stolen goods…would they? Her nerves started bouncing and she stood up. Better to concentrate on the books she needed and get back to the hostel.

She placed the books she wanted to take to the Garza's on the table. She'd ask for permission to transport them from the building tomorrow. Exiting the archive room, she waited in the recess of the door. Five minutes later the security guard exited and locked the same door as every other time she'd left the archive room.

He entered the elevator and rode it up. Once the light showed the elevator stopped at the main floor, she tiptoed to the door and pulled out the newest tool in her survival vest—a lock pick given to her by WIA. The instructor only had to show her twice and she'd unlocked every door in the building.

She inserted the pick, tickled the tumblers, and the lock clicked. Inhaling, she twisted the knob and swung the door inward. Banks of surveillance monitors filled one side of the room. Why wasn't there a person down here watching the monitors? And why did the front door security officer come down here? Scanning the bank of scenes, she noted each row was a floor in the building. The fourth floor with the offices had the fewest cameras and they were all situated in the hallway. Some of the museum rooms had several cameras from various angles. The basement had a camera in the hall and one in each room.

The books she'd left on the table in the archive room were visible. Had he been watching her movements? Anyone who watched the surveillance footage while she'd been here would know exactly what she was looking up and it hadn't all been for a paper.

A shiver rustled up her spine. Was he reporting to someone what she researched?

A monitor brightened. The light came on in the storage room. The same person she'd watched on the videos stood in the middle of the room then walked to a crate. A shipping label was applied and the person moved to the wall under the camera.

All she'd have to do was read the label, and she'd know where the artifacts are being shipped to.

Isabella waited in the room watching the monitor go black then exited and hurried to the storage room. She punched in the numbers on the lock and rushed into the room. As soon as the lights came on, she moved across the floor to the crate the person had labeled. This was why no one thought anything about where the crate was going. It read: British Museum, Great Russell St. London, England, U.K. The missing artifacts were going to a renowned museum.

The whole thing became more and more of a puzzle. Was someone at the British museum knowingly purchasing stolen artifacts? There wasn't a notation to anyone specific. She stood near the crate contemplating all the facts she knew and trying to formulate a hypothesis.

Scuffing sounds behind Isabella caught her attention. She turned and caught a glimpse of Alphonso moments before he pulled the crate across the hole.

Chapter Nineteen

Tino rubbed a hand over his face as he settled down on the bed that hours ago had held the dead body of Cezar. He knew the house staff had put new coverings on the bed and had cleaned out all of Cezar's belongings, but a chill still rippled up his spine. As Garza's new righthand man he had the only single room for employees, but he'd also had to go farther than he'd ever had to go before to play his part. His gut clenched and bile rose into his throat.

With the help of Manny, the most sadistic guard in Garza's employ in Mexico, he'd tortured the two bikers and discovered they were working for the Alvarez brothers and Cezar had been the one feeding them information. What he and Garza didn't understand was the route had been changed after Cezar's death. So who, using Cezar's name, told them of the change? And they discovered, which Tino already knew, Cezar was not killed by the Alvarez brothers. The two bikers had been stunned when they heard he was dead.

Once Garza had the information he wanted, he told them to take the bikers heads and leave them on the Alvarezes' doorstep. Tino left that detail to Manny. The man drove off with the severed bodies and heads and a maniacal grin on his face.

Sitting on the bed rehashing the events, yet trying to not remember the gory ones, he wished he could lose himself in Isabella's sweet concern and tantalizing body. Many more days like today and he'd walk away without any regrets or doubts. If he didn't, he would be such a vile wounded man he wouldn't be worthy to love Isabella.

He stared up at the ceiling and wished his querida was in his arms. He smiled at her outrage over his commenting she was not his partner. They had become inexplicably connected during their time in Guatemala.

His eyes closed, his breathing slowed, and he dreamed of dancing with Isabella at their wedding. She was dressed in a white dress and he in a white suit. He could smell her exotic scent and hear her wonderful childlike laugh.

The beep of his phone shot him to a sitting position. He rubbed a hand over his face and groped the items on the small table by his bed. Cupping the phone, he hit the button with his thumb, noting Rico's number and answered. "*¿Sí?*"

"Your bird hasn't roosted."

Rico's cryptic statement ricocheted around in his head bringing him immediately awake. He looked at the time. Three a.m. She should have been tucked into her room at the hostel unless she was researching. But what? "She could still be in the museum."

"She isn't."

Anger took hold. "How do you know?"

"I have a security guard in the building. He checked. She is not there."

"¡Coño! Did she leave Garza's?"

"Sí. I picked her up myself and dropped her at the hostel. My person saw on the tapes she arrived at the museum at eight but did not leave."

Tino's chest squeezed making breathing hard. He didn't want to discuss this where someone could hear, but he also knew Garza would have his head if he left now. ¡Coño!

"From your reaction I take it she does not usually disappear." Rico's controlled voice didn't help the frustration buffeting Tino's temples.

"The only time she has gone missing is when someone abducted her." He knew she was resourceful but that didn't lessen his anxiety. "I'll meet you behind the museum in twenty minutes."

"I did not call you to have you run out on your mission. I called for information that might help me find her." Rico's voice turned hard and commanding.

"Start at the museum. She has been looking into stolen artifacts. If she is missing, she either found the way they have been taken and they are on to her, or she is following a clue."

"You'll stay put and let us see what we can find out?" Rico might have asked a question but Tino heard the directive in the words.

He exhaled. A hard feat considering the guilt clogging his throat. "Sí, but call me as soon as you know anything."

"I will. Do not ruin the last six months' work. No woman is worth it."

The phone went dead.

"Yes, this woman is," Tino said as he pulled on his pants and grabbed his Glock. He exited the compound, slid into the DEA car, and headed for the hostel. He'd search her room and see what he could find that might lead him to her whereabouts.

~*~

Isabella waited three minutes before moving the boxes and following Alphonso into the tunnel. To avoid his discovering her, she didn't use a light but followed the soft glow of his flashlight beam. He moved swiftly. She pursued as quickly and quietly as she could without a light, but every turn he made tossed her into darkness when she lost the slight glow of his flashlight.

Her toe connected with a hard object and she fell. "Shamutz!" Her hands stung and her knee and toe throbbed, but she popped up and caught a glimmer of his light turn down a tunnel to the right. Isabella placed her hand on the right side of the tunnel and continued, slower than before. Her hand fell into openness and she turned.

There wasn't a glow ahead of her. She'd lost him.

Slowing her breathing and listening intently she hoped to catch a hint of where he might be. A faint scuffing sound came from ahead. She dug into her vest and pulled out her LED light. Muting the light with her fingers she hurried down the tunnel. If she saw a glimmer of Alphonso's light, she'd click hers off.

She chewed on her bottom lip, tossing about the pros and cons of continuing or turning around. Her chase so far had taken thirty minutes so she should be less than a mile from the museum. The stench of sewage grew in the musty air and the ground under her feet grew slicker.

She no longer traveled in tunnels under Templo Mayor, she was in the Mexico City sewer. Panic squeezed her chest. She'd been so intent on watching Alphonso's light she didn't pay attention to the turns or the distance between them to get back to the museum. But how was she to get out of the vast maze of underground tunnels that made up the city's waste system?

Manholes.

There had to be a way for city workers to get in and out of here. She directed the LED beam to the ceiling and began walking, moving the beam back and forth from side to side searching for a ladder to the surface.

Ten minutes passed when she caught sight of a metal ladder leading up. Isabella stuck the light in her mouth, grasped the rungs above her head and stepped up onto the bottom rung. Creaking echoed through the silent darkness as she felt her body tipping backwards. Before she could release the ladder and hop off, she landed on her back and popped the back of her head on the concrete.

Stars danced in her head as air rushed out of her lungs. Everything went black.

~*~

Her roiling stomach hit her, forcing her eyes open and her mind to reconstruct what happened. She rolled to her side to sit up, shoving her hand into a slimy, stinky sludge on the sewer floor. This was more than she could take. Her stomach heaved and the small amount of content left from her meal a long time ago, joined the sludge. The unexpected slap of concrete had her back and bottom stinging.

She repositioned her glasses, found her flashlight, and peered up at the holes in the cement where the ladder had hung. "Next time I'll try it before putting all my weight on the dumb thing."

Pushing to her feet, she swayed and leaned against the wall. "I have to get out of here. No one knows where I am." She started forward. Her watch had a tracking device from the WIA but they weren't allowed to use it unless an operative was believed in danger. While her father had her tracked continually before she became an agent, she'd made him promise to only use it as he did with other operatives.

She trudged on, keeping the light beamed upward. There had to be another manhole soon. Another ten minutes past and she spotted a ladder and a cover at the top. This time she grabbed the rung and hung all her weight. It held. Then she jiggled her body to see if the bolts would slip loose. Nothing.

Elation propelled her arms and legs up the metal rungs to the heavy metal cover. Grunts and a shoulder helped to move the disc to the side enough so she could squeeze out. The manhole appeared to be in an alley.

She stuffed the flashlight into her pocket and straightened her glasses as she stared down the empty street. "Where am I?" She pushed to her feet and spun in a slow circle looking for something familiar. She walked to the end of the alley and spotted a skyline that looked familiar.

Off to her left over the tops of the buildings she thought it was the Catedral Metropolitana. The historical site near her hostel and Templo Mayor. Walking toward the two tall towers of the cathedral, Isabella chastised herself for thinking she could follow someone who knew their way around the tunnels. She should have known better. She had to stop thinking she was Indiana Jones in a fictional movie.

A block closer to the cathedral the traffic picked up. With the night crowd carousing the streets, she had to prove she wasn't a victim, which was hard since she looked and smelled like some rat that had crawled out of the sewers. It was the only way to keep from being mugged or worse. She shifted her shoulders back and looked at people without seeming confrontational. If she walked along keeping her eyes to the concrete, they'd pounce on her in a flash. Increasing her pace, but keeping it below a trot to not look like she was scared and running, she stepped into the block housing the hostel and was soon locked inside the building.

Isabella leaned against the door and let her body droop. She'd made a mess of the evening and wasn't sure how to fix it. With slumped shoulders and slow steps, she climbed the stairs to her second story room and slid the key card through the slot. She shoved the door open and stepped inside.

A hand covered her mouth as an arm banded around her middle. Anger didn't give fear a chance to emerge. She kicked backwards and hissed when she missed her mark.

"Querida, it is I, Tino. Where have you been?"

Tino's low seductive voice siphoned her fortitude. She spun in his arms, tears streaming down her face in relief and shame.

Tino hugged Isabella to his beating heart. When he'd heard the door latch click, he wasn't sure who was entering. He'd hoped it was the woman in his arms, but he couldn't be sure of anything anymore. The stench that came through the door could have been anyone. Tears dampened his T-shirt. He held her away from him. "Are you hurt?" He peered at her using the faint light from the moon to search for wounds.

"Yes. No. Not really."

"Querida?" He'd never witnessed her so sad and trodden upon.

"I messed up. I should have known better." She pulled out of his arms and stalked across the room only to pivot and stalk back. "I shouldn't have followed him. I should have come back here and called the curator and my father." She stalked away from him and back again. "Now they know."

Her anger and words sliced fear into his chest like a machete swing. "Who knows? What have you done?" Was it Garza? Had he somehow discovered her true identity?

"Whoever is stealing the artifacts." She stopped in front of him. "I discovered how they are doing it. There is a tunnel from the digging in Templo Mayor. Only it also connects to the sewer system. They came in and put address labels on crates, and they were sent to the buyers without anyone noticing."

Tino grasped her hand and led her over to the bed. He gently urged her to sit. "Where were they sending the crates?"

"That's what doesn't make sense. They sent it to a prestigious British museum. While I was standing in the storage room contemplating the address, Alphonso, of the Bohu gang, came back and saw me."

"¡Carajo! The Bohu gang? How would they know which artifacts to sell?"

"Exactly. It doesn't make sense. It would take someone who knew something about Aztec history to know what was worth the risk." Isabella unbuttoned her vest and slid it down her arms.

"How did you get away?" Tino didn't like thinking about her in danger. He didn't know who this Alphonso was, but if he were part of the Luis Bohu's gang he had to have a mean streak.

"I guess he figured he could get away from me in the tunnels."

The indignation in her voice made his lips quirk. "And he did."

"What do you mean?" He gathered her hand into his and watched the emotions playing across her face and knew her mind was spinning behind her introspective stare.

"I followed him into the tunnels, lost him, and ended up in the sewer." She scratched her disheveled hair and sniffed her hand, making a face. "When I realized I'd never find him, I started looking for a way out. I found a ladder to a manhole, but the ladder gave way. I fell backward, hitting my head. I think I was out for a time."

"Querida. You should have never followed." He drew her into his arms even though the stench of her was hard to ignore.

She pushed out of his arms. "I know. It was stupid and impulsive to think I could follow him and see who he was working for."

Tino rubbed a hand up and down her arm. His insides were twitching thinking about the danger she'd put herself in. "How did you get back here?"

"When I came to, I found another ladder. This time I tested it. When I climbed out, I used the Catedral Metropolitana towers to guide me back to the hostel."

"But this Alphonso, he knows you saw him?" Fear for her safety had tripled if the Bohu gang would be after her too.

She ran her hands over her head and winced. "I can't be certain. I don't think he'd say anything. It would make him look bad to have allowed me to see him. He's not really gang material."

She looked so forlorn, Tino wanted to treat her like a child.

Her wide pupils peered into his eyes. "I should have turned everything into father and let them handle capturing the leader. I probably ruined their chances of ever catching the person now."

"Querida, all that matters is you are safe." Tino kissed her cheek. She turned and he captured her lips.

Isabella pulled out of the kiss. "What are you doing here?"

"Rico... Aiiyii, I better call him." He pulled out his phone and hit the speed dial for Rico.

"¿Sí?" Rico's angry tone validated he knew Tino had slipped out of the compound.

"Dr. Mumphrey is back in her room."

"And you know this how?"

"I am sitting beside her. And will head back to the compound now that I know she is safe." Tino kissed her knuckles and winked at her.

"You may have jeopardized your career with DEA and your life with this infatuation you have for that woman." Rico's tone had softened to that of a concerned friend.

"Sí. But she is safe." Tino closed the phone and drew Isabella into his arms. "Querida, I must go. I do not wish to leave you like this but I risked much by coming here."

She gasped. "Tino, you need to worry more about you. I'm not in as deep as you are."

Isabella kissed him drawing his thoughts to more pleasant things. When he would have lingered, she drew out of the kiss and his arms. She stood, pulling him up beside her. "Go. I don't want you in any more danger because of me."

He kissed her forehead. "Querida, you have done all you can for your mission. For me, get on a plane tomorrow and put yourself far from here."

"Karyme Garza is expecting me—"

"You owe them nothing. Send a message saying a family matter came up and you had to go home." He feared for her to get tangled any deeper with the drug lord and his wife.

"I will after I check into one other thing I dug up."

If she had looked anywhere other than straight into his eyes, he would have packed her clothes and forced her onto the next plane. "Does this have to do with your mission?"

"Yes, I need to gather more information from the museum about the names of the people I believe might be part of the smuggling."

He relaxed. "Once you have that you will be on a plane back to your university?"

She placed a brief kiss on his lips and pushed him toward the door. "Yes."

As Tino exited the hostel he had a bad feeling she was not going to stay away from the Garzas.

Chapter Twenty

Isabella woke, dressed, and packed all the information she'd acquired so far and her written report in a box and carried it downstairs.

Alphonso's cousin was at the desk. Did he ever leave?

"Would you see that this is shipped out today, por favor?" she asked.

Felix peered at the address and smiled. "Sí. This is for the work you are doing?"

She smiled. It was addressed to the university but attention to a local operative who would pick it up and send it to her father.

"Yes, I'm just about done with my research." She noticed the restaurant wasn't as full as the day before. Smiling, she walked in and took a table near a window. The hovering waiters took her order and arrived with it before she had time to consider her day. Once the food sat in front of Isabella, she ate and let her mind flip through the information she'd filed away last night after Tino left and she'd showered and scrubbed her vest.

She'd made a list of items she wished to check today. At the top of the list was a visit to Director Bastante. She hoped to get him talking about dig experiences and see if he left out the fact he had been on several with Karyme Martinez Garza.

Deep in thought, she didn't notice the person until he sat in the chair across from her. She sat down her cold drink and smiled. "I heard you were looking for me last night. I didn't know I was that popular."

Rico didn't smile back. "You have become a liability to our mission. I cannot have my only operative in the organization I am after run off to find you when you disappear."

Isabella's breakfast soured. "If you hadn't called him, he wouldn't have come looking." She knew it was a poor excuse, but if Tino hadn't known she was missing he would have stayed at the compound.

Rico ran a hand over his face. "True. It was poor judgment on my part to call him when I was told you had disappeared." His gaze roamed around the room then landed on her. "You are a weight around my neck. I have been told to make sure you finish your job and return home."

She held her breath. Had her father called in the DEA to help keep her safe? She should find comfort that he cared, but all she could think was he didn't believe she could do her job. That burned and sizzled in her chest. Why did he allow her to become an agent if he didn't have faith in her skills?

"I'm sorry you feel that way. I told Tino I'd finish my work today and head home so both of you can do your jobs and not have to worry about some lame anthropologist making your job harder." She stood, tossed some coins on the table, and left.

Fury at her father for making that man think she was incompetent had her shoving the door open and marching down the street to the museum. Men! She'd prove to them all that she could do her job and she didn't need them babysitting her. The people and exhaust filled air barely penetrated her thoughts as she stalked into the museum and punched the button for the top floor and the offices.

If she didn't find out what she needed by the end of today, she'd move out of the hostel, find somewhere neither Tino or Rico would look for her, and do some surveillance on the two people she believed were the brains behind the thefts.

~*~

Tino groaned and rolled out of bed. He'd managed to get back in the compound without being detected, but he'd only had two hours of sleep and his mind was groggy. Not a good situation since Garza would want a full account of the attempts on the shipment. Diego stepped out of his room as Tino exited his. Their gazes met and looked away. They had said little last night. Diego had made himself scarce knowing Garza wanted information from the two they'd brought in.

Tino hadn't filled Rico in on the heads that were left for the Alvarez brothers. There were some things better left to the DEA's discovery. He entered the kitchen, rolled two tortillas together and grabbed a cup of coffee. It wasn't as late as he'd thought, but that didn't mean Garza wasn't in his office awaiting a full report. Tino nudged Diego and nodded for him to follow.

They stopped outside the office. Muffled shouting could be heard behind the door.

Diego took a step back.

Tino shook his head. "His anger can't be against us. We saved his shipment."

Diego visibly relaxed and nodded.

Tino rapped on the door.

"Entrar!" The tone was close to a growl.

Gripping the handle, Tino twisted and pushed the door open.

Garza stood with his back to the door and staring out the window. He didn't turn around. "There is no need to give me details about last night. I want you to find out who in this house leaked the change of shipment." He turned and his eyes burned with anger. His red face made a fascinating contrast to his quivering mustache as he pointed to Diego and the door.

Diego didn't bat an eye as he slipped out the door.

Tino waved a hand toward the locked door holding all the drug lord's secrets. "Who besides you has access to that room?"

The drug lord stalked toward him. "Yesterday, you, my wife, and myself were the only people in there after I'd changed the route." His gaze drilled into Tino's eyes.

"Then if it was not you or I, it was your wife." Tino was braced for a blow.

Garza shook his head and stalked across the room. "Karyme would not ruin a life she has grown accustom to. There has to be someone who is entering without our knowledge." He spun. "Get Julio to set up cameras in that room. I want to know who is the traitor." Garza peered intently. "And no one other than you, Julio, and I are to know about the cameras."

Tino nodded and headed to the room full of surveillance monitors. He'd only set foot in the room once before. When Cezar had shown him around the compound. Taking over Cezar's position had given him carte blanche to any area of the house. He frowned. All but the locked room. But if the room would have a camera set up, DEA could use the tapes to nail Garza.

He walked into the room. Julio and another were reading technology magazines and toying with a device on a counter. The far wall was an abstract mural of monitors. Anarosa was in the kitchen, Hadda was laying out señora Garza's clothes. The drug lord's wife walked out of her bathroom in a robe and stepped behind a screen to dress. Maids were moving about the house cleaning and several of the security team were milling about from room to room. The camera in the tower was pointed down the street.

"Julio, I have a message from Jefe for you only."

Both men jumped at his voice. With sheepish grins they looked up.

"Ray, go see if Anarosa has any of her sweets for us." Julio nodded toward the door. When the other man left, Julio put the magazine down and centered his full attention on Tino. "What does señor Garza want me to do?"

"He requested surveillance cameras be set up in both his offices."

Julio narrowed his eyes. "He keeps those areas private."

"He is trying to catch the person telling his business to his rivals." Tino turned to the door. "You can talk to Jefe yourself if you do not believe me. I am only doing what he asked me to do." He walked out the door. He understood the man's reaction. Garza had been hard to get all these years because of his paranoia and his ability to not have any recordings of his actions.

His phone vibrated. Peering at the name he grimaced. Rico must have heard about the heads. From here on out he would have to stay clear of Rico and Isabella. It was the only way he could convince Garza of his loyalty and get the information to bring the man down.

~*~

Isabella walked into director Bastante's reception area. Today his secretary had hot pink nails and stilettos.

"I'd like to see Director Bastante, por favor."

"He is busy. I could make you an appointment for eleven."

From the blank eyes and stiff smile, Isabella determined the woman wouldn't let her in even if she said it was an emergency.

"Those are great looking shoes." She stared at the woman's pointy-toed shoes on even pointier four-inch heels. "What brand are those?"

They talked shoe brands with Isabella faking her knowledge and moved onto the secretary's favorite nail salon. Ten minutes later, the office door clicked.

Isabella feigned interest in the method used by the woman's manicurist to apply the colored stones to her nails as the door opened. Holding her breath, she just about choked when the feminine voice she heard was Karyme Garza's.

There was nowhere to hide, and if she did, the secretary would rat on her. So, she stood and pivoted away from the desk.

She witnessed the surprised expressions on both Karyme and Bastante's faces when they spotted her. She also noticed Karyme's eyes flared a moment before softening and she extended her hands.

"Isabella, you are still coming today to help with boxing the artifacts?"

"Yes. I wanted to ask Director Bastante's permission to bring along some books from the archive room which will help us determine the authentication of the items you wanted me to look at." Isabella drew the list of the books she'd placed on the table in the archive room from her vest pocket. She handed it to Bastante.

"Then I'll see you this afternoon." Karyme did a finger wave and walked to the elevator.

Isabella kept her eyes on the woman as she stepped into the conveyance and the doors closed. The caring, sympathetic impression she'd first harbored about the woman no longer matched. This woman was calculating and dangerous.

She returned her attention to the director. He was also watching Karyme. The desire in his eyes and yearning on his face, almost made her laugh. Isabella had no doubt the woman was using the man's infatuation to her advantage.

He shook his head and stared down at the list. "What do you need these books for?" His curiosity came through in his voice and drawn together eyebrows.

"The Garzas have some items that they believe were not

authenticated correctly. I want the books to check against the items."
She wasn't going to say a word about the possibility the items they had
could be worth a fortune not only in money but in knowledge about
the Aztec. She couldn't leave here until she knew the truth about those
pieces. If they were the valuable pieces, they should be in a museum to
be studied not in the hands of a drug lord.

Bastante peered at her. "Have you seen these pieces?"

"No. I believe they were to let me look at them today."

He handed the list to her. "Take the books. I'd be most interested
in knowing what you learn."

She didn't miss the innuendo that he would be questioning her
further.

"Gracias. I'll bring the books back tonight." She left the fourth
floor. There was no need to question Bastante. Watching the two of
them when they exited his office told her what she had planned to ask.

The elevator door opened at the basement, and she strode down
the hall to the archive room to pick up the books. The door to the
surveillance room stood ajar. The only person she ever saw coming
from the room was the night guard. Was there someone on duty during
the day?

She pushed the door open slowly. Delgado was replaying the tape
of her disappearance the night before. Isabella closed the door.

The click of the lock spun Delgado around. She stared down the
barrel of a handgun.

Chapter Twenty-one

Isabella's heart pounded in her chest and her ears. He'd hired her, why was he pulling a gun?

As quickly as her frightened mind asked the question, the barrel dipped toward the floor.

"Dr. Mumphrey, I thought you were…" Delgado placed the weapon on the counter beside him. "I'm sorry. I was just reviewing the tape of you disappearing. I didn't know who was sneaking up on me. For all I knew it could have been someone to get this tape."

Shaking her mind out of its frozen state, she took a seat beside the curator. "Why haven't you given the tapes you gave me to the police?"

"I do not know who is stealing. It could be someone who pays the police to look the other way. That is why I contacted WIA. I knew I could not depend on the local authorities." He pulled the tape of her disappearance out of the machine. "How did you disappear?" He nodded to the tape in his hand.

"There is a tunnel from the archive room that connects with the sewer tunnels." It still bugged her she'd lost Alphonso. She could still turn him in but…She wasn't ready to tip her hand just yet.

He shook his head. "Is that how they take out the artifacts?"

"No. They label crates. I witnessed one of the members of the Bohu gang put labels on two crates."

The man's attention heightened. "Did you see what the labels said?"

"Yes. They were addressed to the British Museum."

"Attention who?"

"No one. That's the odd part." Isabella felt as puzzled as Delgado looked. "I'm sure the Bohu gang was only being paid to put the labels on. Someone else, who would have access to what was in the storage room and the precise box, would have to give them the information." She pushed out of the chair. "I'm going to get the books I set out in the archive room and then talk with the person who labeled the boxes. I may be able to get information out of him."

Delgado shook his head. "You should not go to the Bohu gang alone."

"I know where to find him that won't be near the Bohu gang." Isabella left the surveillance room and stepped into the archive room. Her senses pricked.

The books weren't stacked as she'd left them. Someone had been in here inspecting the books. Who? When? Why? The more she learned, the more questions she had.

She pulled a folded tote bag out of a pocket in her vest and shoved the books in the bag. As much as the tunnel called to her, she wanted to talk with Alphonso before the car came to escort her to Garza's. She'd check out the tunnel tonight when there was less chance of running into anyone.

Leaving the museum, she made note of the guard on duty. Did he ever go home? Between this guard and Felix at the counter in the hostel she was beginning to think people around here didn't have lives outside of their work.

Stepping inside the hostel, she was surprised to see another clerk behind the counter. The name printed on his badge was Marco. Since her arrival it had always been Felix.

"Is Felix here?" she asked when the man looked up from a check list.

"No, señorita, he has two days off." He smiled. "May I help you?"

Figures, just when she wanted to ask him to contact his cousin, he has his weekend. "No." She tapped a finger on the counter. "Unless...do you happen to know Felix's cousin Alphonso?"

"Sí, he hangs out here and helps." Marco put a hand on the phone. "Would you like me to call him?"

"Yes, but just say you have a customer who would like him to do some shopping." She slid a five-dollar bill across the counter and listened as Marco informed Alphonso he had a customer needing assistance.

He replaced the phone. "He can be here in fifteen minutes."

"Gracias. I'll wait for him in the restaurant. Send him in there without giving away who I am, por favor."

Marco nodded and went back to his check-list.

Hauling the tote bag of books, she took a booth where her back would be to Alphonso when he entered the restaurant. She wanted to be between him and the door when he realized who waited for him.

~*~

Tino and Garza were in the surveillance room with Julio studying the camera angles in the offices when señora Garza returned home. Garza didn't seem to notice his wife, but Tino watched her. She was mad. Her nostrils flared and her steps were determined. Something upset her while she was out. Where had she gone?

"These are good angles. We should see who enters and what they do." Garza straightened. That's when he noticed his wife's return as she climbed the staircase. "Remember only you two and I know about these cameras."

Tino and Julio nodded. Garza left them. Tino watched as he ascended the stairs. What he wouldn't give to stay in here and see what the two discussed. But as the two met in the upstairs hallway, the camera on them went blank. He glanced at Julio. The man didn't seem to find this odd.

"Why did that camera go blank?" Tino asked.

Julio shrugged. "I made a device Jefe can push and it blanks out whatever camera he is closest to."

That was how the man had privacy in a house full of cameras. And how he kept conversations unrecorded.

Tino left the room. He had to warn Hadda about the cameras. He was sure she didn't give information to the Alvarez gang, but he didn't want her gathering intel for the Bohus and get caught by Garza. If she did, it would be one more innocent's death on his conscience.

He found her in the pantry off the kitchen. Her mother had her back to the room as she stirred something spicy on the stove. Tino slipped into the pantry, placing a hand over the girl's mouth and one around her arms to keep her from giving away he was with her.

"Shhh…" he whispered as she started to struggle. "I'm here to warn you. Do not sneak in the office and gather information for Luis. Garza had security install hidden cameras today. He is looking for a traitor."

Tino released Hadda. She spun in his arms. Her wide frightened eyes reminded him of a cornered kitten.

"I have to get information for Luis," she whispered.

"No. Not anymore unless you want to die." Tino heard footsteps coming to the pantry. "Forgive me," he said, pulling her into his arms and kissing her.

Anarosa pushed into the small pantry and whacked him upside the head with a wooden spoon. "Leave my girl alone! You are too old!" The woman smacked him again before he could squeeze by her and out of the kitchen.

He headed straight for his room to wash out whatever had been on the spoon, it was stinging his scalp. He'd warned Hadda, now they just had to wait for the other informant to make a move. The downside was waiting would give him too much time to wonder what trouble Isabella was conjuring. Did she send off the report and head back to Arizona or was the stubborn woman going to stick her nose somewhere that would get her deeper into his mission?

~*~

A minute after Isabella saw Alphonso pass by the restaurant window she heard footsteps approaching. The moment he turned and saw her, his face lost all color and he started to retreat. She sprang to her feet, blocking his way.

"Have a seat Alphonso. We need to talk." She waited, wondering if he would bolt or sit.

He let out a huge sigh and deflated onto the bench seat.

"I have a lot of questions for you. If you answer them, I won't turn you in for labeling the crates."

His eyes flashed with surprise before his eyelids fell to half-mast. "I don't know what you're talking about."

"Play dumb all you want. I can have you arrested and hauled a long way from here if that's what you want." She took a sip of her juice and waited. He seemed to be mulling over her words.

"Why haven't you turned me in already?" His suspicious tone

made her chuckle.

"Because I don't believe you're as bad as the group you hang around with. Give me some answers, and I'll not press charges."

He slumped back against the booth and played with a spoon. "What do you want to know?"

"Who told you about the tunnel to the storage room?"

An air of superiority changed his features and straightened his spine. "I found it when I was down in the tunnels taking lunch to my father one day. I told Luis about it and then six months ago Luis gave me instructions to put labels on certain crates in the storage room." He glanced around the room and leaned closer. "I don't know who he told, but they pay American dollars for me to put the labels on the boxes. Until you showed up last night it was easy." Alphonso scowled at her.

Isabella returned the scowl with a smile. "Sorry, I have a knack for piecing together puzzles. Any idea who is paying you in American dollars or slipping the information about the crates to Luis?"

He shrugged.

"How do you know which crate to put the label on?" If he wouldn't talk about the people involved maybe she could figure it out by learning all about the process.

"They give a general area and markings I look for."

Excitement tingled the hair on Isabella's arms. "What did the last markings look like? Did you cover them up?"

"I'm not supposed to cover them up."

"No, that's how the person on the other end knows which crates to pull from the regular shipment." Isabella made a mental note to call her father and have him see who at the British museum had been at archeological digs with Bastante and Karyme Martinez.

"What markings did you look for this time?"

"You're going to ruin this for me, aren't you?" The young man came as near to a pout as she'd ever seen on a man.

"Do you want to end up in jail? If you are smart enough to find the tunnel, time and again, and find the boxes, you are smart enough to find a good paying job that will keep you out of jail." She leaned closer. "From what I hear jail in Mexico isn't very fun."

Alphonso paled and shook his head.

"What did the markings look like?"

"Do you have a pen?" He scanned the nearly empty restaurant.

Isabella pulled her journal and pencil out of her inside vest pocket. She opened the book to an empty page and slid it across the table.

As he carefully made the lines on the page, Isabella watched a rendering of the Aztec sun unfold. When the sun was finished, Alphonso drew lines to split it in thirds.

The meaning was clear to her. The boxes contained artifacts from the Triple Alliance. The same time period of the artifacts the Garza's wanted authenticated. This couldn't be a coincidence. Someone on the dig was telling them what was found and then marking crates with the items the Garza's wanted. She doubted the labeled crates ever made it out of Mexico City. Someone was pulling them from the trucks and relocating them.

"You know what this means?" Alphonso asked in an awed whisper.

"Yes. But you mustn't tell anyone what I asked or what you told me." She pulled her journal back across the table and tucked it into her vest pocket.

His eyes narrowed. "Are you really an archeologist?"

"No, I'm an anthropologist. I study Native Americans. Their cultures and languages." She glanced at her watch. The car would be arriving soon to take her to the Garza's.

Isabella stood. "We didn't have this conversation, and if you want to get on the respectable side of the law—" she handed him her university business card—"give me a call in a couple months. We're always looking for young people to help with our studies."

She strode out of the restaurant and sat where she could watch the traffic and people outside the hostel. Her stomach bubbled with excitement and dread. If the Garza's had any inkling she was here to discover the missing artifacts, she could quite possibly not walk out of their house tonight.

Chapter Twenty-two

Tino cursed as he pulled up to the cantina where Luis Bohu spent his time when not dealing in illegal activities. Rico sat in a car across the street from the cantina entrance. Tino had ignored all his superior's calls, trying to wash his mind of Manny's glee in beheading the Alvarez gang members and their glazed eyes as the heads were loaded into a box to be tossed at Raul and Jorge's door.

Rico followed him into the cantina. It wouldn't look out of place for them to enter together since that was how Luis found them the other night. What Tino didn't want was a pissing match with his superior. He was here to tell Luis to call Hadda off. If the man cared for her as much as it appeared, he'd listen to reason.

Tino walked up to the bar. "Is Luis around?" he asked the bartender.

"He left about an hour ago." The man glanced toward the door. "But today is your lucky day."

Tino peered in the mirror behind the bar. Luis and three thugs strode across the floor toward him. Rico had planted himself in a booth not too far away.

Pointing at the bar in front of him, Tino indicated he wanted a drink. The bartender placed it in front of him as Luis tapped him on the shoulder.

"What are you doing here? I do not like you hanging around. It's bad for business." Luis motioned to his men to move forward.

"This is the last time you will see me. If you listen to reason." Tino dumped the fiery tequila down his throat and motioned for Luis to walk closer.

The man narrowed his eyes and placed his hand on the handle of the pistol in a shoulder harness under his unbuttoned shirt.

Tino nodded for him to come closer.

Warily Luis stepped up to him.

In a low voice, Tino said, "I warned Hadda to not gather any more information for you. But she was rather adamant she had to. If you do not want her death on your hands call her off."

Luis moved closer, his nose nearly touching Tino's. "No one will kill her. You are the only one who knows what she does and I can kill you without anyone caring."

Tino sighed heavily and shook his head. He knew of someone who would care. Right now, he wanted to keep an innocent girl safe. "I'm trying to help you and Hadda. Garza installed surveillance equipment in his office this morning to catch the person stealing his route information."

Luis stepped back, yanked a phone from his pocket, and pressed one number. He spoke into the phone. His soothing tone and words revealed he had called Hadda.

With his job accomplished here, he headed for the door.

"Wait!"

Tino stopped and slowly pivoted toward Luis.

The man walked quickly toward him. "I owe you for keeping Hadda a secret."

Tino waved him off. "I may need a favor sometime. Keep that thought." He walked out of the cantina and didn't even flinch when Rico ripped open the passenger door to his SUV and slid into the seat.

"What the hell are you doing?"

Without even looking at his boss, he pulled the vehicle away from the curb and started driving. "What are you doing climbing into my car? If someone other than the Bohu gang members saw this it could jeopardize everything." He stared a moment at his superior with the anger and disgust he'd been bottling up.

"Did you have anything to do with the heads left on the street in the Alvarez distrio?" The disgust in Rico's voice echoed in Tino's churning gut.

"Not directly," he said through clenched teeth.

"Not directly? What the hell does that mean? Did you know of the killings?"

Tino gripped the steering wheel. His knuckles ached but not as much as his conscience. "They were the ones trying to intercept Garza's shipment the other night. He had me bring them in." He squeezed his eyes shut, forcing the images out of his mind.

"Hey!"

The steering wheel jerked to the right. He opened his eyes and found Rico holding the wheel.

"What kind of crazy stunt was that? You trying to kill us both?" Rico's eyes were big and round as he tried to watch the road and Tino.

"I-I have done many things undercover I'm not proud of but the end result was worth it. What Garza ordered was…" He straightened his back. If he didn't get that man behind bars, he could do the same to anyone. Hadda, Isabella. *Coño*! He had to shake off the horror and stay focused.

"I did not kill the men, nor did I behead them. Garza has a sadistic monster on the payroll who loves to torture and mutilate." He glared at Rico. "He wanted to send a message to the Alvarez brothers."

Tino released his grip on the steering wheel as he drove in a circle and filled Rico in on the reason they couldn't get Garza on tape and about his latest attempt to catch the person responsible for spilling his routes.

"There is only one person who could be responsible and it doesn't make sense." He spun all the information he had around in his head. There was only one person. But why would she try to bring down her livelihood?

"Who?"

"Señora Garza. She is the only other person with access to that room."

"Not if the maid is getting in." Rico pointed out.

"I need to see how she has been getting in. That could open it up to another possibility." Tino parked two blocks from Rico's car. "I do not know what will happen if the informant is caught. I will try to inform you of what I know."

"Your actions last night both for Garza and then jeopardizing your cover by running to the doctor have shifted my faith in you." Rico opened his door and leaned on the down window. "Do not do anything else that will have me pull you from this investigation. We've worked too hard to have it blown now."

"I plan to stay away from Isabella until this is finished. She promised to head home." He knew her promises were well intentioned but she rarely followed through. Something he would have to teach her to work on.

Rico narrowed his eyes. "You really believe she will walk away when she knows the danger you are in?"

Tino grinned and shook his head. "No. But she will keep a low profile. She is too smart to be found by either of us if she wishes to disappear."

His boss shook his head. "I do not know. She grew angry with me this morning."

"What did you say?" ¡Coño! All he needed was Isabella out to prove something other than her mission which was wrapped up.

"I believe I chose the wrong words. I wanted her to think you had sent me to tell her to go home." He dipped his head. "I believe my words struck a nerve. She said she was leaving and not to worry about her and stormed out of the hostel."

"That is not good. What exactly did you say?" Tino couldn't figure out what would have ignited her anger.

Rico's face reddened. "I said she was a weight around my neck and I had been told to help her finish and get back home."

"¡Coño!" Tino gripped the steering wheel. Knowing Isabella, she took that to mean she couldn't do her job and her father had butted in. "I will have to find her and set her straight or she could place herself in the middle of a drug war."

~*~

Isabella alighted from the car that picked her up at the hostel. She scanned the area trying to appear as if she wasn't searching for anyone. There were more men stationed about the complex. Not a good sign.

She walked up to the door and gripped the brass knocker, rapping it against an Aztec sun.

The young girl, Hadda, answered the door. "Señora is waiting for you upstairs."

"Gracias." Isabella wore her vest today. If there was trouble, she wanted to be prepared. She gripped her tote bag with the reference books and ascended the stairs, turning right. The door to Karyme's room full of treasures was open.

She stepped through, and Karyme straightened her body. She'd been leaning over a table inspecting an item.

"Ah, Isabella. You are right on time. I was just scraping shavings off this piece to send for carbon dating." Karyme pulled latex gloves off her hands and walked around the table.

"Do you send samples of all your finds for carbon dating?" Isabella tried to infuse her question with enthusiasm when all she really wanted was to see the pieces they believed from the triple alliance.

Karyme nodded as she placed a plastic bag into a padded envelope. "I send everything that I need dated to help me solve what it was used for. Sometimes knowing the time period helps." Holding the envelope, she walked to the door. "I suppose you are excited to see our real treasures."

Isabella reined in her excitement. "I'm here to help you determine the origin or authenticity of whatever you wish. But this will be my last day. I've been called back to the university. One of the other professors had an accident and is unable to teach. They want me to fill in." When have you become so talented at lying?

"You are leaving so soon?" Karyme turned.

Isabella would have believed concern etched the woman's brow if not for the calculating look quickly shielded behind lowered eyelids.

"Yes. I received the call this morning. I told them I'd be on the plane back tomorrow. I didn't want to leave you without possibly giving you some guidance on the artifacts you believe are part of the triple alliance." If she kept repeating the lie, she just might also believe it.

"Then we should not waste time. Come." Karyme led her back down the stairway, through the ballroom, and outside to stairs that went to a basement under the ballroom.

Descending into the darkness, knowing the woman walking ahead of her had many ulterior motives; Isabella's heart banged in her chest and whooshed blood loudly in her ears. Trying to slow her heart and mind to listen for a trap, she reverted to her yoga and taekwondo breathing techniques. Slowly, inhale as one foot stepped down and exhaling as the next.

The musty smell reminded her of the tunnels under the city. Could this basement have a tunnel that led to some hide-away?

With her breathing normal, she heard Karyme's downward movement stop. Wondering if the woman was preparing to harm her, Isabella stopped at what she hoped was a distance greater than the woman's reach.

Sound, like a hand brushing the wall, rustled to her right. A click snapped in the darkness and dim bulbs cast a welcome but faint light in a rectangular shaped room with bare dirt walls and hefty beams.

"You did well in the dark." Karyme's tone indicated she'd expected Isabella to not follow.

"I've been on several digs and know how to get around in the dark." She shivered remembering the bat-filled cave she and Tino had encountered when fleeing the narcos.

"Then you won't have trouble with the next place we go." Karyme shoved two crates to the side, revealing a tunnel like the one at the museum, and picked up a high-powered light. "When we have items that we wish no one to steal we keep them well hidden."

Isabella watched the woman duck and enter the small opening. Would walking in there and learning where a drug lord kept his most prized possessions make her expendable? No one knew where she was. Her skin prickled. But not going would be cowardly, and she would never know if the Garzas had found something of significance. Logic said turn around and head for Arizona, her mission had been accomplished. Her heart and yearning for knowledge wanted to see the artifacts and help Tino.

Ducking, she held the bag of books in front of her body to fit through the small opening and stood on the other side. Karyme stood twenty feet ahead, looking toward her.

"I was beginning to think you had changed your mind." The gleam in her eye chilled Isabella's skin more than the cool damp air in the tunnel.

"Just trying to decide if I was a dead person after you showed me the whereabouts of your artifacts." Her bluntness had caught her enemies by surprise before. She hoped this time was no different.

Karyme laughed. "I knew you had to be a strong woman to have made it this far in your career at such a young age." She pivoted and started down the tunnel. Over her shoulder she said, "Your health depends on how valuable the artifacts turn out to be."

Chapter Twenty-three

Tino's chest squeezed so tight it shoved all the air out of his lungs
when he rounded the house and saw Isabella follow señora Garza
down the veranda stairs and disappear. He rushed to the spot and
discovered a door that had to lead to a basement. He hadn't even
known there was an area under the house.

He reached out to grasp the handle on the door.

"Rodriguez! What are you doing?" Garza stood on the veranda
that concealed the basement entrance.

"I thought I saw this door close. I was going to see if that was how
someone was gathering information." He straightened, drawing his
gun from his holster to give more credence to his belief.

"No one entered that door. It has a coded lock. Get up here, I have
a job for you." Garza strolled across the veranda to the ballroom.

Tino glanced at the door and saw the touch pad to the right of the
door. Did Garza know his wife and Isabella were down there? Or was
he clueless to what his wife did? He prayed Isabella learned more
defensive moves when she joined the WIA, and if the other woman
tried anything, Isabella could out fight her and get away.

Pain in his gut had to be an ulcer starting from all the worry his
little dove caused him. He climbed the stairs to the veranda and
entered the ballroom. Garza's steady pace down the hall meant one
thing. They were meeting in the office. Which one was anyone's

guess. If he couldn't take care of Isabella, he wanted to get the information DEA needed and finish his mission. Then the two of them would get the hell out of here and never set foot outside the U.S. It was too dangerous for them both.

He strode down the hall, through the outer office, and entered the usually secured office. What was Garza planning now?

"Shut the door." Garza fumbled with something in his pocket.

It was most likely the gadget Julio had told him about that scrambled the security equipment. He needed to get his hands on it and enter this room to gather the data for DEA.

Tino turned from shutting the door. Garza paced to the white board with the routes marked and back to this desk.

"I have changed the route for tonight's shipment three times. And now you will drive to the south of town and use a pay phone in a cantina to send this final route to the driver." Garza handed Tino a slip of paper.

He didn't look at the note, just shoved it in his pocket.

Garza narrowed his eyes. "If this shipment gets stolen I will know the traitor is either you or the driver."

"Sí." Tino didn't like being sent away from the compound knowing Isabella was under the building but he had no choice. Not if he wanted to finally put his revenge in motion.

"¡Vamos! I want that shipment moving as soon as you call. Then you sit along the route outside of town and wait for it to pass you. Then follow it to the destination." Garza slammed a hand on the desk. "If there is any interference call me. I will send out Manny to deal with them. And if I discover you are the leak. I will send Manny after you."

Tino straightened his back and stared straight into the drug lord's eyes. "I am not the leak. I have nothing to fear from Manny." He made sure the man saw he had no fear and leisurely headed to the door. Once outside the room, he exhaled and headed to the garage. If this shipment was intercepted there would be more dead bodies lying around. And one of them would be his.

~*~

Isabella couldn't believe the excellent shape the two-foot-tall statues were in. They were the carved symbols of the three leaders who made up the triple alliance. The quality of the carvings proved they were made by the same craftsman. But she had yet to find any writing or symbolism that marked them as having made an alliance. That was the marking that would make them invaluable to collectors and museums.

She stretched her neck and back. The past two hours she'd gone over every carved inch of the three statues as Karyme watched her.

"These are magnificent carvings of Itzcoatl, Nezuhualcoyotl, and Totoquilhauztli, but I can't find any conclusive markings that reflect the alliance they made." Isabella pulled another book out of her tote bag and flipped to the pages she'd marked about the alliance.

She tipped the first carving off the spinning pedestal and placed it carefully face down on the blanket that had been wrapped around the artifact. On the bottom of the statue a faint image was etched in the stone.

"I need better light." Isabella couldn't control the excitement in her voice. If this was what she thought and it was on all three…Her mind flipped through all she'd read about the eagle and coyote symbols in Aztec culture.

"Here." Karyme leaned close as she handed the high beam light to Isabella. "What have you found?"

"I may have found the connection." Yes, her eyes had seen correctly. It was a coyote, the symbol for warriors and warfare, on the head of an eagle clasping a serpent; the symbol of the Mexica Valley people.

Leaving the statue tipped, she tipped the next one. Her heart raced as the faint etched lines appeared. Swallowing to push her thundering heart back into her chest, she placed the last statue on its face, closed her eyes, and opened them to see the same symbol on the bottom.

"These are priceless," she whispered and felt the sting of her hair being pulled.

Karyme's lips were drawn back in a nasty sneer as she held Isabella's face inches from hers. "You will not tell anyone of this."

Isabella had a pretty good idea who señora Garza didn't want to know about the artifacts, but she couldn't show her knowledge. "I-I won't tell anyone." She cringed at the pain in her scalp and pushed her eye glasses tighter on the bridge of her nose, trying to portray the nerdy anthropologist the woman thought her to be.

"As you have seen there are many men in my husband's employment who would not think twice about putting a bullet through your head. If you keep this knowledge to yourself, you will live." Karyme released her hair. "Pick up the books. You will return them to the museum and leave on the next plane. You are not to speak of this to anyone." She narrowed her eyes. "I have friends in all the archeology circles. If I get wind of this discovery, I will send someone to hunt you down."

Nodding, Isabella didn't doubt the woman's threats. She shoved the books back in the bag and slung it over her shoulder.

Karyme handed the lantern to her. "You go first."

The sentence told Isabella what she'd suspected. The basement was connected to tunnels that led…where? A trip to the city maintenance for a look at maps of the underground tunnels was in order. If the woman was worried she'd sneak out that way, she should be able to sneak in.

As she formed a plan for the next day, she walked back out the small tunnel opening.

Karyme pushed the crates back in place and propelled her toward the basement stairs. "Leave the light here." She took the flashlight and clicked the overhead light off.

The shock of the darkness wiped out Isabella's sense of direction momentarily.

"Go."

The stern command by a woman who only days ago she'd thought could be a friend, powered Isabella's feet forward. She found the first step with her toe. If she fell and broke her neck, no one would know where she was or what happened to her. Panic settled in her chest like a vice squeezing her lungs. The woman behind her wouldn't think twice of dragging her body back into the tunnel and leaving it. She was as hard and power hungry as her husband.

A hard shove on her back propelled Isabella forward. Her heart raced as her feet moved to keep her from falling head first into the darkness.

That thought sent her on cerebral calisthenics. Was Karyme helping Bastante to break down her husband's business so she could order Bastante around and be the lord? Garza would never allow the woman to rule, no matter how much he loved her, but Bastante… He was under Karyme's spell.

Isabella's hands smacked against the door. She turned the handle and shoved on the metal.

Karyme moved past her, glanced around, and grabbed her arm, pulling her out. "Hurry."

The woman shut the door quickly and ushered her into the ballroom. "Open your books and see what you can come up with to tell my husband about those carvings you were so fond of on your first visit." Karyme strolled out of the ballroom.

Isabella walked over to the statues she'd wanted to run her hands over the first time she saw them. They weren't the artifacts stolen from the museum. She had a feeling that theft was masterminded by Bastante. And possibly, Karyme, given the items she had hidden in the tunnel. But Bastante knew nothing, nor was he suspicious of what Karyme had. How would she have gotten her hands on items before the museum? Another puzzle to investigate.

When Alphonso got back to her several things would be cleared up.

After spending the last hours with the alliance statues, she knew these pieces in front of her were carved by the same hand. They would have all been found in the same dig. But where?

Señor Garza entered the ballroom with his wife trailing behind him. "I understand you have discovered something about my latest pieces of art."

Isabella shot a glance behind him to Karyme. What was she to say, they match the statues in the tunnel under your house? From the glare on the woman's face that comment would get her killed.

"From the style of the carvings and the detail to the faces, I would say they were carved in the early 1400's and tell a bit of the story of the triple alliance." Grasping at small details, she directed señor Garza's attention to the coyote symbols. "These were statues carved to tell of wars and victories over the enemies."

"Excellent!" Garza turned to his wife. "Did you hear that Karyme? We have some work that could be traced to the triple alliance."

"That's wonderful!" Karyme flung her arms around her husband's neck. "I knew those pieces were special when they arrived." The two hugged and Karyme shot Isabella a narrowed warning glare.

Hadda entered the ballroom. "The doctor's car has arrived."

Isabella thanked all the deities she'd read about and started across the ballroom.

"Will you be back tomorrow to tell us more?" señor Garza asked.

She pivoted and stared straight at Karyme. "I told your wife I won't be here tomorrow. I've been called back to the college to teach for an injured professor."

Señor Garza's eyes now narrowed. "This is sudden."

"The university called me this morning. I'll be on a plane tomorrow." Isabella crossed the fingers hidden behind her tote. "It was a pleasure meeting both of you." She spun back around and willed her legs to keep an even unhurried stride to the door. Once out, she didn't plan on setting foot inside this house again. At least not with the owners' knowledge—and not really the house—the basement.

Chapter Twenty-four

Tino sat beside the road waiting for the drug shipment to go by. He'd followed all of Garza's directions with one small change. He'd called Rico and told him to follow the shipment and discover where the drugs were held until they were distributed. But not to move on the building for a day or two or Garza would know it was Tino who supplied the information.

Sitting in the dark watching the vehicles zip by, all he could think of was Isabella. What did she discover today? Why did señora Garza take her into the basement? That scared him more than Garza finding out he was DEA.

He flipped open his burner phone and hit the button for Juanita. One. Two. Three rings. ¡Coño! Why wasn't she answering? Had something happened to her?

Six rings.

"Hello?" Out of breath but alive, Isabella answered.

His heart started beating again. "Querida, where are you? When you did not answer… I saw you go into the basement with señora Garza and all kinds of things—"

"I'm fine. I was packing."

Relief rushed through him like a surge of adrenaline. "That is wonderful. You will no longer be in danger, and I can wrap up what I am doing."

The silence on the other end stood the hair on his arms at attention. "Querida, you *are* going back to Arizona?"

"No. I told the Garzas I was, but I'm just moving across town to the other museums so I can research in anonymity."

"Why? What more do you need to know?" The vehicle with the drug shipment flew by. He shifted into drive and charged onto the highway behind it.

"I've discovered more unaccounted for items, and I believe this is more than stealing artifacts."

His head throbbed from trying to keep his attention on the vehicle and the conversation. Especially when the conversation was so unpleasant. "You know how they were stolen. You have accomplished your mission."

"But there is more and it could be more damaging than the stolen artifacts. I believe someone is trying to take over Garza's empire."

"Sí, everyone who he does business with." Tino didn't need her getting mixed up with the drug wars going on.

"Someone on the inside."

Her softly spoken words zinged to his brain. "Who?"

"His wife."

Two motorcycles sped onto the road, following the drug shipment.

"¡Coño! We'll discuss this later. Call and tell me where you end up." He slapped the phone shut and sped after the thieves. There was no way anyone other than the driver could have tipped off Garza's enemies of the changed route. Now, he had to capture one of them so Garza didn't believe he was the traitor.

~*~

Isabella hung up the phone and stuffed the last of her things into her suitcase. She traveled light. A small suitcase and her backpack. She'd already called a taxi to take her to the airport. From there she'd take a taxi to the Marriott where she and Tino had spent such a pleasurable night. It was within walking distance of the National Anthropology Museum. Before leaving on this mission, she'd arranged with WIA to get credentials as an anthropologist to request records from the Templo Mayor museum if she couldn't find the information at the National museum that she needed.

Felix was still off duty when she checked out. "Would you give this to Felix when he comes to work?" she asked, handing the clerk a sealed envelope. She wanted Felix to call the phone Tino gave her when he returned to work. She needed a way to contact Alphonso. His knowledge of the city's tunnels would help when she took photos of the three statues in the Garza's possession. It was risky to pull him into her mission, but she could tell he wasn't gang material. She could get him to the states and into an academic world that would give him options and opportunities he couldn't get being a gopher for a gang.

In case Karyme had someone watching her, Isabella instructed the cab driver where to go as he stashed her suitcase in the trunk of the taxi. At the airport, she tipped the man and headed into the building. She didn't know how far the eyes of the Garzas reached, so she stood in line to get a ticket as she dialed the Marriot's number.

"Yes, I'm Doctor Sanford, and I have a reservation at your hotel. I just arrived at the airport and would like you to send a car to terminal two, por favor."

"We can have a car for you at the arrival entrance in one hour," said a young woman with barely any accent.

"I'll be waiting." Isabella closed the phone and found a spot that was secluded from the main thoroughfare. She'd hide out here watching the people for forty-five minutes then wait at the curb. Standing at the curb for an hour would draw attention to her. Right now, she didn't know who her enemies were.

The phone Tino gave her buzzed. She didn't know the number.

"Hello?" She hesitated to answer a number she didn't know.

"Dr. Mumphrey, you wished me to call you?"

"Is this Felix?" She hadn't expected to hear from him this soon, but she was happy to get started early on her plans.

"Sí."

"I need to contact Alphonso," she said, wondering how she would explain her need of the man's cousin when she was supposed to be leaving the country.

"Why would you need my cousin? Do you plan to turn him into the policia?" The wariness in the man's voice was warranted.

"No. I need him to run an errand for me. I want to send something special home to my boyfriend." She hated lying especially to a man who had so far proven to be honest.

"I will give him your number and he will call you if he wants to help." The phone clicked and silence filled her ear.

"Shamutz!"

A lady walking by stared at her oddly.

She didn't want this number given to Alphonso or anyone. It was the only phone she had for contact with Tino. If Alphonso turned her into the Bohu gang…

This was one time when she needed her mind to function at top form. If the Bohu gang wanted her dead, they'd had plenty of time since she'd spotted Alphonso and talked with him, to kill her. So that meant they either didn't believe her a threat or Alphonso hadn't told them everything. That could work to her advantage. Would they be interested in taking down Garza? She could use that as leverage to get Alphonso to help her. She'd be showing him and the Bohu gang a way to infiltrate the Garza compound unnoticed. She could warn Tino and he could get out when trouble started

With this little nugget of inspiration at the forefront of her mind, she wandered out to the sidewalk thankful there were lights. The people had thinned since she entered the building. A few locals and out-of-towners huddled in little groups waiting for their rides. Aware a single woman made an easy target, Isabella stayed next to the building under the direct light. While this made her highly visible, it also provided protection in the form of that visibility.

A luxury car pulled up to the sidewalk and the driver placed a sign on the dash. "Dr. Sanford".

Isabella rolled her suitcase over to the car. The driver alighted and helped secure her baggage and herself into the car.

"Welcome to Mexico City," the driver said, once he was positioned behind the steering wheel.

"Thank you." She'd already studied the area where she would be staying but she had to play the part of a newly arrived tourist. "Are there many restaurants or shops near the hotel?"

The driver began what sounded like his usual tour guide spiel as they crossed the town and stopped in front of the Marriott. The car pulled into the circle drive. A bellboy opened her door as the driver pulled her suitcase from the other side of the vehicle. He brought it around to her.

"If you ever need someone to drive you ask for Paul." The driver looked her in the eye as if he wanted her to read more into the meaning.

"Thank you, Paul, I will." She held out a five-dollar tip to him.

He frowned and took the money before climbing back into his car.

Isabella had a funny feeling she either embarrassed him with the tip or not getting whatever it was he had implied. The bellboy continued carting her suitcase into the hotel. She hurried after him.

Her throat constricted when the woman, Therese, stood at the counter smiling.

Isabella held out her hand. She gripped the woman's and squeezed slightly. "Hello, I'm Dr. Sanford with the Arizona University. I believe you have a reservation for me."

Therese's eyebrows rose but she released Isabella's hand and checked the computer. "Sí, I have you booked in one of our terrace rooms." She glanced up from the computer monitor. "One key or two?"

The woman remembered she was here before as Mrs. Konstantine. Isabella, smiled. "One, por favor."

Her phone rang as the woman took her fake identification. "Hello?"

"Dr. Mumphrey, it is Alphonso."

She glanced at the woman to see if she could hear her caller. Therese appeared to be engrossed in making a key card.

"Can I call you back in ten minutes?" She smiled at the woman as she handed over the key card.

"Sí. But what is this about?"

"I'll tell you when I call back. Ten minutes." She pushed the off button and pocketed the phone as she handed over the WIA credit card with her fake name. She signed the paperwork as Mary Sanford and picked up her bags. "Gracias." Isabella nodded to Therese and headed to the elevator.

Once in a room reminiscent of the one where she and Tino made more memories, she dropped her bags and pulled out the phone. Searching recent calls, she hit dial on the call from Alphonso.

"¿Sí?" He answered on the first ring.

"Are you alone?" Isabella asked, hearing loud music in the background.

"Vamos," he said and the music grew more distant. "Sí, why are you calling me?"

"You know the tunnels under the city, and I need your help to get photos from a hidden room off the tunnels." Isabella knew it was foolish to toss her whole scheme out to him but she believed she knew him well enough and his confidence and interest that he wouldn't run his mouth to the wrong people.

"Where is the hidden room?" His skeptical tone swirled worry in her stomach.

"I'll tell you tomorrow if you can bring me a map of the tunnels in the north hill area."

A whistle trilled in her ear. Isabella pulled the phone back and wiggled her ear.

"There are not many tunnels in that newer residential area. How do you know of a tunnel?"

Her nerves were vibrating. He was speaking bolder than she'd perceived him. Had she been wrong in thinking he would be grateful for her help?

"Bring the maps to the Museo Nacional de Anthropologia E Hisotria tomorrow at ten. Ask for Dr. Sanford, and I'll tell you more then." She hung up before he could ask more questions.

Her hands shook knowing she was setting up a caper that wouldn't be condoned by her father, WIA, or Tino. She had been sent here to find out who was stealing. She'd given them the murky films of Alphonso, who if he helped her would have to have his identity hidden from not only who she worked for but the Garzas. She'd pulled him into a dangerous situation. First rule she'd learned at WIA was not to draw in innocents.

She showered, slipped into her tank top and boxer shorts, and placed both her phones on the bedside table. If her father called to find out where she was, she'd have to tell him the truth. If Tino called, she'd discover what he knew about señora Garza and try not to spill what she had planned. She feared he would expose or hurt his mission if he tried to stop her. She used the logic her escapade had nothing to do with drugs or señor Garza and shouldn't compromise Tino.

Just keep telling yourself that.

Chapter Twenty-five

Tino forced the two motorcycles off the road, but fearing there would be more attempting to hijack the drugs in the SUV in front of him, he stayed with the vehicle. He ran the events of the last few days over in his mind as Isabella's soft voice whispered, "It's someone inside."

He'd watched señora Garza's return the other day. She'd been upset and it didn't have anything to do with her nephew's death. Why did she take Isabella into the basement? He'd have to investigate down there when he had a chance to slip away.

Lights blinded him as a vehicle on the side of the road flashed their high beams on the drug shipment vehicle and himself.

"¡Coño!" He grabbed his sunglasses from the dash and crammed them on his face in time to stop his vehicle from rear-ending the SUV. Tino opened his door without turning the vehicle off and crept to the far side, working his way into the shadows behind his car, and slipping into the darkness at the side of the road. Four armed men surrounded the SUV with the drug shipment as a fifth man walked boldly up to his deserted vehicle.

"¡*Vaciar*!" The man yelled telling his accomplices the car was empty. The heads on the men surrounding the SUV swiveled like owls as they scanned the darkness looking for him.

Tino remained hidden in the darkness beyond the vehicles' lights, until he reached the vehicle with the blazing lights. This pickup was empty as well. He flipped the bright lights off. Shouts and gunfire rang out. Bullets pinged off the pickup.

Drifting back into the darkness along the road, he watched as the tires on the Garza SUV squealed and the vehicle charged down the road. Flashes and the rat-a-tat of guns revealed the banditos taking aim at the vehicle.

Either they were fools or just that pissed. Garza's drug vehicles were bullet proof. That's why the men remained inside while the banditos had surrounded it. If they stayed inside nothing could happen to them or the shipment. Which led him to wonder how the other shipments were taken so easily? Someone had to have been inside the vehicle. If the driver had been the snitch, he would have opened the door and not sat in the vehicle.

Coño! This bit of information put him back in Garza's crosshairs as the traitor.

A round of gunfire echoed through the night ricocheting off his vehicle and ending with a chorus of hisses as the air escaped his tires.

This was just getting worse. He either had to get back to their pickup and get out of here before they shot at him or call for someone to pick him up and have no proof he wasn't the one who targeted this shipment.

Only one thing to do. He sprinted back to the assailants' pickup, jumped in, turned the key, and slammed the pickup in reverse as his foot shoved the accelerator to the floor. A volley of bullets shattered the windshield. He whipped the vehicle around and sped down the road in search of the drug shipment.

Once the Garza SUV was in sight, he punched in Garza's number and waited. After the fourth ring the drug lord growled into the phone.

"This had better be good news."

"I stopped two attempts at the shipment—" Garza cursed "—it is inside the city limits now and should make it to the warehouse safe." Tino wondered if Garza had figured out who the traitor was. "I am driving a vehicle that tried to detain us. I will bring it back to the compound, and we can figure out who it belongs to."

"Good. I need solid proof. It seems surveillance cameras cannot catch the traitor." Garza disconnected.

Tino followed the shipment to the warehouse and spotted Rico and another in a car two blocks back when he headed for the compound. After the adrenaline pumping evening he'd had, there was a person he wanted to see. He punched the number for Juanita and listened to the rings.

"Hello?" Isabella's sleepy voice hardened his miembro.

"Querida, where are you? I must see you tonight." He couldn't hide the longing in his voice.

She inhaled and he could envision her cheeks darkening in a blush.

"I would like nothing more, but is it safe for you to come to me?" The worried tone made him smile.

"I will be safe. Tell me where you are."

"You'll find me on our terrace bed. But don't go through the lobby, Therese is there and she remembered me. I'm checked in under Dr. Sanford."

"I'll be there in thirty minutes." He tapped the phone and pressed his foot down on the accelerator. He would need to stash the pickup at Garza's compound so no one became suspicious of it sitting on a side street near the hotel.

~*~

Isabella shook the sleep from her foggy mind. Tino was coming! She flipped the light on beside the bed and sat up. Checking her breath, she ran in the bathroom and brushed her teeth. What happened tonight to bring him to her? He'd made it clear they had to remain apart yet here he was coming to her. Something happened.

Worrying only made the minutes tick by slower. When she'd pulled out her journal to find something to distract her, a light tapping at her door, drew her attention. She stumbled out of the bed covers and across the room.

With an eye pressed to the peephole, she studied Tino's profile as he scanned the hallway. The latch clicked under her hand, and Tino pushed into the room, gathering her into his arms and closing the door with his foot.

His lips devoured hers and set her heart to hammering. Heat swept through her, rampant and all consuming, while her hands crept under his shirt and skimmed across his hot skin. His scent trickled into her senses and her body responded to the scent of *her* man. His kisses moved down her jaw to her neck and lower.

Isabella tipped her head back. "What happened?" she asked, not allowing her heated body to rid her mind of the questions she'd listed while waiting.

Tino halted his descent and sighed. She pulled his head against her chest.

"When will this be over?" she whispered, kissing his temple.

"Soon. Rico will raid the warehouse in two days, and I will bring the DEA the information they want." He pulled from her embrace, taking her hand and leading her to the bed. Tino urged her to sit. "Tell me why señora Garza took you into the basement."

He began shedding his clothes. Isabella kept her gaze on his hands slowly revealing more and more of his toned body.

"She—I don't believe señor Garza knows of them—has three statues that could be worth millions to collectors and historically the biggest find in the Mesoamerican culture."

Tino stopped undressing and peered at her. "Could?"

"I'm not positive they haven't been tampered with to make them appear to be the find of the century." She'd been thinking about the three statues a lot. While they were definitely carved during the time of the triple alliance, she'd never come across any mention of the marking on the bottom. That was why she wanted to do more research. If there was a chance the marking was real, it should be mentioned somewhere. It would have been noted in another carving telling of the making of the statues or from an archeologist who came across another piece from that period.

His eyes narrowed as he shoved his pants and jockey shorts down to the floor. "What are you planning? You have completed your mission. You must go home." Tino grabbed her upper arms, drawing her to her feet. "Mi pichon, you must leave before you are discovered."

Sadly, she shook her head. "I can't let that woman pawn a fake off to some unsuspecting collector or museum."

"But if you suspect they are fake then others will also." His arms encircled her, drawing her flush to his bare chest. "Querida, do not put yourself in danger."

Isabella pushed out of his embrace. When in his arms she wanted to forget everything else, but she had a strong sense of right and couldn't allow Karyme to dupe anyone. "I have to—" She stopped. Tino wasn't here to quarrel and that isn't what she wanted either. If he didn't know what she was up to he wouldn't worry.

"I will be careful." She grasped his hand and fell back on the bed, dragging Tino on top of her. "Show me some Latin loving."

"I will love you, but this discussion is not over." Tino made quick work ridding her of her tank top and shorts.

The tenderness and care he took to pleasure her, filled her heart and shot electricity through her extremities, igniting her body and soul. Tino growled his completion and nestled his head on her small breasts, his arms wrapped around her in a tight embrace. Her chest ached with happiness. Soon. Very soon, they could leave all this danger behind and be together as a couple. The thought settled warm and comfortable.

Her eyelids grew heavy and she started to fall into the darkness of sleep.

Ringing and Tino pushing off, tugged her from the bliss she'd drifted into.

Tino stood over the bed, naked, holding the phone he'd given her as it rang again. "Why is this ringing? Only Rico and I have this number."

Isabella shoved hair out of her face and sat up. "I gave the number to someone who is helping me." She didn't want to lie to Tino but from past experience she knew he wasn't going to like that she'd taken it upon herself to discover the truth about the statues.

"Shall I see who?" Before she could even attempt to grab the phone, he pressed a button. "Hello?" He frowned. "Sí, this is Doctor Mumphrey's phone. And who is this?" His eyes darkened and narrowed. "Why are you calling her?"

Isabella jumped across the bed, snatching the phone from his grasp. "Alphonso, I'll call you back." She snapped the phone closed and peered at Tino. His face had darkened with rage. His hands fisted at his sides.

"When were you going to tell me about Alphonso?" A muscle in his jaw ticked.

Isabella drew in a fortifying breath. Tino had never been this angry with her. "When I told you about the tunnel leading from the Garza's basement."

"What tunnel? And what does that have to do with Alphonso?" He stood by the bed, his arms crossed, staring down at her like an Aztec god. His body was definitely adulation worthy.

"Alphonso knows the tunnels in the city. He's the one who was labeling the crates at the Templo Mayor basement."

Tino threw his hands in the air. "Are you loco? You have joined up with the thieves from the museum? How do you know they are not using you to get to the statues?"

"Alphonso is part of the Bohu—"

Tino reached down grasping her upper arms. "You *are* loco. You cannot make friends with gang members. They will turn on you swifter than a jaguar." He tapped her forehead. "For someone so brilliant you do stupid things."

That did it. "I am not doing something stupid." He'd never used her intelligence against her. Her heart ached at the anger boiling in him.

"I will not stand by and watch you make stupid choices. You will never make a WIA agent or any agent when you do not follow the rules."

Isabella snorted. "You're one to talk. All you're using the DEA for is to cover your own revenge!"

Tino pulled on his pants. "My revenge will save many other lives. How many lives will authenticating those statues save?" He shoved his arms in his sleeves and stared at her. "That is what I thought. None. But it could bring about your death. Ezzabella, for the love of God, do not continue this death wish."

Her mind understood his argument but she couldn't let this go. If the statues were real, she wanted to revel in the discovery. If they were fake, her sense of justice refused to let Karyme profit. "I'm sorry but I have to discover the truth."

"I will not seek you out again. I cannot do my job when I am worrying about you. My revenge, as you call it, will help many. It must be carried out." Tino strode to the door. He stopped with his hand on the handle. His gaze swept up and down her body before he sent her a wobbly smile. "Take care querida, I would hate to see one so gifted end her life in suicide."

The door closed behind him.

Isabella stared at the door as her heart thudded in her chest and her mouth grew dry. That was their first real fight. She ran a hand over her head replaying Tino's angry tirade. Her chest squeezed with fear that she may have gone too far this time. Sniffing back tears, she shook her head. No, he loved her, and he would come around once he got past the anger. But he'd made himself clear. He would not help her. She hadn't planned on his help, but knowing he was against the whole caper and felt she was on a suicide mission churned her gastro intestinal juices.

Inhaling three deep breaths, she slowly released the air through her nose and picked up the phone. Why had Alphonso called her at three in the morning?

Chapter Twenty-six

Tino stomped out of the Marriott hotel and slammed the car door. He sat staring at nothing as his mind flashed back over the argument he'd had with Isabella. The woman was a fool to think she could authenticate the statues without someone finding out. Especially, using a Bohu member to help her. Moments like this, he wished she was a softer woman and he could demand she get her skinny ass on a plane and wait for him in Arizona. But she wasn't a compliant woman. She was hard-headed, stubborn, and hell bent to find justice in everything. All the reasons he loved her and couldn't bear the thought of her getting hurt. He slammed his palm against the steering wheel and cranked on the ignition.

There wasn't a damn thing he could do to change her short of having Rico arrest her for interfering in their operation or kidnapping her. The later sounded like the best alternative, but Rico would stay out of their differences, and he didn't have anyone he trusted to not harm her. ¡Coño!

He drove back to the Garza compound his head spinning with what to tell Garza about dumping the pickup and running off and what to do about the stubborn woman he loved.

Lights blazed in the Garza garage. The drug lord himself had a computer on his lap, typing.

He looked up and scowled. "Where have you been?"

"I wanted to see if I could find any evidence where the motorcycles tried to overtake the shipment."

"Did you find anything?"

"No." Tino shrugged. "Have you discovered who this pickup belongs to?"

Garza shook his head. "I have someone searching the records but it appears to be a vehicle stolen in Guadalajara." He put the computer to the side and stood. "Come, tell me everything about the attempt on my shipment."

Tino followed Garza into the locked room. He noted the white board had been wiped clean. Where was the man storing the shipment information now? And how was he to get it before Rico crashed the warehouse?

~*~

Isabella stood at the street corner Alphonso had said would get them into the tunnel leading to the Garza basement. While carousing the night before, he'd looked up some old friends of his father who worked for the city and knew the sewer tunnels. They'd steered him to this area. He'd called her as soon as he'd discovered the information they needed.

That he'd found the information they needed this fast and without leaving a paper trail as she would have had to do had they gone to the city and looked at maps, she was thrilled. Moving this fast would insure the statues didn't disappear before she could take photographs.

Her digital camera was tucked in a pocket of her vest. With the photos she could do a more extensive search and would have proof of their existence if they were to disappear into a collector's hidden trophy room.

Alphonso arrived at the corner five minutes late with a sheepish grin. "I slept in."

"You had a busy night." She noticed the traffic had picked up on the street. "Where do we find the tunnel?"

Alphonso tipped his head and pointed to a manhole cover.

They walked over to the cover. Alphonso scanned the area, bent, and lifted the metal disc. "Go," he said, nodding to the dark hole.

Isabella stepped onto the metal ladder and descended into the pungent darkness. The moment her feet touched solid, but slippery ground, she reached in her pocket and pulled out her LED flashlight.

When the beam lit up the bottom of the tunnel, Isabella was glad she'd packed her boots. The nasty looking ankle-deep water and sludge on the floor gave off a nauseous odor that rivaled the exhaust fumes up above.

"We are lucky it is not the rainy season." Alphonso dropped off the ladder landing beside her with a splash.

"Why?"

"During the rainy season this would be full and overflowing into the streets in the lower areas." Alphonso pointed to his right and started that direction.

Isabella beamed her light up the twenty-foot concrete side of the sewer culvert. "You mean sewage washes into the streets?" She'd heard of such conditions in smaller towns but this was the capital.

"Sí. Our ancestors built on lakes and we continued to do so. When it rains this area fills with water."

"Let's hope we get out of here before any storms come along." Isabella picked up her pace, moving Alphonso along at a faster gait.

"Why do you think we can get into the Garza compound?" Alphonso asked.

"I was in a tunnel that started at their basement yesterday. I noticed it continued." Isabella knew she would have to tell Alphonso everything in time, but right now, she wanted to only give him bits and pieces to keep him interested and not trying to outwit her. As they walked, she marked the wall every fifty feet with a photoluminescent marker. Just a small dot. She wanted to be sure she could find her way back should she and Alphonso need to part.

Alphonso stopped at an indent in the wall of the sewer.

"What's that?" Isabella stepped up beside her guide.

"This is a doorway into an old sewer tunnel. If Garza dug a tunnel to exit his property, in the case of a raid or to smuggle things in, he would have built it into the old unused sewer system."

It made sense. The Mexican drug runners were known for their tunnels to get merchandise into the states.

Alphonso spun the round handle and pulled the door open. Isabella stepped through shining her light on hard-packed, earth walls. This tunnel was a third the size of the concrete one they just left. The air was stale, musty, and held a faint reminder of what the tunnel had once been used for. When Alphonso closed the door, she made a box of four dots with the marker on the door.

They continued to their right. Alphonso had a high beam light he shone on the walls along their left side.

"How do you know where to find the tunnel?" she asked.

"All I know is what my father's friend said about finding a man-made tunnel along this section one day when he was checking the tunnel for cracks. The unused tunnels are monitored. The heavy traffic that crosses over them causes them to crumble more and more each year."

"Did he check the tunnel out?"

Alphonso stopped and faced her. "You are the only person I have met who does not belong to a gang yet insists on sticking your nose into matters that could get you killed."

A chill slithered down her spine. She looked him square in the eye. "Did you tell anyone else about this?"

He didn't look away. "One person. My cousin. If we did not return, I wanted him to know where to send help."

Isabella released the breath of air she'd been holding and smiled. "You don't belong in a gang. When we get through with this, I want to take you to the states. I can get you into the University of Arizona. You can live without having to worry about gangs."

He pivoted and continued down the solid dirt tunnel. "We haven't completed this yet."

That one sentence hung over her head like an anvil ready to crush her. They had to complete this without a hitch.

Thirty minutes later, Alphonso put a hand up and disappeared to his left through a hole in the sewer wall.

Isabella followed.

This was the man-made smaller tunnel. Alphonso had to hunch to walk in the tunnel. She had only an inch of clearance for her head and ducked to avoid any unseen obstructions that might be hanging down. The corridor was wide enough to carry boxes but would be close quarters if too many people were trying to pass one another.

Alphonso slowed and crept quietly forward. Isabella stayed on his heels. He whispered, "I am going to turn the light off. It looks like the tunnel widens, maybe a room."

Isabella turned her light off as well. They shuffled forward in darkness. She used the sound of his breathing and shuffling feet to stay a short distance behind him. The only offensive odor in this tunnel wafted up from her boots. The solid dirt walls gave off an earthy, musty scent.

The floor dropped, and she fell forward into Alphonso's back. She used him to push herself upright. His light came on and the three statues stood on the table as they had the day before.

Elation warmed her from her head to her toes as she stared at the carvings.

"What are these?" Alphonso put his hand out to touch the nearest one.

"No! Wait." She pulled latex gloves from a pocket. "We don't want to leave any trace of our visit here."

He took the gloves and stared at her. "What don't you have in that vest?"

She smiled. "It contains everything I'll ever need in any situation."

"Do you have a cart in there to carry these out of here?"

"We aren't taking them. We came to photograph them." She pulled her camera out of her vest. "Hold your light up and shine it down toward the first statue." He did as she requested. "A little more to the left, please." She snapped four shots of the statue. "Move to the next one." She snapped four of it and four of the last one.

"Now, we have to tip them. I need photos of the bottom."

Alphonso tipped the first one onto its back. She zoomed and focused on the etched figure on the bottom. Then she took one of the whole base and the etching. By the time she finished the first one, Alphonso had the next one ready for her to photograph.

"You make an excellent assistant," she said, taking the last photo of the third statue.

He replaced the three statues and turned to her. "Why is it so important to sneak in here and photograph these?"

"They may be very important to Aztec history or they could be fakes. I needed photos so I can do research and discover the truth about them." She tucked the camera back in her pocket and headed for the tunnel.

Alphonso followed. "Why not ask the Garza's to allow you to research them? If they showed them to you, they must want your knowledge."

A cold chill rippled down her spine. "Señora Garza showed them to me yesterday. I'm not sure why, because I told her I was leaving today for the states and couldn't help her with whatever she wanted."

She heard his footsteps behind her and felt him gaining on her. Isabella pressed against the wall to let him pass. But he stopped in front of her.

"She is toying with you if she allowed you to see these and you believe they are fake." Alphonso shook his head. "We could have both just walked into a set-up."

"What do you mean?"

"If she showed you that room and those statues yesterday, she had a reason. I bet there are surveillance cameras and now she has you in there taking photos of her statues. If she had been looking for your trust, you just showed her you cannot be trusted."

His words slapped her to her senses. She *had* walked straight into the trap. "Did you see a camera?"

"No, but I was not looking for one." He looked back the way they'd come. "Do you want to go back and see?"

"No. I'd rather get back to the anthropology museum and see what I can find." She pushed him toward the sewer tunnels. Had she just completed a suicide mission as Tino had said?

Chapter Twenty-seven

Tino sat in the Garza kitchen chatting with Anarosa waiting for Hadda to return from an errand. He had to find out how the girl got in the locked room and gathered the information for the Bohu gang without being caught. Before he'd stopped her, there hadn't been surveillance cameras in the rooms, but she would have been picked up on a hall monitor going into the offices.

He had to get into that room and gather all the evidence that would bring down Paolo Garza and his operation. His future depended on taking out the drug lord. Tino's knuckles ached from the tight grip he had on the glass of milk. Breathing slow, in and out, he relaxed his hand and smiled at the cook when she turned to him.

"You are too old for my Hadda," she said.

Her comment caught Tino off guard. "What?"

"I know what goes on around here. With Hector gone you think you can turn my daughter's head." She narrowed her eyes. "I see the way you are always watching everyone. You do not fool me."

Tino put the glass of milk down and wiped a napkin across his mouth while he gathered his thoughts. She'd witnessed him kissing Hadda the other day when he warned the girl about the new cameras. It was no wonder motherly concern made her testy toward him.

He raised his hands. "I do not know what you are saying. Hadda is a cute kid. I have no notions about your daughter."

"Then why did you ask me where she was and sit in my kitchen? You have not wasted time in my kitchen before."

"I have a question for Hadda about Hector. We are still trying to figure out who killed señora Garza's nephew." He stood, ready to leave the room, when Hadda hurried in, tying her apron as she entered the kitchen.

"Sorry, I am late…" Her eyes widened when her gaze landed on Tino.

Tino stepped toward her, grasping her elbow and directing her toward the pantry. He'd determined there wasn't a camera in the small confines and knew exactly what anyone who saw the video feed and Anarosa were going to think.

Hadda was a quick learner, she smiled at him though a bit timidly and walked into the area without a struggle.

"Hadda?" Anarosa questioned.

"It is fine, Mamá," Hadda called back as Tino closed the door, pressing them close together so they could speak quietly.

"How did you get into Señor Garza's locked office without the surveillance cameras seeing you?" Tino asked without any preamble.

Hadda trembled under the hand still holding her elbow.

"I am not here to get you in trouble. I need answers. However you got in, is how other people are getting in. It could have something to do with Hector's death." He rubbed a hand up and down her arm. "Hadda, I don't want to expose you to señor Garza but if I don't get him answers soon, he will start cleaning house, and I will give up you and anyone else I need to keep alive. If you can help me point to someone else, your name will not pass my lips."

She exhaled and sighed heavily. Her internal battle filled the dimly lit area with indecision.

Finally, when he'd about given up hope of getting anywhere with the girl, she raised her chin and stared into his eyes.

"Señora Garza had Julio make her a remote like señor Garza uses to block the video. I took it from her hiding spot and used it to enter the locked room." Her eyes glistened with tears.

"How did you know the hiding spot?" It would seem the drug lord's wife was even more cagey than her husband knew.

"I was cleaning her closet one day and found the compartment. There was also a key. I realized it went to the locked room and mentioned them both to Luis. It was his idea to find out about the shipments and tell him."

Anger at the gang leader tightened his grip on the girl's elbow, she winced and he dropped his hand. "You think Luis loves you. But to put you in that kind of danger, he does not love you. If he loved you, he would take you away from here not throw you to the lions."

Tino searched her weeping eyes. "Bring me the remote and the key tonight and I will take you away from here."

She shook her head. "No! I cannot leave Mamá and Luis."

He grasped her upper arms. "How long do you think it would take before the Garzas figure out it has to be a staff member who is the traitor? If you disappear the same time I do, they will think you ran off with me."

"I will give you the remote and the key, but I will not leave. They will not harm me."

He stared into her eyes. "How can you be so sure?" It was that moment staring into her eyes, the connection struck him fully. He was looking into Paolo Garza's eyes. Once he made the assessment, the other similarities stood out like beacons.

"Does señora Garza know who your father is?"

She shook her head. "No. My father is very generous to my mamá and I, but señora Garza believes it is because my mamá and grandmamá have worked for the Garza family many years."

"I would not be that sure. She is more shrewd than you think. Why did you withhold knowledge of the remote and key from your father?"

"I wanted to help Luis. Father would not let me marry anyone who can't bring me to a higher status. With extra product, Luis can make more money."

Knowing this new information, Tino wasn't sure he could trust Hadda to get him the remote and key and not tell Garza. There was only one safe thing to do.

"When you get the remote and key leave them under the cloth near Guadelupe at the shrine in the dining room."

He wouldn't answer her puzzled expression.

"Hadda?" Anarosa called outside the door.

"Go." Tino urged her to the door.

Hadda opened the door and stepped out. Anarosa scolded her

daughter as he exited the pantry. The woman sent him a scathing glare. He smiled back and headed to the office. It wasn't the Bohu gang who tried for the shipment last night. He also wanted to know who Garza suspected.

~*~

Isabella hunched over the open book reading about the Triple Alliance searching for clues to the statues in the Garza tunnel. Her back ached, her eyes ached, and her stomach had been rebelling for the last hour. Nothing had come up about the statues or the markings. Her gut told her Karyme was planning to dupe either an unsuspecting Aztec artifact collector or the archeological world. Granted her scheme would be refuted, but not before she had rocked the academic world and profited.

She leaned back, thinking the woman probably set up an account somewhere exotic that she planned to retire to. How maternal was Karyme? Would she leave her daughters to their father's care so she could live the life of luxury on an island? She hadn't witnessed the woman with her children so she had no clue to her maternal instincts. The employees all seemed to like her.

Her stomach grumbled. Isabella closed the book and pushed away from the table. She hadn't had any trouble getting into the research section of the National Anthropology Museum with her fake identification. There was one more book she wanted to take a look at, but she wouldn't be able to concentrate if she didn't get something to eat.

Rounding the end row of shelved books, she couldn't retreat before Director Bastante spotted her.

His eyes narrowed as he walked toward her. "Dr. Mumphrey, I thought you headed home yesterday?"

The title of the book he held flashed at her like a neon sign. It was the volume she wanted to look at next. "I—my flight was delayed."

"Why are you over here when you could have any of these sent over to Templo Mayor?"

She boldly stared into his eyes. "I could ask you the same, director."

His gaze flew over her left shoulder and he cleared his throat. "I was over here on business and thought I'd look something up rather than bother someone else with finding the book and sending it over."

Her stomach growled. "If you'll excuse me, I missed lunch." Isabella walked past the director, keeping her eyes forward even though every nerve ending in her body danced with the need to see if he found her stack of research books. If he did, he would know she was looking up the same thing he was. The book he held in his hands proved he and Karyme were together in the scam with the statues. Did Garza know his wife and her possible lover were scheming behind his back?

Chapter Twenty-eight

Tino started to pass the powder room but heard an irate female voice. The venom in her words stopped him, and he listened.

"What do you mean?" She sucked in air. "She was supposed to leave today not be snooping around. Where? How?" The woman's heel tapped sharp and resounding as if she'd jammed her heel down to squash a bug. "I will take care of her. That woman has been trouble since her arrival."

The handle on the door jiggled. Tino stepped across the hall into the laundry room and listened to the click of high heels moving down the hall toward Garza's office.

What had Isabella done? It was clear Karyme was talking about his querida. She was the only person he knew in the Garza circle that had told them she was leaving today. His gut soured and his mind flashed over everything Isabella had said last night. Had she gone through with her plan to return to the Garza basement through the tunnel? Had she been caught?

There was only one way to find out. He strode down the hall to the office. The door wasn't completely closed. Angry voices seeped around the edges.

Tino rapped hard enough to sting his knuckles. He needed the sting to penetrate the numbness the woman's words had injected into his heart.

"Entrar!" Garza roared.

Tino pushed the door open and stepped through. The man and woman in the room stood several feet apart their arms crossed over their heaving chests, glaring at one another. The air was charged with their animosity.

This was his first glimpse of anything other than love emanating between the two. From each one's formidable stance, he believed this wasn't the first time they had locked horns.

"I want that woman taken care of. Either you do it or I will." Señora Graza's venomous words froze Tino's heart with fear.

He forced his expression to remain blank as his mind worked feverishly to find a way to warn Isabella.

"She is too smart for her own good, I agree, but to kill her?" Garza remained with his gaze locked on his wife.

The two stood discussing Isabella as if he wasn't standing eight feet away.

"She has seen too much." The woman slowly shifted her gaze to Tino. "Have him take care of the matter."

Garza walked away from his wife and sat behind his desk. Once seated, he peered at Tino. His dark assessing eyes sent every nerve in Tino's body tingling. He had to reflect someone who would do anything for Garza. He had to be the one to go after, Isabella. It was the only way he could guarantee her safety.

"Send for Manny."

Garza's command dropped Tino's stomach and dried his mouth. The sadistic Manny would torture Isabella before killing her.

Tino shook his head. "Do you want to leave a mess? I can take care of the matter in a tidy manner."

Garza tipped his head to the side, narrowing his eyes. "You were squeamish when Manny took care of our shipment thieves. I do not think you could kill a woman."

He'd only killed one other woman. It had been self-defense, but he had to prove to the drug lord he could to this. Isabella's life and his future depended on it.

"I do not like messy killings. A broken neck, clean bullet hole; it does not matter man or woman. It is the blood and guts, the mess Manny makes, I cannot stomach." Tino rubbed his hands together as if he relished the idea of breaking Isabella's neck.

"I do not care who you send. I want it done today. She has been snooping and digging up things that I wish to remain hidden." Señora Garza paced the office, her heels clicking on the tile floor like cat claws.

Garza continued to study him. Tino decided to look too aggressive would make the man suspicious.

"It does not matter to me. Only if you wish the woman to disappear quietly with no trace." He focused his gaze on the agitated woman. She'd stopped pacing. She studied her husband as her fingers played with the edge of her sweater.

"I always prefer no trace when I need a person to disappear." Garza met his wife's gaze. "My wife wishes Dr. Isabella Mumphrey to disappear."

Hearing Isabella's life meant so little to the two angered Tino, but he nodded and left the room. He'd let his fury loose once he was out of the compound gates and heading to warn Isabella to get the hell out of the country.

~*~

Isabella sat in the small restaurant at her hotel waiting for Alphonso to arrive. She had to go back to the tunnel and get one of the statues. It was the only way she could keep Karyme and Bastante from profiting until she had finished her research.

The theme from Indiana Jones played on her phone. *Daddy*. If she didn't answer he'd have agents swarming the city looking for her. Taking a deep cleansing breath, she pressed the button.

"Hello, Daddy."

"Where are you? Your report arrived but no one has seen you."

The reprimand in his voice only added a pinch more guilt to her conscience.

"I've come across a possible scam." She held the phone away from her ear as her father let loose expletives she was sure he usually only used around his men.

"You're not sanctioned to pick up your own assignments. Get home on the next plane or I'll send a team down there to bring you back."

The line went dead. Well, now she wouldn't have to deal with him for twenty-four hours. She slipped the phone into her vest pocket as Alphonso stepped into the restaurant. He sauntered over to her table and plopped on the opposite chair.

"What do you want me to do now?"

She leaned forward to whisper. "We're going back into the tunnel and take one of the statues."

His eyes widened and he leaned back. "You are loco." He peered into her eyes and shook his head. Slowly, he leaned over the table so their noses were only six inches apart and whispered. "You cannot walk into a drug lord's tunnel and steal from him. We would be dead before we made it back to the main tunnel."

"If your gang comes up with some kind of a distraction that would have security busy, we could have the statue and be on our way to the U.S. before Garza knows the statue is missing." She smiled and emitted as much confidence as she could muster. There was no doubt in her mind Bastante had told Karyme about the encounter in the library, and they would move the statues to keep her away from them. But if she and Alphonso headed there right away, she could get one before they were moved.

He continued to stare at her. "You are one loco chica."

She smiled. "You're not the first person to say that." Her thoughts traveled to Tino and their fight. Sadness squeezed her chest. She couldn't ask him to help her. He'd made it clear his revenge was more important than her desire to ferret out the truth.

"Can I count on you to help me?" She grasped his hands. "I don't have anyone else, and we need to move quickly."

Alphonso's cheeks reddened. He withdrew a phone from his pocket and hit a number.

She listened as he asked someone if they felt like causing trouble for Garza. She detected a hesitancy when he said in an hour. It was a suicide mission to go at the Garza compound with such short notice.

Isabella glanced at her watch. The evening traffic would soon be creeping through the streets. They needed to hurry. She tapped the face of the wristwatch. Only eight months ago she'd discovered her father had her whereabouts monitored through a chip in her watch. Something he had upgraded every year on her birthday without her knowledge. Now that she was a WIA agent it was mandatory to have the chip on you at all times. This knowledge made going into the tunnels easier.

She had to smile. If Daddy waited to hear from their man in

Arizona that she hadn't arrived with the reports, he was adhering to her wish that he only use the tracking device if he couldn't contact her.

Alphonso slipped his phone into his pocket. "My leader isn't happy to go at Garza without proper preparations. We worked for months to plan getting in during the last party."

Isabella stared at the young man. "You were the ones who killed Karyme's nephew?"

Alphonso nodded and leaned forward. "He was hurting Hadda to get her to help him spy on his uncle. Luis does not like his women hurt."

Comments and things she'd witnessed while at the compound now became clearer. Hadda had to be the traitor in the mix. Did Tino know this?

"I asked them to cause a confusion in an hour. We must hurry to be at the entrance to the room when they start, so we can grab the statue and be to safety before they realize what has happened."

Isabella nodded and followed him out of the building. He opened the door of an older small import and she slid in. Taking a deep breath to calm her jittering nerves, she prayed no one got hurt from her need to discover the truth.

Chapter Twenty-nine

Tino pounded on Isabella's door in the Marriott hotel. She hadn't answered either of her phones and now she wasn't answering the door. He tried the burner phone he gave her one more time. A faint shrill buzz came from the other side of the door. ¡Coño! Was she in her room and hurt? Had someone else already played out Garza's orders? A maid slowly pushed a cart into a room at the end of the hall.

He ran down the corridor.

"Miss, please, I need you to open a door. I think something has happened to my friend. She was not well and now I can hear her phone ring and no one answers the door." His urgency must have swayed the older woman. She shuffled down the hall. He ran ahead of her and stopped at Isabella's door.

The woman opened the door and he burst in. He rushed through the main room, noting her suitcase and backpack on the chairs. The bathroom was clear of any personal items. Her bags were packed for departure. Where was she?

"Gracias," he said to the woman, urging her out of the room against her protest.

Where could Isabella be? He dug through her belongings. Her vest was not packed. The tunnel. If she entered that tunnel, she would walk right into the hands of the people who wanted her dead.

Tino punched in Rico's number. "Isabella is in danger. I will get the key to the locked office for you and hand it over, then I will be through. I have to find Isabella and keep her safe." He disconnected and headed to his SUV. He would gather the key from Guadelupe and follow the tunnel in hopes of running into Isabella before she committed suicide.

~*~

Isabella had insisted they stop at a hardware store and purchase two dowels, several yards of canvas and a staple gun. As Alphonso drove to the manhole to enter the sewer tunnels, she made a gurney to use to pack the statue. It was rolled up and easy to carry by the time they parked and exited the car.

Without scanning the area, Alphonso moved the manhole cover and they both climbed down. Her dots remained from their last visit to the bowels of Mexico City. Knowing the route, they moved faster and stood outside the small room with a few minutes to wait for the Bohu gang's diversion.

"How will we know they are out there?" Isabella whispered.

Alphonso shrugged. "We have to believe they did not run into problems."

She leaned her back against the cool dirt wall and breathed in the earthy scents. If this was a dig and they were excavating the statues for the first time, her adrenaline would be pumping just as fast, but she wouldn't have panic squeezing her chest. She was stealing an artifact. And not just from a dig but from a drug lord's wife.

Fear sparked in her chest and constricted her throat. She worked hard to swallow the spit pooling in her mouth. How had an easy assignment to discover thieves ended up with her working with a thief to steal? The logic of this befuddled even her clockwork mind.

"It is time." Alphonso took one end of her gurney sticks and led her into the room. "Which one do you want?" he whispered.

"The closest one," she replied also in a whisper.

They spread the canvas gurney on the ground and carefully placed the two-foot stone carving onto the canvas.

Isabella turned around, grasped the dowel handles, one hand also clasping her flashlight, and walked back into the tunnel. She kept moving as fast as she could with the push-pull of the gurney handles and sway of the statue in the canvas hammock.

She spotted the old sewer tunnel at the same time voices echoed in the smaller tunnel.

"They have discovered the missing statue," Alphonso said, pushing her to move faster.

"Don't push. I'm hurrying." She stepped into the old sewer.

"Go left."

She hesitated. "But the way out is to the right."

"Sí. That is the way they will expect us to go. To follow the marks you made." Alphonso walked past her in the wider tunnel, taking the lead.

She had no option but to cling to the handles and follow him with her flashlight illuminating half his back and the tunnel to his right.

"Turn off the light. They will see it," Alphonso said, stopping when they had traveled around a corner.

She doused the light and stood. The eerie drip of water was soon muted by the scuffing of feet and voices. Her heart pounded in her chest and head nearly masking the sounds of their pursuers. Using yoga breathing techniques she stilled her heart and listened to the retreating sounds.

"You're right. They went the other way," she whispered aware that sound carried well in these tunnels. "Now what?"

"We follow this until we find a way out." Alphonso tugged on the dowels as he started forward.

Isabella followed and after shuffling in the dark for several more turns, she flipped her light back on.

"Gracias. I was having problems moving in the dark. We have lost them. Even if they backtrack, they would not believe us to be this deep or know the tunnels." He looked back at her and winked.

"What are you not telling me?" His wink didn't bother her. She could see it was the mischief of a boy. But his reference to the tunnels made her suspicious he knew exactly where he was taking her.

"I have studied these old sewer tunnels in case I was caught labeling the crates at the museum. I know how to get there from any spot in this city as long as we stay in the old sewer."

Relief slacked the tension in her arms and her steps moved freer. They would soon be back at the museum. They could crate this statue in the storage room and hide it until she could put a label on it and have it sent to her university.

"I knew you were the right person to help me."

They stopped an hour later to take a break. Alphonso pulled a small flashlight out of his pocket.

"I need to check the walls for markings to figure out exactly where we are. Will you be okay here by yourself?" The backlight of the flashlight showed his concern.

"I've been in worse situations. Go find our way out of here." She handed him an energy bar and waved him off as memories of her ordeal with bats in a cave in Guatemala sent shivers down her back. There were no bats in this tunnel. Rats, yes. She could deal with rodents without wings. She inhaled the musty tunnel air and slipped a hand into a vest pocket and pulled out a small bottle of water and an energy bar.

The statue had to weigh close to two hundred pounds. She was glad she'd thought of the gurney while waiting for Alphonso to arrive at the restaurant. The conveyance made carrying the carving much easier. And if they took the tunnels all the way to the museum and artifact room, they wouldn't have to worry about a way to cover it while packing it in public. She'd been mulling that problem over as they'd made their way to the three statues.

Skittering came from the direction Alponso had headed. The moment his light came into view, six rats raced toward her. She pushed to her feet and smashed her body against the wall, clenching her jaw to keep from screaming. Rats didn't usually cause terror, but the size and the number overrode her good sense as they scampered by ignoring her.

She'd barely regained normal breathing when Alphonso walked up to her and put a hand on her shoulder.

"Are you okay?" he asked, peering into her eyes.

"Yes. I-I've never had that many large rats run at me before."

He grinned. "They will only hurt you if they are hungry or you are hurt. Come, I know where we are." He picked up the front of the makeshift gurney and headed the direction he'd just returned from and waited for her to gather her end.

She turned off her flashlight and grabbed the dowels. "I'm ready."

They used Alphonso's light to show them the way through the sewer.

~*~

Tino's fingers wrapped around the key and remote tucked under the cloth cushioning the figurine of Guadelupe as gunfire and yelling broke loose. He pulled his gun out of the shoulder holster, wrapped the key and remote in a small cloth from the table and shoved it into his holster, pulling his shirt closed and hooking a couple of buttons.

Pounding feet rushed from all areas of the house as Garza's men ran outside. He followed, wondering about an attack in daylight. His forward momentum stopped as someone grabbed his arm. Tino spun to confront the person and found Karyme Garza. Her eyes were wide and dark; her breathing came in small hisses.

"You were told to kill that woman." She threw her hands in the air theatrically and then pointed toward the ballroom. "Take men and go after her. She just stole one of my statues from the basement."

Tino didn't know whether to smile or grimace. Isabella had used someone to distract while she stole a statue. But how and where had she gone? And how could he catch up to her and keep her safe?

Before señora Garza started hand selecting his help, Tino spotted Diego and Cruz. Two men he felt he could control.

"Diego, Cruz! Come on!" He ordered and headed for the basement. He threw open the door ignoring the men's questions.

In the basement, he discovered the small opening. Hunching over, he stepped through and stopped. The men both bumped into his back as he stared at the size of the statue Isabella had stolen. What was the woman thinking? How would they cart something of that size through the tunnels? ¡Coño!

Diego grabbed his arm. "What are we doing?"

"Someone stole one of these statues and señora Garza wants us to find them." If Diego and Cruz hadn't heard señora Garza wanted Isabella dead, he had a chance to get the statue into the two men's hands and take off with Isabella.

He pushed out of the small chamber and into a tunnel just wide enough for a fair-sized man to travel as long as he ducked his head. He stopped as the dark folded around them. "Cruz, go back into the basement and find a light." Tino stood in the darkness, listening to Diego breathe and straining to hear movement ahead of him.

Light grew behind him and Cruz arrived with a small flashlight. The beam was weak but enough to keep them from stumbling about and getting disoriented in the dark. He pressed forward but not at a speed that would catch up with the thieves or at least he hoped not.

They moved out of the smaller tunnel into an old dirt culvert that was three times the size of the tunnel. Across from the opening, Tino spotted a shiny dot.

Diego saw it at the same time. "They left a trail." He took the light from Tino and started down the tunnel. "Here's another one! They went this way!"

Tino lingered behind the other two as they commented on the thieves' stupidity to have left such an easy trail. Stupid wasn't a word he'd use for Isabella. Was it possible this was a ruse to draw them the wrong direction? He hoped so, but for him to go the opposite direction wouldn't get him close to keep her from harm. However, he had no idea which direction she headed.

He didn't have a light so he couldn't take off opposite Diego and Cruz. He decided to follow the two men and the dots and see where they came out. The only other tunnel Isabella told him about led from the museum storage room. He'd ditch Cruz and Diego once they surfaced and head to the museum to follow that tunnel.

Chapter Thirty

Isabella's arms burned and her fingers ached trying to stay wrapped around the dowels. The statue now felt like five hundred pounds. She didn't want to sound like a whiner but she also didn't want to drop the statue.

"Alphonso, can we take a break?"

He stopped and she moaned as they eased the gurney down. With her back to the tunnel wall, she slid down to sit on her haunches and pulled out her water bottle. She took two mouthfuls and handed it to her co-conspirator. He smiled and swallowed two hefty swigs.

"How much farther do you think?" She unbuttoned another vest flap and poured a handful of almonds in her hand and passed the bag to Alphonso.

"If we did not take a wrong turn, we should be nearing Templo Mayor in an hour." He popped some nuts in his mouth and chewed, smiling down at her.

Isabella put one almond at a time in her mouth and chewed thoughtfully. In the dark and quiet as they walked, she'd contemplated how much more to tell the young man who had put his life in jeopardy to help her. There had to have been surveillance cameras in the room to have people chasing after them so fast, and he was now on tape stealing from the drug lord.

"I meant what I said about getting you and the statue out of here." She took the bag of nuts he held out to her.

He shook his head. "I will not leave my family."

Fear gripped her stomach, causing a nauseous wave to ripple through her abdomen. "I just put you in Garza's crosshairs. I'm so sorry."

His lips curled into a wobbly smile. "You did not hold a gun to my head just as Luis did not force me to label the crates. I do these things for the thrill. I am sure my family can hide me until things have settled down."

Isabella thought of Tino's words about her committing suicide. If anything happened to Alphonso she would label herself a murderer. "You could go to school in Arizona for a few years while you wait for things to calm down." She had to convince him to leave with her, and then she could get him protection through WIA.

"We will see. Right now we have to get rid of the evidence."

"True. Once we get in the museum, we can crate it up like the other artifacts. Then I'll go back later and put a label on it."

Alphonso's eyes sparkled with mischief. "You are becoming a good thief."

"Please! If my bosses knew, I'd be out of a job." It was true. She had no doubt she'd lose her tenure at the college and her father would toss her out of WIA for going beyond the mission. But she couldn't let something this valuable—if it truly was—get into the wrong hands.

She stood up and they both resumed their ends of the gurney. One more hour and her arms would get a reprieve.

~*~

Alphonso proved to be correct. After another hour of agonizing pulling and jarring on her arms, they set the gurney down and he shoved on the crates concealing the passageway. He didn't reveal the opening slowly. He walked up and shoved at the crate in front of the opening. Before Isabella comprehended the light shouldn't be on, Alphonso disappeared through the hole and a man she'd never seen before stepped into the passage. He grabbed her roughly, dragging her into the storage area.

Director Bastante had a revolver pointed at Alphonso. He shifted his attention to her. His dark eyes narrowed and his mouth straightened into a line of disapproval.

"Dr. Mumphrey, it is a shame you have become such a nuisance. I have read your papers and hold your writings and great knowledge of the Mesoamerican people in high esteem. It will be a sad loss to your community." He waved the revolver, motioning the man holding Alphonso to move toward Isabella and her captor.

His words weren't lost on Isabella. She understood he planned to kill her. That is if she didn't thwart his efforts. Their only chance was to get back into the tunnel and hide from Bastante and his men in the maze of passages.

She glanced at Alphonso. It was the first time since meeting him that he not only looked scared but baffled. What was it about this situation that puzzled him? Did he know it was Bastante that paid the Bohu gang to label the crates?

"If you shoot us here, you're going to leave a mess." She glanced at the surveillance camera and its blinking red light. "Not to mention the fact it will all be on tape."

Bastante laughed and waved the weapon. "You forget I have access to the cameras. The tape of this incident will be gone before anyone even notices you and your friend are missing, just like the ones that disappeared from the surveillance room." His eyes narrowed as he glared at her.

He knew she took the tapes.

"What do you mean?" Alphonso's voice rose an octave. "You told me to help her. You said get her and the statue here and you'd pay me three times what you paid Luis."

Betrayal ripped through Isabella. She jerked out of her captor's grasp and turned on Alphonso. "You only helped me to take money from this bastard!" She slapped the young man hard across the face. "I should have known from the first time you tried to rob me that you would never be anything other than a thief." Her heart hammered in her chest. She had no one to count on but herself to get out of this mess.

Her mind quickly grasped the fact that after wrenching loose from her captor he'd yet to regain his hold. Without a second thought, she pivoted and ducked into the tunnel. Gunshots pinged off the concrete walls. She scrambled over the statue and into the darkness. After packing the thing for hours, she hated leaving it behind, but her survival instincts kicked in. It was her or justice and right now she wanted to live to enjoy life with Tino.

She shuffle ran through the tunnels using her hand on the side to keep a forward motion. When her hand dropped into nothing, she swiveled into that tunnel. Every connecting tunnel she came to, she turned down and didn't stop until her breathing became loud and her rubbery legs refused to carry her any farther.

Her breathing slowly returned to normal and she listened for anyone following her. The only sound in the tunnel came from skittering rats.

Using her LED light, muted behind her fingers, she found an area where digging had made a rectangular indention in a wall. She sat on the edge and pulled her body all the way to the back and curled up. She'd wait for morning and find her way to the surface. From there she'd mix in with the visitors and find Tino. He was the only person she trusted.

~*~

Tino heard gunfire as he slipped into the basement at the Templo Mayor museum. Rather than rush to the storage room, he hid in the dark recess of the research room doorway and waited. Within minutes Bastante, another man with a revolver, and the kid, Alphonso, hurried out of the storage room.

"I can find her, I know those tunnels," the kid said. "Didn't I bring her to you?"

Rage started to build in Tino. Isabella had trusted the kid and he led her into danger.

Bastante backhanded Alphonso, knocking him into the armed man. "I shouldn't have to buy your loyalty."

If the kid led Isabella to the museum, then she must have gotten away in the tunnels. He willed the trio to leave so he could get into the storage area and the tunnel. For once his prayers were answered as the three moved down the hall and into another room.

Tino ran to the door they'd left ajar and entered a large room full of crates, packing material, and artifacts. He spotted the toppled crates and the gaping hole in the wall. Without a thought to the darkness, he plunged into the tunnel. His foot rammed into a large heavy object and he barely held his balance in check. Kneeling down he ran his hands over the cold stone and realized it was the stolen statue. The fact reinforced his belief Isabella was in the tunnel somewhere.

He passed the statue and continued into the darkness with his right hand on the wall. His steps became sure and he moved into the inky darkness, straining to see but knowing it was futile. The wall disappeared from under his hand. Tino stopped and waved his hand and arm around. A tunnel. If Isabella was stumbling around in the dark like I am, she'd use the same method of travel. She would also take as many turns as she could to thwart anyone following her.

Tino turned down the tunnel to his right and continued in this fashion. After taking several bisecting tunnels, he stopped to listen. A faint, familiar jasmine-laced scent wiggled through the dank, mustiness of the dirt tunnel.

"Ezzabella, where are you," he whispered, yearning to have her in his arms where she was safe.

He continued forward and the soft scent seemed to grow in essence. "Ezzabella?" He whispered.

"Tino?"

The softly spoken question accelerated his heart. "Sí. Where are you?"

A soft light illuminated Isabella's face and the silhouette of her body in an earthen box.

"Querida, I'd feared…" he let the words fade as he knelt in front of the opening and drew his woman into his arms. She trembled and burrowed her face into his neck. "Querida, I am here now. We will find a way out."

He grasped her head and found her lips. He deepened the kiss, wishing to chase away the salty tears he tasted. Her arms slid up around his neck and he pressed her body close to his. Body to body, lips to lips, the connection between them was more than physical or he would not have known to take the same route as she in the dark.

Easing out of her embrace, he continued to cradle her head in his hands as he whispered. "Do you know if anyone followed you?"

She nodded. "I heard him behind me until I ducked down a side tunnel. After that I didn't hear him again."

"Good. We can hope he has traveled a long distance down the tunnel." He kissed her forehead. "Do you have any idea where we are?"

"I think we're not too far from where they've been digging. The marks in this indention feel a bit jagged like it hasn't been that long ago that something was extracted from this spot. The smell is cleaner, more earthy and not so musty. There must be a surface opening close by." Her hands slipped under his shirt and T-shirt but couldn't climb to his chest because of his holster strap.

"Why did you remain here and not go to the surface?" He released her face and drew her hands away from his skin. He relished her touch but not when he needed to keep his wits about him.

"I was going to wait until morning when I could mix in with the visitors. For all I know Bastante has positioned men around Templo Mayor waiting for me to pop up."

He should have known she would remain calm and consider all the angles.

"Now there are two of us. We need to get out of here so I can deliver something to Rico and we can get on a plane."

She squeezed his hands. "But you have to finish your job. And the statue—"

He kissed her and waited for her body to relax before he released her pleasing lips. "Once I deliver what I have to Rico, my mission is through. And that statue can remain in the tunnel. You can write up a report or whatever you need to do to make known its existence." She started to protest. Tino placed a finger on her lips. "Shhh… No more talk of going back for the statue. You are safe, and we are going to start our life together far from Central America."

Tino folded his hand around one of Isabella's and drew her to her feet. "Come. We will find a way out of here and contact Rico."

Isabella switched on her flashlight, and Tino walked beside her down the tunnel until they spotted a wooden ladder leading to a circle of muted light.

"I will go up first. They are not looking for me. No one even knows I am in this tunnel." Tino squeezed Isabella's hand, then released and grasped the wooden rungs of the ladder. He climbed up until he could poke his head through the hole. Carefully, he rotated his head to peer in all directions and check for people lurking about. The only people he spotted were couples strolling along the sidewalk near the hostel.

He moved farther up the ladder and climbed out. He stood near the hole keeping watch as he waited for Isabella to appear. Her head barely appeared before she was standing next to him, slipping her hand in his.

"Come." He kissed her temple and moved toward the street behind the museum. He ushered her into the shadow of the building at the same moment he caught a glimpse of a man standing not far from where they'd emerged. It didn't appear the man had noticed them. He remained in his place not moving in their direction.

Tino hurried Isabella along the shadows and continued around the building and to the end of the block. He wasn't taking any chances Bastante didn't have the man power to have surveillance within several blocks of the museum. The director had manned up to take down Garza. Tino could care less who won that battle as long as DEA took down the winner.

He had to call Rico and set up a meet. Tino stopped, holding Isabella with one hand and punching in Rico's number with the other.

"Maño. I have what you want." Tino smiled at Isabella. And he had what he wanted.

"Are you on foot?" Rico asked.

"Sí. You will have to come to us." Tino scanned the street. "And make it fast. I want to get Isabella far from here." Standing around this close to the tunnels wasn't safe. "Meet us at Salón España." He punched the off button and started briskly walking. "Come. We will fill our bellies while we wait for Rico."

"That sounds good. I've missed several meals today."

Tino draped an arm over Isabella's shoulders, drawing her close to his body to give anyone passing by the illusion they were two lovers on a stroll. He rubbed his hand over the heavy fabric of her vest. With her vest she was easy to spot. "You should take your vest off. It makes you stick out."

Her steps hesitated. "But how would I keep it with me?"

He stopped, unbuttoned her vest and turned it inside out before draping it over her arm. "Just hold it like a jacket." Tugging on her braid, he pulled the band from her hair and spread her long straight strands down her back and over her shoulders. "There now you look more like a woman out for the evening than a scholar stealing away from death."

Isabella stood on her toes and kissed Tino's cheek. "Gracias." She'd never been so happy to hear a voice as she had when Tino whispered her name in the tunnel. She'd tried to chase away the fear that had started to play "what if" in her head. Hearing his voice calling to her, she'd at first thought she was dreaming or having hallucinations brought on by her fear.

She snuggled closer to his chest as he held her tight and continued strolling along as if they didn't have a drug lord and a greedy museum director after them. Shivers crept up her spine and spread like icy fingers through her chest. How would they get out of this country when one of the most dangerous and influential men was looking for them?

"Querida, all will be fine." Tino kissed her forehead, and they turned down the street leading to Salón España. The crowd seemed double that of the one other time Tino had brought her here. There wouldn't be a place to sit, but then after spending most of the day and part of the night in tunnels sweating from lugging around the statue…It scalded that she had to leave behind her evidence to Karyme's scheme. If only it had been one of her little trinkets rather than a two-foot statue.

Her mind slowly emerged from her irritation to register they were no longer walking. Tino gripped her arm with one hand. She looked down and jerked from the sight of his revolver pointing at her side. Disbelief engulfed her as her gaze sought to find reassurance in his face.

His narrowed eyes spit flints of hatred and his face was cast in a stone scowl. Fear stair-stepped up her spine when she shifted her gaze. The Garzas stood beside one of their limos, the door open like the oven door in Hansel and Gretel.

Tino's phone conversation played in her mind. ... *I have what you want… Sí. You will have to come to us.*

He'd said he was calling Rico, but he could have called the man studying them with a calculating glare.

Isabella hadn't slipped through Bastante's grip only to end up in the Garzas. She stomped on Tino's foot and yanked from his hold. Her feet pound out two strides before her hair caught and jerked her backwards. She hit a solid wall of body. An arm lashed around her arms and chest while the other one circled her throat. She started to scream but the air was cut off.

Everything went hazy and gray before she floated into a black sea.

Chapter Thirty-one

Tino raised his Glock to shoot the brute, Manny, strangling Isabella and was struck from behind. The force flung his weapon into the air and his body into the limo. Someone shoved his nose into the plush carpet and a knee into the middle of his back.

Fear for Isabella had blown his cover. No longer having to keep up pretenses, he struggled to turn his head to catch a glimpse of her. They couldn't be separated. He had to keep her safe. Relaxing, hoping the rata on his back would ease up, Tino slowly breathed in and out and listened. More people entered the car. A female voice, not Isabella's. Several male voices, some grunting. It was a stretch limo with more space in the back than most.

"Go!" Garza ordered.

¡Coño! He hadn't had the chance to give Rico the evidence on him that could get him shot before he could help Isabella. How had the drug lord known they would be at Salón España? Only he, Isabella, and Rico… ¡Coño! Was Rico in Garza's pocket? Was that why it had taken so long to get in good with Garza?

As all the facts started piling up in his head, Tino slowly worked the arm underneath him into his shoulder holster. He had to rid himself of the remote and key.

"Manny, why did you make her blackout? I have questions for

her." Karyme's shrill tone, so unlike her usual calm, bordered on hysterical.

The question gave Tino the hope Isabella was still alive.

"Karyme. Pull yourself together. I will deal with traitors in my own way." Garza's business-like tone told Tino all he needed to know. Both he and Isabella would soon be dead if he didn't think of something.

The little cloth package he'd worked out of the holster was now under him. He pushed his hand along the floor using his body as a shield and shoved the cloth along until it was under his chin. He moaned and pushed his torso off the ground while shoving the cloth, remote, and key between the seat and the wall. A knee came down hard in the middle of his back, knocking the air from his lungs. Black circles spiraled before his eyes and he blacked out.

~*~

Isabella moved her fingers over her neck. She could barely swallow, like something was tied around her neck. "Stop pounding," she tried to say, but it only came out as a whisper and made the pounding increase. The pounding was in her head. Which ached. Hard cold ground supported her curled form. With incredible effort she forced her eyes open one at a time. The flicker of candlelight made ghostly shadows ripple on the wall.

Where am I? Stealing past the pain in her head, she pieced together what she could remember. Bastante had her at gunpoint…Alphonso was a traitor…she scrambled over the statue in the tunnel. Her heart warmed and sped up. Tino found her…they kissed and were headed to meet Rico…Her heart flash froze remembering the feel of the gun in her ribs and Tino's hate-filled eyes. Her first instinct was he betrayed her, but in her heart, she knew that wasn't true.

How had she been so foolish to drag Tino into a mess she'd created because of her curiosity and blind faith in justice? What did he think of her? Was that hostile glare how he felt about her?

This whole assignment she'd put her trust in all the wrong people. Tears burned down her cheek and pooled at her shoulder on the hard floor. Pushing to a sitting position, she sniffed back the tears and waited for her head to stop throbbing from the exertion. The transmitter in her watch would bring WIA, but she had to make sure she stayed alive long enough they didn't show up and find only her body.

Nausea swirled in her stomach, but she fought it off. She leaned her back against the wall and surveyed her surroundings. It appeared to be a tunnel or underground chamber. There was one lit torch in a holder high on the wall. Something in a dark corner of the chamber moved. A groan echoed through the closed-in space.

She wasn't alone. Hope spiraled in her chest. Could it be Tino? Despair stomped on her hope. Would he even want to see her after the mess she'd made?

From the guttural moan, the person was physically worse off than her. But having been duped so many times lately, she'd keep silent and wait for the person to come around. That would give her time to come up with a plan. Slowly, to not start the pounding again, she slid her back up the wall and stood. Breathing deeply, she ignored the round of nausea.

Isabella stepped cautiously—making no sound—along the length of her wall, pivoted to the left, and walked along that wall. There wasn't a door to this room. How could that be?

A glance over her shoulder at the mound on the far wall confirmed no movement. Was the opening near the other occupant? She wished Tino hadn't suggested she take off her vest. The garment had fallen from her arm when someone grabbed her and—she put a hand to her throat—choked her. Tears burned behind her eyes. Crying wouldn't get her out of here nor change her bad judgment.

Another moan, this time louder, bounced around the small area. There was something vaguely familiar about the tone. Was this someone she knew?

Unable to contain her curiosity any longer, Isabella quietly crossed the floor and stood over the groaning person. Dark patches on the clothing and the iron tang of blood in the air revealed the person was badly hurt.

She dropped to her knees and touched a shoulder. It was muscular. She tugged on the shoulder and the body rolled to its back. Tino's bloody, puffy face flopped into the flickering torch light. She inhaled. Her actions did this to him. Guilt stabbed her insides, causing sharp pain. Would he forgive her? Memories of his tender kisses and words of endearment surfaced.

It was up to her to get them out of here. If he didn't want to see her after they were free, she'd have to live with that. This whole assignment she'd gone rogue and that rashness had caused them to be awaiting death.

She leaned close to his ear. "Tino, it's Isabella."

He tried to mumble, but she shushed him and stroked the one place on his face that wasn't bloody or swollen. "I'll find a way out of here. I promise." Isabella bit her lip to keep from crying. Her impulsive actions had caused the man she loved pain. She should have listened to him and got on the plane as soon as she'd figured out how the artifacts were stolen.

Tino's hand dug at his shirt. She grasped his hand to still his motions and felt more than his skin under the clothing. Raising his shirt, she spied what looked like her vest. How could she have not listened to a man who was so skilled? Tears burned the back of her eyes. His quick thinking would get them out even if it was her handiwork. She kissed Tino soundly on his puffy lips.

"I don't know how you got this, but we'll get out now." She pulled the vest out and slipped into it. "Rest," she said and with her LED light in hand, began a thorough search of the chamber. There had to be a way in and out. On her hands and knees, she crawled along the walls and found what she was looking for. The crack between the floor and the wall was larger. This had to be the opening. It was on the wall opposite Tino and the same as the torch.

She couldn't reach the handle of this light source to snuff it out and conserve it for later if her flashlight gave out. By the dimming glow and charred remains she'd only have an hour more of light from that source. That was if their captors didn't come back in the meantime.

This wasn't a time to second guess. Every move had to be made with logic. She was their only hope of getting out and there was no way she'd allow her bad choices to bring about Tino's demise. She reached into her vest pocket and pulled out her first aid kit. Extracting three ibuprophen tablets she crossed to Tino.

"I found the way out, but it might take me a bit to find the trigger to open the door." She raised his head, pushing the tablets between his swollen lips. "These will take the edge off the pain. I'm sorry they beat you up." A lump formed in her throat. She swallowed, holding back the tears burning behind her eyeballs. "I'm also sorry I didn't listen to you and get on a plane. This—" she waved her arm to encompass Tino and the room, "—is all my fault. If you never want to see me again once we get out—"

Tino barely moved his head and his hand touched hers. She peered into his eyes. The dark blue orbs held pain but no recrimination.

She turned her lips up into a smile as her heart raced. He didn't hate her. "We aren't going to let them win." Isabella pulled a small flask from a vest pocket. From the meager sloshing, there would barely be enough water to wash the pills down. The flask touched Tino's lips and he opened, allowing the measly drops of water into his mouth.

Isabella gently settled his head back on the floor. "Rest, so you can walk out of here when I get the door open." She started to rise. Tino caught her wrist. His fingers didn't dig in, they held her gently.

"Get…out…you." His hand fell away, but his eyes focused on her. The earnestness in their dark depths brought back her nauseous state.

"Rest. We'll discuss this later." There was no way she was leaving him behind. Not when this whole mess was her fault.

She dropped to her knees at the crack she'd found and pulled out her survival tin. Ever since discovering a video on how to make a survival tin, she never left Tucson without one. The lid flipped up revealing all the items she needed to get her and Tino out of here. Bypassing the several yards of nylon string, two magnetized sewing needles, a Fresnel magnifier, safety pins, and two feet of aluminum foil folded into a small square, she picked up one of the X-Acto knifes and used a piece of the folded-up duct tape to secure the blade to her journal pencil.

With finesse, she slid the blade into the crack and gently ran it along the floor and then up the side. This would discover the size of the door. She didn't like forcing the blade along the crack, so she eased it out to where the tip of the blade glided along easily. On her tiptoes, she followed the crack as high as she could reach, praying the latch wasn't higher than the length of her arms. Dropping to her knees, she started across and up the other side of the door.

She stepped back and ran the beam of her LED light along the faint line that now defined the door. There had to be a latch along one of the sides. Switching off the light, she flipped open the tin and pulled out the ten feet of twenty-four-gauge snare wire looped around the inside.

Like threading a needle, she poked one end of the snare wire into the seam at shoulder height. Using a sawing motion, she worked the wire down the seam line. The wire slid back and forth all the way to the floor. A moan from the other side of the room pushed her on. Tino would live, and they would spend the rest of their lives together.

"He promised, and I'm not going to let him renege," she mumbled.

Isabella crossed to the other side of the door and threaded the wire in at shoulder height and began the downward sawing. A foot down the wire caught.

Exaltation bubbled in her chest. She wanted to shout, Hallelujah, but feared rousing their captors or scaring Tino. He'd watched her motions in the beginning until his eyes slowly closed. She hoped the mild pain pills had helped him rest.

The easy part had been finding the latch. Now she had to figure out how to trigger it. Using the X-Acto blade she dug divots in the door where she discerned the latch to be. Once she'd dug several divots spaced three inches apart, she pulled the survival tin from her pocket and plucked out a small signal mirror. It wasn't as sharp as the blade but was larger and could dig at the stone in wider grooves.

The torch light grew dimmer, but she didn't want to waste the battery in her flashlight. She glanced over her shoulder at Tino. He remained in the same position she found him in. Staring hard in the dim light, she saw his chest rise and fall. There was little she could do for his condition other than the pills she provided and getting him out of here.

When the torch sputtered out, she continued carving until the scraping sound changed pitch. Isabella fumbled in her tin for matches and a one-inch candle. She lit the candle and held it up to where she'd continued working in the dark. The flame reflected on a piece of metal one inch wide.

She placed the candle on the small ledge carved in the stone and began chiseling the limestone away from the metal bar. The mirror caught on something. Her spirits soared at the discovery of a nut on the end of a bolt. That had to be the handle on the other side that opened the latch. Placing the mirror against the bolt, she pounded on the edge with the tin. Millimeter by excruciating millimeter the bar moved. Lifting her arm for one more blow on the mirror, she felt the huge rock door swing away from her.

With shaking fingers, she replaced the items into her tin by waning candlelight. She peered into the darkness toward Tino. She'd wait to disturb him until she had an idea of what was on the other side of the door.

Isabella pushed on the door and peered through the crack. Light shone in the same undulating pattern as in this room. More torches. Where were they? Listening, the silence gave her pause. Were they completely alone? Had they been left here to die? Why would the Garzas make a scene of taking her and Tino in front of the Salón España then dump them here?

None of this made sense.

Giving the door another shove, she stepped into a chamber larger than their prison. Tremors goose pimpled her skin. A carving of Huitzilopochtli killing his sister Coyolxauhqui could only mean this room was set up for human sacrifice. The red coloring on the five steps up to a raised dais with two chairs sent her scurrying back into the smaller chamber.

"Tino, can you stand? We have to get out of here, they plan…" She couldn't say what she saw as their end if she didn't get them out of here. She'd been a sacrifice victim before and didn't plan on having it happen again.

"Tino?" She pulled on his arm and he moaned. "We have to go, now."

"Save yourself." His voice was barely above a whisper.

"No. I'm not leaving here if you don't come with me." Tears spilled down her cheeks. "You promised me a future, and I'm not letting you back out." She hauled him up to a sitting position. "We may not get far, but if we can hide until help comes, that's better than sitting here waiting for the Garzas to return and use us for a sacrifice."

Tino groaned and shoved to his feet. His body hurt all over. He'd wondered why señora Garza called off Manny before the sadist slit his throat. Now it became clear. She planned to use him as a sacrifice victim. His mind was moving even if his body was having a hard time remaining upright.

He pressed his puffy lips to Isabella's hair. She should leave him. She could move faster without him. "Go," he said hoarsely and tried to push from the arms locked around his middle.

"No! I'm not leaving you here."

His lips hurt as a smile tried to form. She was one strong and loco woman. He'd heard her muttering as she worked. About his promise and he was going to live up to it. Her determination and his knowledge would get them out of this. Together they would survive. "Then hurry."

He felt her urgency as they left the small chamber and stepped into the larger room. His gaze landed on the red stairs leading up to the chairs. This didn't fit the Garza he knew. The man was greedy and wanted the power of a drug lord, but he'd never figured the man for a zealous fanatic that would re-enact human sacrifices. His instincts about people were rarely wrong.

"Hurry." Isabella half carried him through the larger chamber to a doorway.

Through the doorway a tunnel ran both right and left. Fear gripped him. Which was worse; staying and trying to outwit their captors or becoming lost in a maze of tunnels?

"Querida, this is not good."

"Shhh, I need to listen." She cocked her head, and he felt her breathing slow and become imperceptible. "This way." She turned them to the right.

"How?' he whispered.

"I paid attention when the traitor Alphonso led us through the tunnels. This direction is off the old tunnel because you can't hear the sound of water. The new tunnels drip and slosh."

"Why the old tunnel?" As he moved, his bruised muscles slowly eased and warmed.

"It's drier and the signs are easier to read." When total darkness folded around them, she clicked on a flashlight. They shuffled along, with him gaining a little more balance and strength as they continued. A tunnel loomed to the left. Isabella leaned him up against the wall and ran her hands along the right side. Using a corner of her vest she scrubbed at a spot and nodded.

It hurt to smile but he couldn't stop the upward motion of his lips knowing his grabbing the vest she found so comforting had gotten them out of another tough spot. He'd received two more kicks for falling on the vest and not getting up until he'd shoved it under his own shirt. Manny was so set on inflicting pain he didn't notice the vest was no longer on the floor where Karyme had tossed it after taking Isabella's journal. He made a mental note to get the book back. It held everything important to Isabella.

"We are not far from the Garza's house. They must have built those two chambers believing no one would ever be walking around down in the old sewer."

"Can you get us away? Some place safer." He was in no shape to ward off any attackers. The need for revenge of his family disappeared when he saw Manny choking Isabella. She was alive, and he was going to keep her that way, so they could have a life together.

"If I have the streets memorized correctly, we can keep straight on this line and we should come out close to the Marriott." She shoved up under his right arm pit like a crutch and they started down the tunnel.

"We must get out of here to some place safe. I believe there is more going on here than drugs and stolen artifacts." His senses also believed Garza was being played by many of the people around him. If Hadda was his daughter, she too, could be in danger. So many people were depending on him and he could barely put one foot in front of the other.

Chapter Thirty-two

Tino's weight bore down heavier and heavier. Isabella propped him up against the wall, holding him upright with one hand while she worked to find the directions on the wall. They had to be getting close to the Marriott. It was going to be hard to get in without someone noticing the shape they were both in. But she couldn't call anyone. They'd both been stripped of their phones. The phone Tino gave her was in her room. She could call Daddy and have help within hours. She hated to pull in the WIA. It was Tino's assignment to take down Garza, but if he really did call Rico and Garza showed up, that meant Rico couldn't be trusted.

The markings confirmed her assumption. Now to look for a manhole. She allowed Tino to slump into a sitting position and wandered on down the tunnel with the beam of her light pointed to the ceiling. The beam glanced off a round metal disc. There was the way out. The next problem was whether or not the rusted rungs protruding from the wall would hold not only her but Tino.

She counted her steps back to Tino, hoisted him up, quivering the muscles in her legs and arms, and tried to count her steps as they shuffled back to their only escape from the sewer.

"Tino? Tino, you're going to have to help me. I can't pull you up the ladder."

"Querida. Leave me and go for help." He coughed and moaned.

"No! You will buck up and climb this ladder. When I get you in the hotel room then you can become the whiny, wimp I always knew you were." She grabbed his hand. "Sit here and shine the light up so I can see. I'll climb up first and shove the cover to the side. Then I'll come down and we'll both climb up."

"Won't hold." His gaze slid up the wall.

"It will. Keep the light steady." Her conviction was as much for herself as for Tino. She walked over to the wall and grasped the rung in front of her face. Raising her legs, she hung there waiting to see if the metal held her weight. It passed. If this one—which would have been in the water more than the rest—was solid, they should all be. She placed a foot on the bottom rung and began her ascent of the wall. At the top, she used one hand and her shoulder to push on the cover. Grunting and perspiring, she slowly inched the heavy metal disc to the side and stuck her head out. They were on the far side of the Anthropology Museum at the edge of the park.

Finally, something was going their way. She descended the ladder and roused Tino. "Come on. We're at the edge of Reforma Park."

Tino stood, forcing his muscles to respond. He had to get up the ladder. It was the only way to get Isabella to safety. His muscles, bones, and insides felt like several days had passed as he pulled and Isabella shoved him up the ladder. His arms shook, and he didn't think he could hang on a moment longer. Isabella gave him one more push on the butt and his head cleared ground level.

Aching and cursing, he forced his arms up onto the street and rested, propped on the walkway. Several people strolled by watching him emerge from the bowels of the earth. Had they been their Aztec ancestors, they would have welcomed him as a god. But his beaten and bloody face only had them hastening away.

It took considerable effort, but between his weakened condition and Isabella forcing him upward, he finally rolled clear of the hole and she landed on her back beside him.

"You really have to start carrying your own weight." She kissed his cheek and lay beside him gasping.

"Sorry." He wanted to say so much more but even the effort of talking wore him out.

She stood. "Come on. I'll get a taxi to take us to the hotel."

Tino leaned on Isabella as she hailed a taxi. She opened the door and pushed him in before sliding in beside him.

"Marriot, por favor," she said, and he dropped off to sleep.

~*~

Isabella's heart thudded and elation slipped a near hysterical giggle from her lips as the taxi pulled up to the Marriott's front doors. Her WIA instructor, Sean Gunderson, stood in the lobby of the Marriott. She waved him over and within minutes two other men helped her carry Tino up to her room.

"He needs a doctor." She smoothed the hair off Tino's forehead as she took a seat on the bed beside him.

One of the operatives with Gunderson spoke into his cell phone.

She looked up at her instructor. "How did you know I was here?"

"Therese is an operative. She was told to let us know if you didn't return. I had already landed when she called saying you'd been gone over night and someone had searched your room."

"I knew there was something about her I trusted." Isabella smiled. That was one of the few people her gut had been right about.

"Where have you been and what happened to Konstantine?" Gunderson took off his jacket and rolled up his sleeves.

"I'm not sure what happened to Tino. We were headed to hand over something to Tino's superior and we were snatched by Garza and his wife. Someone nearly choked me to death, and I woke up in a small chamber with Tino. He was beaten badly. I found a way out of two chambers built into the old sewer tunnel not far from the Garza home. The one"—she shivered—"appeared to have been used to kill people. It looked like blood stained the stairs leading up to two thrones." She clutched Tino's hand.

Gunderson patted her knee. He knew how she'd almost been a sacrifice victim in Guatemala.

"Anyway, I'd spent enough time in the underground tunnels lately that I figured out how to get back here."

Her instructor's right eyebrow arched and his lips quirked into a smirk. "And why have you been spending so much time in the underground tunnels?"

Her stomach squeezed and a sigh whispered over her lips. She would have to face someone with all the things she'd done under the auspices of doing her job. It might as well be this man rather than Daddy.

"I guess you've read my report on how the artifacts were stolen? I also stumbled onto some statues that are either more valuable than any other Aztec artifact yet uncovered or a case of fraud. I wanted to determine which and used the tunnels to steal one of the statues. Only I chose the wrong accomplice and ended up turned over to Bastante, who I think, is part of the statue scheme."

Gunderson crossed his arms. "Where did you lose the statue?"

"In the tunnel just inside the storage room at the Templo Mayor museum." She tipped her head and moved her fingers over Tino's forehead. "If DEA closes in on Garza's house, they'll find the other two in a tunnel off the basement."

Gunderson pulled out his phone and punched in a number. "Hello, Fred." He walked away, and Isabella directed her attention to Tino.

"Why did they beat you?" she softly said, rising to get a wash cloth.

"Because I didn't kill you and wouldn't tell them how I know you." Tino grasped her hand when she returned to sit on the bed. "I didn't want to put the gun to your side. But I'd been sent by Karyme to kill you. Seeing them at the spot I'd set up to meet Rico, I could not control my anger. I thought by pretending I'd caught you, they would let us slip away believing I would execute her wish." His pain-filled eyes clouded even more. "I should have caught on to Rico sooner. He did things that were risky and harmful to informants. Now I fear Hadda could be the next to fall victim to Karyme."

Isabella shivered thinking of how she'd thought the woman was kind before seeing the dangerous side seep through her disguise. The vile side of Karyme that would have watched as someone killed her. "Why is Hadda in danger?"

"She is Garza's daughter by Anarosa."

Gunderson returned with a man carrying a black bag. "This is Dr. Hardy. He's paid well for his discretion."

The man walked up to Tino and ushered Isabella away. She walked over to Gunderson. "We need to talk," she whispered and walked into the outer room with Gunderson following.

"Karyme Garza ordered Tino to kill me. And one of the Garza goons nearly strangled me to death. But the person Tino is most worried about is a girl in the staff at the Garza house. Her name is Hadda and her mother is Anarosa. If we can find a way to get those two out of there, the DEA might have some reliable witnesses to help build their case against the Garzas." She could see by Gunderson's shuttered eyes he didn't care what the DEA did. Or that two lives might be in danger. It would be up to her and possibly Tino to get the women out of that household.

"I'm here to close the thefts and bring you back." Gunderson's phone trilled. He looked at it and walked away talking.

The doctor walked over and stood beside her. "The patient has bruises, contusions, and some knife cuts but as far as I can tell without x-rays it is all mostly muscle and tissue damage, nothing internal. I did sew up two gashes on his abdomen that he'll need to watch that he doesn't rip the stitches out." He held up a small bottle. "These are eight hundred milligram ibuprophen. He can take one every five to six hours for the pain." He looked back at the bed. "I gave him one already. When it kicks in, it would be a good idea to scrub him in a shower. From the smell, I'd say he's been in the sewer and that will make all his open cuts susceptible to infection."

Remorse hit Isabella in the solar plexus. She should have thought of the risk of infection. She'd been so anxious to pour out her thievery to Gunderson she'd not taken care of Tino properly.

"I'll get him cleaned up right away. Thank you, doctor." She shook hands with the man and returned to the bed. Because she'd been in the sewer as well, the smell hadn't registered. She looked over her shoulder to the main room where Gunderson and his men were all huddled together. They can deal with the theft and the statues. Tino would be her task.

She strode to the bed and picked up Tino's hand. "Come on. It's time for a shower."

One eye opened and the side of his mouth that was the least swollen twitched.

"I think you like the idea well enough to help me get you up." She winked at him and working together he sat on the edge of the bed and then stood.

Isabella didn't say a word or even look back as she helped Tino into the bathroom. She closed and locked the door before she eased him onto the toilet lid and began stripping him.

Her heart ached at the sight of the bruises, gashes, and stitches on his torso and limbs. "Who did this to you?"

"Manny, the man who nearly strangled you to death." Tino tentatively touched her throat. "I tried to shoot him and someone took me out from behind."

His dirty smelly clothes were in a pile on the floor.

"Can you stand in the shower by yourself until I get in?"

His eyes brightened. "Sí." He rose to his feet and stepped under the already steaming water.

Isabella quickly undressed and joined Tino. "The doctor said you should be thoroughly cleaned." She lathered a wash cloth with the hotel soap and started at his head working her way down his body, stealing herself when her scrubbing made him flinch. A moment of pain would be far better than becoming sick from infection.

Even though she washed him with a caregiver mind set, her hands caressed and massaged the intimate areas on his body with care. By the time she knelt at his feet washing away the sewer stench from his ankles and toes, she knew the pill the doctor gave him had eased his pain.

His hands massaged her head, before urging her to her feet. The minute she stood, he cradled her head in his hands and kissed her tenderly. Within seconds the soft kisses turned ravenous as his tongue tangled with hers and their bodies meshed. She forgot about his ravaged body and reveled in the ecstasy his kisses and heated caresses did to her body and soul.

Tino immersed himself in the emotions only this woman could bring out in him. He'd made his decision while lying on that cold stone floor and watching her find their escape. He would resign from the DEA as soon as they set foot back in the U.S.

The warm water running over their heated bodies soon cooled. Tino reluctantly, eased his embrace and dropped kisses along her face. "I wish to leave this place. To take you home and spend our lives together."

Isabella leaned back, peering into his eyes. "Is this a marriage proposal?"

He tried to read the emotions in her eyes, but her body snuggling against his, told him as much as any sparkle in her eye.

"Yes, querida, it is a marriage proposal. I want you in my life." His hand cupped her cheek as he watched her eyes. Her mind was spinning. He could tell by the concentrated stare in her green/gold irises.

She eased out of his arms. "What about your job?"

"I will resign as soon as we land. I no longer wish to chase drug lords or my family's revenge." He placed a hand over her left breast. "You are all I care about. Making you happy and keeping myself alive to enjoy life with you."

Her gaze searched his for a moment before she smiled and jumped, looping her arms around his neck and nearly bringing them both to the shower floor.

"Then I accept."

Her answer and deep, intoxicating kiss chased away the pain and filled his heart with warmth and contentment. Two things he'd been missing for the last eight years.

Pounding on the door, angered him. It had to be the men from WIA.

"¿Sí?" he called not releasing Isabella. She turned off the water.

"I need to speak with the two of you. Now." The man's voice didn't sound the least bit embarrassed. More irked.

"We'll be right out," Isabella said, grabbing towels from the shelf above the toilet.

"We cannot put on the dirty clothes and I do not have any clean ones here." Tino dried his hair and wrapped a towel around his waist.

Isabella's cheeks reddened. "And my clean clothes are in my bag in the other room." She dried her hair and wrapped the towel around her chest. The bottom barely covered her cheeks. "Stay in here. I will bring your bag to you then I will have clothes delivered from a store for me." He made a mental note to also have Isabella pick out a ring before they left. He wanted her to arrive in the states with his ring on her finger.

He opened the door and was relieved to see that only the man in charge remained in the room.

Without the hot water and steamy thoughts washing over and through his body, the muscles stiffened quickly making his movement jerky and re-igniting spasms of pain. He walked over to Isabella's bag and hauled it back to her in the bathroom. He kissed her cheek, and then faced the man standing with his arms crossed and scowling.

"I've heard about you from Isabella's father but that doesn't mean I have to like or trust you."

Tino shook his head. "I do not know you and I do not like or trust you. So we are even. The only thing I care about is getting Isabella back home safe." He stepped by the man and picked up the room phone. He asked the desk clerk to have a set of men's clothing and shoes his size sent up to the room as soon as possible. He put the phone down, and Isabella walked into the room dressed in jeans, a t-shirt and sneakers. Her damp hair was in the usual braid. She wasn't wearing her glasses which made her eyes appear even more exotic.

"What did you need to talk to us about Gunderson?" she asked, stopping beside Tino, grasping his hand, and drawing him to sit on the couch beside her.

"DEA raided the Garza compound. They found the locked room and all the evidence to bring down Garza, but they only apprehended the staff. Garza, his wife, and his underlings were nowhere to be seen."

Isabella squeezed Tino's hand. He felt her fear vibrate through their linked palms. He was pretty sure Garza would head out of the country but would his crazy wife go without taking revenge on Isabella?

"Hadda and Anarosa, the cook and her daughter, are safe?" Tino asked.

Gudnerson shook his head. "They found the cook with a nasty hit to the head. She's in the hospital and the girl is missing."

Tino looked at Isabella. Her eyes widened as she peered into his. They couldn't leave until the girl was safe. Isabella squeezed his hand. She'd help him.

"What is the DEA doing to find Garza and the girl?" Isabella asked.

"Nothing. They are confiscating everything in the Garza house and contacted local authorities to stop Garza if he tries to leave, but I'm sure he has all the local law enforcement on his payroll."

Isabella released Tino's hand and stood, fisting her hands on her hips. "What is WIA doing about the missing girl?"

Gunderson snorted. "Nothing. She doesn't have anything to do with the missing artifacts. And that tunnel you told me about…it's been sealed off. We didn't find any evidence of carved statues."

A knock on the door sent Gunderson to answer it.

Tino pulled Isabella back down on the couch beside him. "We must find Hadda," he whispered.

Isabella nodded. "We have to go back into the sewer and find those chambers. I'd bet my vest Karyme has her."

Chapter Thirty-three

Gunderson returned with a package. It was the clothing Tino had requested. He took the package into the bathroom and dressed. He would have preferred Isabella help but knew he had to keep moving to remain limber. If their suspicions were correct Hadda was in Karyme's hands and needed their help.

What he didn't understand was where Garza had gone. Why wasn't he helping his daughter or his wife? While working for the man, he'd sensed a commitment to his immediate family.

He stepped into the bedroom and found Isabella alone. "Where's the WIA?"

"I told him to do another sweep of the museum for the statue and to bring in Bastante." She smiled. "It was mainly to get rid of him so we could go find Hadda."

Tino hugged Isabella. "You know I would prefer you go with him, but I need your intelligence and knowledge of the sewer tunnels to get me back to those two chambers. That has to be where Karyme has the girl."

"You know I won't leave you now. And I've deduced the same thing. There was a significance to those chambers and I have a feeling Karyme uses them to sacrifice her enemies." She slipped into her vest.

Tino inhaled the pungent sewer aroma. "I cannot believe you

waited so long to shower."

Tears glistened in her eyes. "I almost got us both killed by not believing in you. Once I realized I'd been a fool, I only wanted you safe. Smelling like a sewer didn't matter."

She sniffed and put a hand on his cheek. "Will you be able to handle going back down there?"

"Sí. But I will need another revolver. Mine has disappeared." Tino frowned, remembering he couldn't count on getting help from Rico. He could think of only one person who would lend him a weapon. "Come. We have a stop to make."

He grasped Isabella's hand and led her out of the room and hotel. They hailed a taxi and Tino leaned forward, "Cantina Roja, por favor," he said, directing the man to take them to Luis Bohu. He had to make the man see giving him a weapon and not following would be the best for Hadda.

The taxi pulled up to the cantina. Tino slowly unfolded his stiffening body and helped Isabella exit the cab. They stood on the busy sidewalk as the taxi pulled away from the curb.

"How will we get to the manhole cover?" Isabella took his offered hand and followed him into the dark interior.

"The same place I am getting a gun." Tino stood a moment allowing his eyes to grow accustom to the darkness. The music was a bit subdued from his first visit to the establishment.

Walking forward he was met by two of Luis' ratas. "I wish to speak with Luis," he said, drawing Isabella close to his side.

One of the men retreated through the spattering of customers. Tino kept an eye on him as he moved to the farthest corner of the room. "We do not have time for this," Tino said, pushing the man in front of him to the side and heading the direction the bearer of his request disappeared.

He spotted Luis as the man bent to speak to the gang leader. Luis peered their way and frowned. Tino continued. He ached all over, but he couldn't show any weakness. To do so could bring harm to Isabella.

At the table, he motioned Isabella to slide into the booth and he followed her.

"I do not wish to speak to you," Luis said through clenched teeth.

"If you really care about Hadda you need to listen." Tino leaned over the table to keep the conversation low and away from any overly curious ears.

Luis dropped the anger and leaned his crossed arms on the table, leaning closer. "What do you know?"

"We believe Karyme Garza has her and we believe we know where." Tino nodded toward Isabella who squeezed his hand under the table. "But her men took my weapons. I need you to give me a revolver and us a ride."

Luis peered at Isabella. "I know you. Alphonso said you were a friend of his." His eyes narrowed. "He's disappeared. His cousin has been calling me asking if I know anything."

Isabella shivered. Had Bastante killed Alphonso? Even though he turned on her, she hoped he hadn't come to that. "Yes, we met at the hostel restaurant one day. Alphonso was helping me with something that may have put him in danger."

Luis's faced darkened. "Are you the one who asked him to help you in the tunnels?"

Remorse lodged in her throat. She swallowed and nodded. "Yes. Only he led me into a trap. I managed to escape, but I don't know what happened to him."

Foul words exploded from Luis and his guards lunged forward. He waved them away. "Was it that backstabber Bastante?"

Had the museum director pulled something on this man as well? "Yes. Was that the person who had you labeling crates in the museum?" This was the one thing she didn't know. Who the person was behind the labeling?

"Sí. The last shipment he did not pay us. He said there would be no more and he did not have to pay us. Who would we complain to?" Luis glared daggers at the knife that appeared in his hands. "We have been planning a way to get our payment. Alphonso said he had the way. Then he disappeared."

"This is interesting, but the longer we sit here the greater the chance we will not get to Hadda in time," Tino cut in. "I need a gun, and we need a ride." He stared into Luis's eyes. "And it has to be you who helps us. I trust no other."

Luis stood. "Follow me."

Tino slid out, pulling Isabella out behind him. She fell into step beside him as they followed Luis out a back door. Once outside, Luis turned to his guards. He instructed them to remain.

"In the car." He opened the door of a small SUV and slid behind the driver's wheel.

Tino held the door open for her and she climbed up into the back seat. Tino took the passenger seat in the front and Luis sped out of the back alley and into the congested street.

"Where do you need to go?" Luis asked, deftly navigating the busy streets.

"Do you have a revolver in here?" Tino asked before Isabella could speak.

"Sí."

Tino looked over his shoulder. "Tell him where we need to enter the tunnels."

Isabella leaned between the two front seats. "We need a street north of the Garza compound about three blocks that has an old sewer entrance."

Luis nodded and headed toward the Garzas.

Isabella hoped she'd judged the distance about right. She remembered spotting an entrance off the sewer tunnel like the tunnel that went to the Garza's basement when she and Alphonso were in the tunnels. She was focused on getting Tino out earlier but she believed they came into the sewer tunnels at that spot. It was a fair distance from the Garza tunnel, but easy enough access, she could see Karyme having it installed for what she now assumed was carrying out sacrifice rituals with people she wished to get rid of.

The idea she could have thought highly of this woman at their first meeting filled her mouth with bile. How had her instincts been so wrong?

Luis stopped the vehicle. "We are three blocks from the Garzas."

Isabella hopped out of the vehicle. Tino opened his door. "Stay here and get your gun. I'm going to find a manhole." She jogged down the street two blocks and didn't find a cover. She pivoted and found Tino and Luis in a heated conversation. Leaving them to their head butting, she jogged the other direction and found a manhole. It was into the new sewer, but she could find a portal into the old sewer. Isabella knelt down and worked the lid loose.

By then Tino and Luis noticed her and came over.

"I will go with you," Luis said.

"No. Isabella and I know what we are dealing with. If Hadda is still alive we will bring her back here. You wait. She will want someone she cares for waiting for her." Tino waved to the open hole.

Isabella dropped her feet and legs into the hole. The damp, foul odor of the functioning sewer wafted out. She found the ladder and descended into the darkness. Her feet sloshed into the slick sludge and the stench grew around her. She clicked on her flashlight and waited for Tino on the raised ledge on the side of the cement culvert.

When he stood beside her, they both looked up. Luis peered down into the hole.

"Do you think he'll stay?" Isabella asked, moving down the tunnel.

"I hope so. He could get someone hurt if he follows us." Tino walked beside her. She flashed the beam of the light along the wall, until she found the portal into the old sewer.

"We do not know what we are going to find." He touched her arm. "Are you even sure this is the way to the chambers?"

The concern in Tino's voice helped ease the tiny beads of doubt skittering around in her brain. He might be in pain and injured, but he would protect her with every ounce of muscle and skill he had.

"Yes, we have to get into the old tunnel." She turned the round handle, sucking the seal loose, and pulled on the door. They stepped through and Tino helped her pull it closed.

"We might need to make a quick get-a-way," he said, stopping her from sealing it shut.

"Good idea." The light caught on the metal plate with the name of the street. The direction they walked and came through the door etched in her mind as she determined which direction they needed to go. "This way." Isabella turned to the left. The older tunnel had drier, less pungent air. She inhaled deep and set her mind picking through the street map she studied the first week she arrived in Mexico City.

Faint voices floated down the tunnel toward them. Isabella stopped and listened. They didn't grow closer. She placed her lips on Tino's ear. "I think the voices are coming from the chamber."

He nodded. Shining the light down only a few feet in front of them, they continued down the tunnel until she could see the faint flickering glow from the torches in the chamber. She clicked the flashlight off and continued quietly. Tino moved past her, a revolver in his hand.

At the opening, they paused listening.

"I know you have told your father lies about me. I have seen you two whispering." Karyme's voice wasn't as controlled and cultured as usual. She was flustered and veering toward excitable. That wasn't good for whoever she was talking to.

"Karyme, my queen, this girl is not going to tell you anything. It is time." Bastante's voice held authority and conviction. Isabelle gripped Tino's arm. He and Karyme were working against her husband.

Tino moved to the edge of the doorway and peered in. He backed up and placed his mouth on her ear. "They have Hadda. They are all in white robes. Karyme and Bastante on the chairs. Hadda at their feet with her wrists and ankles tied."

Isabella put her hand around her survival tin. She would need a blade to slice Hadda's bindings. Her mind raced through the images she remembered of the chamber. Other than the chairs there was no place to hide. They had to make the room dark to have the advantage. How many torches were there and where were they located?

She tugged on Tino drawing him down the tunnel away from the doorway.

"We need a plan," she whispered into his ear.

He nodded.

"There is nowhere to hide in that room. You can't go in shooting. We don't know if someone has a gun. There were two torches in that room. One on either side of the door. We'll have to go in at the same time, grab the torches and snuff them out. I'll go for Hadda if you stay by the door, so I can find the way out in the dark."

He shook his head. "I will go for Hadda."

"No. You need to have your hands free in case you need to use the revolver."

He shook his head. "It will be dark what will I shoot at?"

"What if they have another light source hidden? If the lights come on, you'll need to protect us."

Tino's hand roughly cupped the back of her head, and he drew her face to his. "I do not like this but can come up with nothing better." He kissed her with the intensity she'd grown to love and released her.

Hand in hand, they crept back to the doorway. Tino pushed her to the opposite side.

"Please, do not hurt me. I will not tell anyone."

Hadda's scared voice was all Isabella needed to chase away her fear. The girl's only hope was in their hands.

Tino nodded and they both rushed into the room, grabbing the torches. It took Isabella a second longer to rub her torch out on the dirt floor. In that second, she saw who stood behind Karyme's chair. Her heart squeezed with fear for them all.

Chapter Thirty-four

Now, she understood everything. Rico was the person really working with Karyme to take down Garza and not for the DEA. How had he gotten so high up in the organization? She shoved that aside for later. Before noticing Rico, she'd set in her mind where Hadda knelt.

Moving in the darkness and listening to scuffling coming from the dais above Hadda, Isabella rushed to the girl's side. Hadda emitted a cry before Isabella could stop her.

"Shh, I'm here to help you get loose," Isabella whispered in the girl's ear. The scuffling continued as she dragged Hadda across the dirt floor away from the dais. Feeling down Hadda's body, she found the rope around her ankles and sliced at the hemp with her X-Acto blade. The small blade, while sharp, took small slices. The rope finally fell free when a bright light flashed on above the dais.

Isabella shielded her eyes, waiting for them to become accustom to the bright light. Removing her hand, her body froze. Bastante, bloody and still, lay on the dais at Karyme's feet. Her hands and a wide blade knife dripped blood. Red droplets spattered her white robe. The glow in her eyes and triumphant smile on her lips frightened Isabella more than anything she'd ever witnessed before. Even the insane zealot Virgil as he was plunging the obsidian dagger toward her hadn't brought on the terror the sight of this woman brought.

Hadda shoved her body against Isabella, reminding her she had more than herself to get out of this mess. Tino! Her gaze caught sight of him slumped on the ground by the door. Rico stood over him smiling.

Shamutz! She was Hadda and Tino's only hope.

Rico raised his head. His gaze bore into her like a laser. His displeasure to see her was as palpable as the iron tang of blood in the air. In fact, he looked worried. Finally, something she might have control over. It appeared this was yet another man who feared her intelligence.

"Karyme is insane. You need to get her some help," Isabella said, standing and drawing Hadda up beside her. Her hope was to get near Tino and figure out how to get all three of them out of this.

"I am not insane!" Karyme said in a commanding voice. "I give gifts to the gods and they in turn give me the things I want." Her eyes glassed over. "They brought me Paolo who allowed me to continue exploring the ways of the Aztec and gather the means to give my thanks to the gods." She shook her head. "I thought he was worthy but he wasn't." She dropped the knife, point down, into Bastante's body. "I was close to attaining everything I want,"—Karyme peered at Rico and smiled seductively— "until she,"—Karyme pointed toward Hadda—"discovered my Paolo was her father."

Karyme stepped over Bastante's body as if it wasn't even there and stalked toward them. Isabella pulled Hadda behind her. The iron tang of blood preceded the woman. How could she keep the girl out of the woman's hands?

"Don't come any closer. You are not absolved from your actions. You don't have all three of the Triple Alliance statues so their shield won't protect you." She grasped at the hope Bastante had kept the statue she'd stolen to keep Karyme in line.

The woman stopped. Her forehead wrinkled in confusion.

"I've been researching." Isabella swallowed to ignore the taint of the lie she was about to spout. "As long as the statues remain together all those who believe in the alliance who are within the triangle of the three Temples are safe. The statues no longer are together. We are all doomed."

Karyme's eyes narrowed. She glared at Isabella.

"I know you took the third statue. I will have Manny work you over until you beg to tell me where it is." Karyme reached a hand toward Isabella as if to snatch her.

Isabella sliced the woman's arm with the blade in her hand.

Karyme screamed and came at her like a wild beast. Isabella swung her arm again, slicing at the woman.

A gunshot echoed in the small room, mingling the acrid scent of gunpowder with the tang of the freely flowing blood.

Karyme slumped to the floor. Her body sprawled at Isabella's feet, bloody, her wild eyes staring up at the ceiling.

Inching away from the vile woman, Isabella's hand shook as she raised an arm to hide her nose and eyes from the gut roiling smells and sight. Hadda pushed against her back as if trying to find comfort. Isabella peered at Rico still standing by Tino, a revolver in his hand.

"She was becoming a liability instead of an asset." His gaze moved to the girl behind her. "Karyme wanted her husband's fortune to use it to become a specialist on her ancestors. I, on the other hand, just want her husband's fortune. I refused to wait by marrying his daughter and having him die an unexpected death. I want it now, while I can enjoy it and all the amenities that come with it."

"Greed is not becoming on you, Rico." Isabella turned to Hadda and began to slice at the ropes on her wrists.

"What are you doing?" Rico lunged toward her as she had planned. She wanted him away from Tino and his attention on her until she could find a way to get the jump on him.

She put a hand on her hip and glared at him. "Do you really think after all this killing and being separated, the Triple Alliance gods are going to allow you to get away with this?" She didn't have a clue if Rico was superstitious or if he believed in the Aztec gods but she'd try that ploy first.

Tino heard Isabella's voice as he gradually gained consciousness. He opened the one eye that wasn't swollen and his body immediately surged with adrenaline. Rico was advancing on Isabella and Hadda. The two women he'd sworn to keep safe. Without moving his limbs, he flexed his muscles to assess what kind of movement he might have. Two beatings in twenty-four hours had reduced his ability to defend even himself.

¡Coño! He hated this. The tang of blood registered. He scanned the room. Bastante lay in a bloody heap on the dais, Karyme sprawled on the floor not far from Isabella and Hadda. What had happened while he was out? The chamber looked like a massacre.

Rico stalked toward the women. He had to do something to distract the man holding *his* weapon. The snuffed-out torch lay on the ground beside him. Tino reached out, caught the handle in his grip and rose. He wanted to run at the man but knew his body couldn't.

Moving one foot and then the other, he quietly walked to within striking distance and swung. The torch clobbered Rico alongside the head, knocking him to the floor.

"Come!" He dropped the torch and grasped Isabella's hand. Shuffle-trotting he led the women out of the chamber.

"This way." Isabella took the lead, pulling him and Hadda along one on either hand.

They only traveled a hundred meters when the sound of footsteps came from the direction they were headed.

"We have to go the other way. We have no weapons." Tino tugged on Isabella.

"But Rico is back there." Hadda's scared voice boosted Tino's adrenaline.

"He is one. The sound coming toward us is many." He expected Isabella to say something, but she only changed direction and headed back the way they had come.

Going by the chamber door, Tino peeked in. Rico was gone. He had to be in the tunnel ahead of them, thinking that was the way they had traveled. Tino stopped.

He pulled the two women close and whispered. "I think Rico is ahead of us, and we have the others coming from behind. We need to find a way out of here before either one finds us."

Isabella clicked on her flashlight shielding the beam with her fingers to give her only enough light to see the walls and look for a way out.

Tino had been in situations like this before. Then he was alone and had only his own hide at risk. Right now, he had the life of the woman he loved and a young girl who was pulled into this because of her birth. He had to keep them all alive even if he was only at fifty percent. Fear for the women overrode any fear for himself.

As Isabella scanned the tunnel, he kept his ears trained for movement ahead and behind them. They didn't want to be surprised again.

With her looking for plaques and doorways they weren't moving as fast as before. The sounds behind them quieted. They probably found the chamber and dead bodies. Which meant they weren't that far behind.

"Here it is," Isabella whispered. Her light shone on the crack of a portal and the round wheel that suctioned the door closed.

Tino walked up and grabbed the wheel, pulling it as hard as his battered ribs would allow without screaming in pain. It barely budged.

"Let me help." Isabella squeezed in next to him and pulled on the handle as well.

Inch, by miserable inch the wheel gradually gave way. The footsteps started up again. Moving closer. They weren't masking their movements at all.

Tino groaned. His muscles burned and seared as he forced them to flex and pull on the wheel.

"We have to move on," Hadda said, the fear in her voice causing it to raise an octave.

"We can't take the chance of Rico having help at the end of that tunnel," Tino huffed between trying to turn the wheel.

"Rico is not a problem."

"Arrh!" Tino growled as he spun toward the sound of Garza's voice.

Isabella clicked the light on and shone it in Garza's face. The man raised up a hand shielding his eyes.

"Papa!" Hadda threw her body against Garza. He wrapped his arms around her.

"Are you safe?"

"Sí. These two got me away from Karyme, but there are others following." Hadda hugged her father.

Tino hated that his enemy was so protective of his daughter—the girl he'd made his promise to keep safe.

"Let me help." Garza pushed his daughter into Isabella's hands and grabbed the wheel. With his help they broke the seal and the door swung open.

"Hurry!" Isabella ushered them through and shoved the portal closed. "Try to turn it enough that it will stay closed. We can't chance it squeaking if they walk by while you're trying to seal it."

Once the portal was closed, Isabella set out down the walkway of the larger culvert to her right using her light at its brightest.

Tino wasn't as nonchalant about being in the company of his sworn enemy. He'd spent years trying to bring this man down and now here he was helping them. The whole idea made his head throb.

"How do you know we don't have to fear Rico?" Tino didn't want to give away his affection for Isabella to this man but at the same time he wanted to make sure he was close to her if the man decided they were expendable. He'd yet to see a weapon on the drug lord but that didn't mean he didn't have one. Tino hurried to catch up to Isabella. Touching her arm, he slowed her steps so he could keep up and remain close to her.

"I found him coming toward me as I was traveling through the old sewer. He appeared wobbly and disoriented. All he said was Karyme and Bastante were dead. I knew he was part of Karyme's obsession and wanted to question him later, so I knocked him out."

"Did you do anything else to detain him?" Tino didn't like the idea of Rico coming to and finding them.

"Papa, he wants you dead." Hadda clung to Garza's hand.

"I knew Karyme was seeing him, but I didn't realize he wanted anything more than to have DEA catch me." His voice softened, sounded weary.

"Your wife was loco." Tino sucked in air when Isabella's elbow jabbed him. "If he did not know she was loco he needs to know. It could be in his other daughters."

"How did you know we were down here?" Isabella asked.

"Luis called me."

"Luis?" Hadda asked in a loud whisper.

"Sí." The heavy sigh that hung in the air around the word stopped everyone.

Tino turned along with Isabella who trained the light on the ground. The father and daughter were silhouettes in the outer ring of pale light.

"I thought you hated Luis." Hadda backed away from her father.

"I do not like someone who uses my little girl to rob me. But he persuaded me that he was only worried about you and that I needed to call off my wife." Garza looked at Tino and Isabella. "He told me you were trying to get Hadda and where you went into the sewer. I climbed into the manhole on the same street closest to the house and headed this way hoping I'd find you."

"How did you know to go into the old sewer?" Isabella's mind was working better than Tino's.

He was still having problems seeing the man as anything other than the man who killed his family.

"Luis. He told me everything he knew." Garza smiled at Isabella. "You are too clever for your own good."

"I agree," Tino added. "We must continue."

A light flashed ahead of them.

"Cut the light," Tino whispered, grabbing the flashlight from Isabella. He pulled her closer to him and away from Garza and Hadda. Let the drug lord protect his daughter. Tino had his own prize to protect.

"There has to be a manhole around here somewhere," Isabella whispered in his ear. "We've traveled far enough there should be one. They have them every five blocks." She grabbed his hand tucking it in a jean pocket. "Stay with me."

Tino shoved his fingers deeper into her hip pocket and followed Isabella. She walked sideways along the wall. The sound of her hands sliding across the concrete wall gave him the visual she was feeling for a ladder in the dark. He also heard the father and daughter following behind them.

The light grew brighter as they continued toward it.

The twang of metal rang through the darkness and the light stopped as if the person behind it listened.

"I found the ladder," Isabella whispered. "I'll go up and move the cover."

"I'll go, those lids are heavy," Garza whispered.

"No." Tino put up his hand, ramming it into Garza's chest. "I do not trust you. You could get out of here and put something on the cover leaving us to these sewer rats."

"Fine. I am the only one with a weapon." Satisfactions purred in Garza's voice.

Tino's teeth ground together, knowing his enemy had the upper hand.

He turned and realized Isabella had already started climbing the ladder. The sound of their followers grew louder as the light coming the other direction lit more and more of the culvert in front of them.

His one solace was that Isabella could get free even if the rest of them didn't.

The grinding of metal on metal meant Isabella was moving the lid. "Send Hadda up," she called down.

Tino grabbed the girl and placed her hands on the ladder rungs. "Go."

"Papa?" she questioned.

"I'll be right behind you."

Tino didn't like the tone. He wasn't staying down in this hell hole with his own private devil. He pushed up against Hadda so he could follow right behind her up the ladder.

He raised his foot to step on the bottom rung and the area around he and Garza lit up.

"Go!" Garza shoved him upward. "Take care of my daughter."

A bullet thunked into the concrete beside Tino. He forced his stiff and battered body to move up the ladder, leaving his enemy at the mercy of whoever shot at them. More shots rang out in the tunnel. The thud of a bullet hitting something soft, like a body, made him look down. Garza held a hand to his middle as the fabric on his shirt darkened.

¡Coño! The man had taken a bullet for him. No... not for him... for his daughter.

Chapter Thirty-five

"Tino!" Isabella screamed hearing the gun shots ringing in the tunnel below. Her heart wedged in her throat as she leaned down trying to see. The light from the attacker wavered and she could see Tino moving up the ladder. Garza stood at the bottom of the ladder shooting at the attacker.

Tino's head and shoulders appeared. She and Hadda grabbed him, hauling him out of the hole. She hugged him tight, her heart pounding. They made it.

Hadda looked through the hole. "Papa?" she called.

Isabella looked into Tino's eyes. She saw remorse in his dark depths. He shook his head.

"Papa!" Hadda shouted down the hole.

Isabella's heart went out to the girl as she put an arm around Hadda. "Come away from the hole."

"But Papa…"

"He was hit. I don't know if he'll come up, but he told me to take care of you." Tino stood. "We need to get out of here. Whoever was shooting at us could come up the ladder."

"No! We have to help Papa." Hadda spun out of Isabella's grip, flinging herself at Tino and pounding on his chest. "You should have helped him."

"I was too far up the ladder to do anything, and he was the one with the gun, not me." Tino grabbed her upper arms and shook her. "He would want you strong. You are the only family your younger sisters have. You will have to care for them."

Hadda stopped abruptly. "Aracela, Maribel, and Jemsa." Her eyes widened and tears flowed. "Their mother and father taken from them. Oh, dear God."

Isabella hadn't lost any family members, but she also hadn't lived as close to her family as Hadda had even if they had thought her only the help. She put her arm around the girl and walked toward the sidewalk. Tino followed beside them.

"Help, por favor."

Garza's strained voice spun them all around. Isabella, followed by Hadda, hurried to the manhole and helped the drug lord out. His midsection was bleeding.

"Can you walk?" she asked, helping him to his feet as Hadda hugged his arm.

"I have to. It is Manny who is after us."

Garza's words sent shivers up Isabella's back. Manny was the one Tino said beheaded the Alvarez men and nearly choked her to death.

Tino took the revolver from the waistband of Garza's pants. "Why is he shooting at you?"

Garza's dark eyes narrowed. "The DEA have raided my house, my wife crawled in bed with a rotten DEA agent, my world is crumbling. Everyone who has ever wanted to be me now wants to take me down. Even my own men." He peered into Hadda's face. "I can get us out of here if you get me to a phone. I have loyal people in Columbia. If we get to my plane, we will be safe."

Isabella saw the twitch in Tino's jaw. Would he let Garza go or make the drug lord pay for his family's demise? There was no time to debate it with him. "Come on. We need to get away from here." She put an arm around Garza's waist and nodded for Tino to lead.

Tino speared her with an angry look, but he didn't say anything. He led them into the shadows of an alley. They walked for several blocks before Garza started coughing.

"We have to get him a doctor," Hadda said, stopping and easing her father to sit on a back stoop.

"Come on," Tino grasped Isabella's hand, pulling her away from the father and daughter.

Isabella dug her heels into the cobblestones. "We can't leave them here."

Tino glared at her. "Do you think he would stay with us if it was one of us who was injured?"

Isabella's heart ached for Tino. His pain ruled his good judgment. "We will take them to a hospital, have WIA watch him until someone from DEA can come take him away." She kissed Tino's cheek. "If you leave him here. he may not die and you wouldn't have closure."

Uncertainty dulled Tino's eyes. "He sent me up the ladder to take care of his daughter while he held the guy off."

Now she understood the tortured thoughts in his mind. How could he turn in a man who saved his life even if he was the man behind his family's deaths? He wanted to leave the man so he could get away. But would Tino be able to live with himself later in life knowing he allowed the man who was responsible for so many deaths to get away.

"We will do what is right by our law's standards."

She returned to Garza and Hadda. "Come on. We'll get a taxi at the next street."

~*~

Garza had passed out by the time they arrived at a hospital. Tino paced back and forth in front of the door of the operating room. If Isabella hadn't made him see reason, he would have left the man in the alley and hoped he'd died along with feeling he'd given the man a chance for saving his and Isabella's life. But deep down, he would have hated himself for having a weak moment and letting the man go.

Isabella had called WIA. It turned out they were the people in the tunnel following them. When she'd contacted Gunderson, he was in the chamber cleaning up the mess Karyme and Rico had made. The only loose end was Rico. He'd disappeared.

DEA would have a mess to clean up, finding out which agents were legit and who was in Rico's pocket.

Isabella walked toward him with Gunderson. Her strength and ingenuity had saved them. He couldn't stop the smile spreading across his lips. Once he wrote up his report about this whole mess, he and Isabella would be on a plane to Arizona. He had plans to ask her father for her hand in marriage and then get her to pick a date.

Gunderson and Isabella stopped next to him. Isabella had her journal in one hand and slid her other hand into his.

"Where did you find your journal?" Tino asked, knowing Karyme had been the last person to have it in her possession.

"I found it on señora Garza's body. I don't think it's anything that needs to be noted as evidence." Gunderson winked at Isabella.

"You two work well together. Not only did Isabella crack the artifact thefts you both brought down one of the biggest drug lords and several small ones." Gunderson slapped Tino on the back.

He winced but held in the howl of pain that lodged in his windpipe.

"Garza is all yours. I have to get this hard-headed Venezuelan to see a doctor." Isabella tugged on his hand. "Come on, I have a doctor waiting to check you out."

"I still have to report to file." Tino followed, knowing he could never resist the woman towing him down the hall.

"This is the age of the internet and computers. You can file it from anywhere. And I'm thinking, my place."

The twinkle in Isabella's eyes eased his stiff muscles. He couldn't think of any place he'd rather be than at her place, learning even more about her and loving her.

Epilogue

Isabella couldn't believe how well Tino fit into her life. He accepted a job with the DEA as a liaison with the border patrol in Arizona. There was only local travel involved and he was home every night. They spent hours together, learning more about one another and planning their future.

There were still several things that were unresolved in Mexico City. Rico never surfaced. All law enforcement agencies were on the lookout for him. The tunnel from the Garza basement was opened and the statues were never found. The third statue that she and Alphonso stole was also missing. The only evidence to their existence was her photos and her word. To her dismay the authorities found Alphonso's body in an alley in the Alvarez distrio. She'd had high hopes for him even if he had been bought to betray her. He was also her only witness to the statues.

Isabella jotted down the names of the people who had knowledge of the statues in her journal and closed the book.

Tino reclined in her bed, reading a magazine, waiting for her. She smiled and sashayed naked over to the bed.

"This is the way I want every night to end," she said, slipping between the sheets and into Tino's arms.

"So do I." Tino kissed her nose and turned serious. "When are you going to turn in your WIA resignation?"

Isabella twisted to turn out the light. Burying her head against Tino's chest, she crossed her ankles and whispered, "The next time I see Daddy."

~*~*~

About the Book & Author

Thank you for reading ***Secrets of an Aztec Temple***. I enjoyed researching and bringing not only my characters, but Mexico City, to life. While I have never been there, I asked people who had to help me portray the ambiance. I read news stories about the city and researched the area.

If you enjoy the book please leave a review. And you may also like book 1, ***Secrets of a Mayan Moon***, and book 3, ***Secrets of a Hopi Blue Star***.

I also have several mystery series. You can find out about them at my website: https://www.patyjager.net

Paty Jager is an award-winning author of 48 novels, 8 novellas, and numerous anthologies of murder mystery and western romance. All her work has Western or Native American elements in them along with hints of humor and engaging characters. Paty and her husband raise alfalfa hay in rural eastern Oregon. Riding horses and battling rattlesnakes, she not only writes the western lifestyle, she lives it.

You can catch up with her at:

Website: http://www.patyjager.net
Blog: https://writingintothesunset.net/
FB Page: https://www.facebook.com/PatyJagerAuthor/
Amazon: https://www.amazon.com/Paty-Jager/e/B002I7M0VK
Pinterest: https://www.pinterest.com/patyjag/
Twitter: https://twitter.com/patyjag
Goodreads: http://www.goodreads.com/author/show/1005334.Paty_Jager
Newsletter- Mystery: https://bit.ly/2IhmWcm
Newsletter- Western: https://bit.ly/2JVGe4j
Bookbub - https://www.bookbub.com/authors/paty-jager

Thank you for purchasing this Windtree Press publication. For other books of the heart, please visit our website at www.windtreepress.com.

For questions or more information contact us at info@windtreepress.com.

Windtree Press
www.windtreepress.com

www.ingramcontent.com/pod-product-compliance
Lightning Source LLC
Chambersburg PA
CBHW051043050726
47592CB00002B/376